Fanny Kemble

Further Records 1848-1883 - A Series of Letters

Vol. I

Fanny Kemble

Further Records 1848-1883 - A Series of Letters
Vol. I

ISBN/EAN: 9783744765541

Printed in Europe, USA, Canada, Australia, Japan

Cover: Foto ©Andreas Hilbeck / pixelio.de

More available books at **www.hansebooks.com**

FURTHER RECORDS.

1848—1883.

A SERIES OF LETTERS

BY

FRANCES ANNE KEMBLE,

FORMING

A Sequel to Record of a Girlhood

AND

Records of Later Life.

WITH TWO PORTRAITS ENGRAVED BY J. G. STODART.

VOL. I.

LONDON:

RICHARD BENTLEY AND SON,

Publishers in Ordinary to Her Majesty the Queen.

1890.

CONTENTS OF VOL. I.

CONTENTS. vii

FURTHER RECORDS.

I HAD hired for this summer a cottage belonging to my youngest daughter, called York Farm, on the estate known as Butler Place, about six miles from Philadelphia and three from the pretty suburban village (town as it now is) of Germantown, in the pleasant villadom surrounding which many of the Philadelphia men of business find an agreeable rural retreat from the city. The house at York Farm, however, not being ready for my reception, I took one for six months in Philadelphia, and until I was able to obtain possession of it, stayed at a country place belonging to a dear friend.

When first my father and myself went to America in 1832, a hired house, lodging, or apartment was not to be had for love or money—nobody let their premises or any portion of them—and in New York, Philadelphia, and Boston we were obliged to live for two years expensively and uncomfortably in hotels. This is entirely changed now, and while I occupied the house I had taken in Rittenhouse Square, my eldest daughter was living in a hired apartment in the city.

My friend's residence was called Champlost, after some place (but I know not where) in France. It was within a few miles of Philadelphia. The grounds joined those of York Farm (my contemplated residence), and a pleasant woodland and meadow path was made, affording a direct and short communication between the two houses, that was called "The Lady's Walk."

Champlost was a small estate of picturesquely varied surface, with bits of fine wood and some noble single chestnut and oak trees, with a bright little brook trotting and singing through one of the hollows. The house stood upon a gently sloping lawn, over which it looked to a sunny prospect of cultivated fields, bounded by a country road, on which the lower entrance opened into a drive through a charming bit of fine wood, which of larger extent would have been called in England a chase. Beyond the house, this road led to the upper entrance on a pleasant lane, known as Green Lane, with pretty private residences on it. There was no flower garden proper at Champlost, but round the house irregular masses of flowering shrubbery, a charming conservatory, and admirable vegetable garden, from all which the fine produce went with profuse liberality to all who could be benefited or delighted by it.

The dwelling itself had for its core or kernel an old-fashioned Pennsylvania country house, to which had been made alterations and additions which gave it a certain quaint and picturesque irregularity exteriorly; in the interior reigned a simple, elegant, exquisite comfort, the perfection of which was proverbial.

Dear Champlost! to me an unfailing refuge from trouble and sorrow, a haven of peace and rest, a home of liberty and love, of the happiest social companionship, and the most devoted and constant friendship, during all the years that I spent in the foreign country, where I married, my grateful blessing rests upon it for ever!

1812, *Rittenhouse Square, January 6th,* 1874.

MY DEAR H——,

I got a letter from you to-day in which you say that one of my last reached you in ten days. The passages of the vessels this way have been very rapid lately, and there should be no delay in the receipt of letters on either side, but while I was at Champlost there may have been remissness on the part of the servants in posting the letters.

You asked me if I have been caring about General Bazaine, but I did not even know of his trial till you referred to it. You speak of having sent me several *Spectators*—one only has reached me, in which I could not find anything which should have particularly induced you to send it, and which I therefore think must have been forwarded instead of some other which had some article in it that you especially wished me to see. I am about to subscribe to the *Spectator* and the *Nation* (the latter the only decent American paper I know), as I think it desirable to know rather more of what is going on in the world than I have been content to do since I returned to America.

As I know nothing whatever of the present condition of France, I cannot speculate as to its future.

I have supposed hitherto that the great national desire
for revenge on Prussia, would probably induce the
French to place a military man at the head of the
government, and imagined that one of the Orleans
princes would perhaps be elected eventually, because
they are all in the Jesuit interest, and that will probably act very powerfully in France, for the Jesuits, as
a body, hate and fear Protestant Prussia, as much as
the French people hate their German conquerors.　A
wise old Russian gentleman, Count Pahlen, told me at
the very beginning of the war that it had been brought
about by the intrigues of the papal government, with
a view to, and in the confident expectation of, the
suppression of the Prussian Protestant influence in
Germany, by the power of the French arms, which
were expected to meet with a very different success
from that which they found in their encounter with
the heretic Teutons. . . .

You asked me if I had a piano.　There is one in the
drawing-room of this house, belonging to the people
from whom I have hired it, and it is in every respect
a sample of the sort of people they are.　It is of
extremely handsome and expensive wood, very elabor-
ately carved, and must have been very costly, merely
as a piece of ornamental furniture; as a musical
instrument it is one of the poorest and most miserable
that are manufactured, being quite contemptible in
tone and power—in short, as bad as a piano can
be.　Moreover, I found it in such a hopeless state of
discord, that it is hardly possible to bring it into tune
at all.　Nearly a pan full of dust was cleaned out of the
interior of it, when I had it tuned, and the keys were

literally begrimed with dirt; the piano, moreover, is not an old one. The tuner, whom I sent for to put it to rights, pointed contemptuously to the carved wood of the case and said, "This is what this piano was bought for." However, here it is, and I have not place for another in the room, nor do I care to afford myself either the purchase or the hire of another, so having had this made endurable, I practise every day after breakfast, still playing and singing my beloved Beethoven and Schubert, with a thousand memories of exquisite pleasure derived from having heard them —oh! how far otherwise executed—in former days and other places. . . .

Ellen (a very dear and devoted servant) made an immense sacrifice in coming with me to this country for two years, and the whole comfort of my daily existence depends so entirely upon her, that I do not think it would be possible for me to live here without her; if I did, I would give up all idea of having an establishment of my own, and betake myself to a boarding-house or hotel, which I could very hardly afford to do at the present wild cost of living here in such houses.

On the opposite side of the square where I live is the Episcopalian church, which was served by my excellent and eloquent friend Mr. Phillips Brooks, until he was called from Philadelphia to Boston, and I go to it frequently for afternoon service, though I now no more hear his admirable sermons. [This gentleman is now no longer a stranger to the English pulpit: he has preached in Westminster Abbey and several other churches, producing everywhere the same profound impression by the fervent eloquence of his noble religious discourses.]

Moreover, half a quarter of a mile on the other hand is the "high-church" church of Philadelphia, to which I went on Christmas Day, saw the altar a blaze of wax candles, heard Handel murdered, and a gentleman trying to intone, who was rather funny, as he did not know how to do it. You see, I have plenty of church privileges.

God bless and keep you, dear.

Ever, as ever, yours,
FANNY.

1812, *Rittenhouse Square, Saturday, January 10th,* 1874.

MY BELOVED H——,

. . . My Christmas present to O—— was three dozen of the finest wine I could procure here. The things I got for him in Dublin were so trifling, that I had quite a misgiving about offering them to him, though, when I mustered up courage to show him the old-fashioned seal I had had engraved with his monogram, and found that he liked it, I was very much pleased and relieved, for really people's presents to each other are on such a magnificent scale here that one hardly knows what to offer them. . . .

I had some very beautiful flowers given to me. M—— sent me, in a magnificent china flower-pot of English fabric (a pale delicate green, with birds, butterflies, and flowers scattered all over it), a large Catalonia jasmine in full bloom. It was Mr. Butler's first gift to me before we were married; and on Christmas Day, M——, to whom I had given it years ago, and in whose gardener's care it has been ever since, sent it back to me in this beautiful vase, and covered with fragrant blossoms, a strange flowering again of former memories—of the *tempo passato che non torna piu.* . . .

The weather here now is perfectly lovely, mild and bright only unnaturally warm for the time of year. I suppose we shall have the rest of our pinching cold (of which we had a bitter instalment while I was at Champlost in November) in the early spring, which I shall be sorry for. Dr. W—— and S—— and their boy dined with me on Christmas Day, and Ellen insisted on hanging green Christmas garlands round the dining-room, but was very unhappy because she could not find a handsome sprig of holly with bright berries to send up on the plum-pudding, for the honour of England.

Mr. S——'s Christmas gift of a turkey does not seem so strange to me as to you. Our old friends, the Mayows, who were Norfolk people, invariably sent us at Christmas a huge turkey, for which kind of domestic fowl, as you probably know, that county is famous. My old and dear friend, William Donne, I know always sends a similar tribute to Arthur M—— from his small Norfolk estate. Here, where I think the turkey is quite as much the national bird as the eagle, people are not unapt to send each other mince-pies of very large size and especially rich and delicate composition. M——, whose cook is famous for their manufacture, sent me one made like a huge tart, and one to Dr. W——, who is a great favourite of hers, and has a tenderness for that unwholesome Christmas dainty. I heard a ludicrous and touching story of an

American diplomatic lady, who received at Christmas, while at her embassy abroad, a huge mince-pie from "home" all the way across the Atlantic. Her husband invited some of their compatriots (exiles like themselves) to dine with them and share this national dainty, but when it appeared on the table a considerable piece of it was missing. The gentleman looked surprised and not altogether pleased, when his wife, with a charming mixture of shame and simple naïveté (as she was described to me), exclaimed, "Oh, George, I couldn't help it; it was so like home!"

I had a very exquisite Daphne Odora in full bloom, brought to me by my dear Dr. Furness's daughter, and some delicious cut hot-house flowers, made up into a very tasteful nosegay, and a quantity more that came in a beautiful glass vase, that looked as if it was growing in a thick bed of lovely moss.

Dr. W——, to whom I had said that I wanted a pair of candlesticks (for this house had no such utensils, and everything of that description that I own is buried in the bowels of a store-room in Germantown, amidst piles of boxes, and furniture, and goods, and chattels, belonging to my children, which will not be opened till we all go out in the country), gave me a very pretty pair of French candlesticks, the one a figure of Doré's Don Quixote and the other of Retch's Mephistopheles. S—— gave me Horace Furness's Variorum Shakespeare, the "Romeo and Juliet" and "Macbeth," the only two volumes yet published, which I wished for very much, but thought too expensive to get them for myself. F—— sent me up from the plantation a barrel of the most magnificent oranges I ever saw, a product of the estate. Half the barrel, I grieve to say, was spoiled in coming, but I got about six dozen of the most superb and delicious oranges that I ever saw that were sound. So you see I had a very fine Christmas fairing.

God bless you, dearest friend.

1812, *Rittenhouse Square, Thursday, February* 5th, 1874.

MY DEAREST H——,

This square is enclosed in an iron railing; it is about as large as Lincoln's Inn Fields, open to the public, and not reserved, as our squares are, for the use of the persons residing in them. There are neither shrubberies nor garden-beds with flowers, but trees, grass, and gravel walks, and it affords a pleasant diagonal short cut across the square.

There is no special post day to write for from the United States now, the number of steamers from every port makes constant letter-carrying to Europe the rule, instead of the limited agency of the Cunard Line, to which we were formerly restricted. There are now three or four lines of steam-packets from Boston, New York, and this place, and they are all letter-carriers between the two continents. I am sorry to say, however, that it is not impossible that some of my letters to you may have been lost. I have had a drunken man-servant, to whose charge the letters were committed for posting, and it is just possible that he may have neglected his duty in this respect, or delayed fulfilling it, or even mislaid and lost the letters. I certainly have been writing to you frequently, and cannot account for you not hearing from me. I have acknowledged the receipt of the *Saturday Review*, and told you that I had liked the article on Sir Charles Lyell's books. very much. . . .

I think it most probable that the L——s will return to England in two years, and that, if I live, I shall go back the summer after next; but I trouble myself not at all with plans of any sort for the future, I am too heartily thankful for the present. My condition is full of causes for gratitude to God, and the days go by with an amazing velocity that suggests the rapidly approaching end of all to me much more frequently than any intermediate plan, prospect, or purpose.

I will certainly endeavour to procure the *Contemporary Review* for December, and read Dr. Carpenter's article on the " Psychology of Belief." It is, I suppose, an essay about which Fanny Cobbe spoke to me once or twice with great admiration and interest. I think he was imparting his views to her before he published them upon these matters.

You speak of the social disorders and disorganization which exist in America quite as much (that is, considering the different circumstances) as in Europe, and ask, Where is social rest to be found ? Nowhere, I rather think, until people are more aware than they are now that prosperity, national as well as individual, is a *moral* and not a material question. Here, in America, the great question of the identity of the interests of capital and labour will, I imagine, be worked out; and here, I suppose, people will first arrive at the conclusion (I mean masses of people, not individuals) which Maurice preached, that *politics* are

christianity, and that no favourable conditions whatever will stand instead, either for individuals or com-
munities, of obedience to God and the teaching of
Christ. It is wonderful for one, who believes this as
I do, to watch how perfectly ineffectual all the liberty,
all the social advantages of the working-classes in
this country are to produce effects, which are moral
and not material everywhere.

I go on scribbling my Reminiscences more or less.
It is an occupation that amuses me, but which I put
aside, of course, very frequently for other things, as I
can always resume it at any time, and am not bound
ever to finish it.

I have now greatly altered the plan upon which I
came to America. My first intention was to take the
York Farm for two years, and go into it as soon as
I arrived here last autumn. This was rendered impossible by the state of the house there, the repairs
and alterations in which could not be completed
before this spring, so I took the house where I now
am till June, when I expect to go out to the York
Farm. . . .

God bless you, dearest H——. You say truly
words can little express a lifelong love, such as ours
has been; but, indeed, what is it that words *can*
express? in spite of which we needs must use them,
and I am ever, as ever, yours,

FANNY.

I am sorry to hear Colonel Taylor thinks of
resuming his laborious position in the house as Whip.

1812, Rittenhouse Square, Thursday, February 12th, 1874.

MY DEAREST H——,

My will was drawn up by my lawyer and general adviser on business matters, and duly signed and witnessed in his office, so you may dismiss all anxiety with regard to its validity from your mind.

I shall try to get the *Quarterly* for the sake of Fanny Cobbe's review of Mrs. Somerville, and I shall try to get the *Contemporary Review* for December with Dr. Carpenter's article, but it is by no means easy to procure these periodicals here. A certain number of them are obtained for regular subscribers, but beyond that there is no general demand that makes it worth any bookseller's while to send for them, as they would probably find no sale.

You are quite right in supposing that the employers of servants here are answerable for much of the inefficiency and bad quality of the service they receive. A good many causes tend to make good masters and mistresses quite as rare as good servants. The old proverb holds good, " Like master, like man." The large and rapid fortunes by which vulgar and ignorant people become possessed of splendid houses, splendidly furnished, do not, of course, give them the feelings and manners of gentle folks, or in any way really raise them above the servants they employ, who are quite aware of this fact, and that the possession of wealth is literally the only superiority their employers have over them. The difference of religion between the Irish servants and their American employers is, I think, unfavourable to a good deal of very serious and sincere sympathy that should pervade a household—a *family.* The total absence of early discipline makes bad disciplinarians of American heads of houses. They are impatient of system, of order, of necessary and legitimate control themselves, and shrink with great cowardice from enforcing them on their own children and servants. The children are allowed to be at once familiar and rude towards the latter. Nowhere in the world, where I have been, is the relation of home dependency and authority so little understood or the intercourse of members of households so wanting in mutual good breeding and courtesy. The institutions which secure freedom all but unbounded to all, the almost inviolability of individual *rights,* cannot by any possibility supply the place of domestic virtues or charities, or the graces of mutual respect and regard that ennoble and sweeten human relationships.

I think the Americans generally (but more especially the women), have a superficial hardness of manner perhaps in some degree of character, and no people appear to me to have so little *civility* as distinguished from humanity and real kindliness in which they are by no means deficient. Their manners to their servants I think far from good, and I have no doubt at all that they are themselves in great measure responsible for the disorder, discomfort, and insubordination of their households. The exceptions (of which there are plenty) prove this to be the case.*

* In England, for some years past, the relation between servants and their employers has been gradually undergoing very important alteration. Orlando's compliment to Old Adam

There is undoubtedly some occasional irregularity in the posting and delivery of our letters, for this

points to some decided deterioration in the *sentiment* of service in Shakespeare's own day—

> "Oh, good old man, how well in thee appears
> The constant service of the antique world,
> When service sweat for duty, not for meed.
> Thou art not for the fashion of these times,
> When none will sweat, but for promotion."

The lifelong service and attachment still to be found in some few families some years ago, is, I imagine, disappearing more and more before the " fashion of these times." Change, for its own sake, is one of the predominating features of the present day, and affects all classes with a restless desire for novelty and excitement, created and stimulated by the increased facilities of locomotion and the comparative ease and cheapness of travelling. No reason is now considered more natural and unobjectionable for a servant's throwing up a situation than feeling the want " of a little change," a motive which my mother would have thought quite sufficient for not engaging any person who assigned it for leaving her place, and would have occasioned as summary a dismissal on the part of my mother as that charming Conservative and exquisite old Tory, Lady Ludlow (in Mrs. Gaskell's delightful book, so called), pronounced to the young woman, who, coming to be engaged as her lady's-maid, said, in answer to the fine gentlewoman's rather deprecatory inquiry, "I am told you can read?" "Oh yes, my lady, and write too." "Oh, go away, child—go away!" being Lady Ludlow's only comment upon this modern excess of education in a maidservant.

Of late years servants are often discharged during the temporary summer absence of their employers abroad, whose return gathers together a new household of new people. This again has given rise to what is called "taking service on a job," destructive, of course, of all personal relation beyond a mere temporary contract of the merest temporary convenience on week I have received on two consecutive days letters of yours, dated the 25th and 27th of January, but the

both sides. I have moreover been assured that a lady's-maid's long continuance in one service was objectionable on the score of her having probably become accustomed to the "habits" of her *mistress*, which title, I believe, is now universally abandoned for that of "my lady." No doubt freedom from some expense and trouble is gained by the very independent modern fashion of ladies travelling without attendant abigails, a practice now quite frequent with young women of perfect respectability and good social position, but which formerly would have been condemned as so *unladylike* as to be impossible, and great surprise and disapprobation would have been excited by the reply of a very lovely young woman of high rank, who, being asked how she had managed to travel abroad without a maid, answered, " Oh, my husband's man valeted me ! "

According to my observation, it is only in England and America that domestic service is considered degrading ; in America it is absolutely held so, and in England compared with other forms of industry. Nothing of this sort of feeling exists on the Continent—French, Italian, and German servants all living upon terms of kindly, honourable, and respectful familiarity with their employers. I have more than once quoted to my English servants Imogen's lovely answer to her unknown brother, who asking her, " Are we not brothers ? " replies, " So man and man should be, but clay differs from clay in dignity whose dust is all alike." Imogen was doubtless quite aware of the social difference which separated (in spite of her blood-instinct) the young Welsh hunter from the princess of Great Britain. I quote Shakespeare occasionally to my servants as next best thing to quoting the Bible to them. My own half foreign blood and foreign breeding has given me a friendly familiarity with my household children—my servants—which, I imagine, until they became accustomed to it, must have puzzled my English maids, and made our intercourse strange and perhaps difficult to them, though I have endeavoured by the most sacred teaching of all, and the Pope's title of " Servant of servants," and the last reached me first. You must ere this have received the account of my domestic tribulations with my poor drunken negro servant, and how he having taken the pledge, I took him back, buying myself off at the cost of seven guineas from an engagement with a Dublin man, who bribed me to take him by saying he had been at Ardgillan (with his master, one Colonel Brownrigg), who came to me *unsober* the day he was to have entered my service. As however my negro had taken the pledge, because his wife had understood that I would take him back if he did so, I took him back, and since then, now nearly a month ago, he has been perfectly steady and sober. I hope with all my heart the poor fellow will be able to keep his vow. He is a Roman Catholic, and brought me his priest's attestation that he had taken the pledge.

I not only should feel the difficulty of house-keeping doubly here, if I had not Ellen to assist me, but I would not attempt to keep house without her.

Prince of Wales's noble motto, "Ich dien," to make them feel how fine a thing true service is. With foreign servants, of whom I have had several, I have never had the slightest em-barrassment from the freedom of my intercourse with them, their own simple self-respect preserving them from the vulgar estimate of service held by our people ; but I have very little doubt that my habit of addressing all my people, men and women, as "my dear" and "my child," must often have sent a shudder through the respectable bosom of my London friends.

My little granddaughter, having heard me speak so to my maid, adopted the same style to her nursery maid, to whom she addressed with great gravity a solemnly serious remonstrance, beginning with, "My dear child, I have told you before," etc., a comical confirmation of the Darwinian theory of monkey descent.

I should go at once into an hotel or boarding-house, and dismiss my other servants. . . .

1812, *Rittenhouse Square, Saturday, February 14th,* 1874.

Certainly, my beloved H——, the "mystery of life" is not to be solved by government, and the sooner people find that out by making their governments as good as possible, the sooner they will discover that the "mystery of life" is individual righteousness and whatever makes most for that. Long ago Milton said that the good government of a state was nothing other than a man's good government. Institutions cannot produce virtues, but they can greatly hinder or help their development. This is the country, above all others, for demonstrating what can, and what cannot be achieved by government for the highest national results; and how curiously, where all external and material circumstances are most favourable, the prosperity even of a nation is shown to be a moral, rather than any other kind of result.

As for your quotation from "Lear," respecting the real superiority in honesty of judges over thieves, I suppose, as you are speaking of the Gladstone and Disraeli administrations, you are simply contemplating the common characteristics of party politics. You know, though I take a very deep interest in certain measures of government from which I expect certain results, and always in the *main* side with the Liberal party as the party of progress, I never desire to know anything of the detail of political measures, lest even those which I think best should lose anything of their intrinsic value to me, by seeing what low, paltry, personal motives and base machinery and dirty hands have helped to bring them about. . . .

I know nothing at all of the probable period—I can tell you nothing—of my nephew's marriage to Miss Grant, I have not seen him since he was a lad of thirteen. . . . I have only come as far as 1832 in my Memoirs, and my letters to you from the provincial towns, where my father and I were acting during the summer of that year.

I have no intention whatever of undertaking any literary work of any sort, but this of my Reminiscences. I have no mental vigour, and not much physical energy left. Looking over my letters, and copying portions of them, affords me a certain amount of quiet amusement and occupation daily. The letters which could have revived any distressing associations were all destroyed when first I received the box containing my whole correspondence with you; and though occasionally, in going back over all my life in those I have preserved, I still find details that sadden me, I have hitherto derived more interest and entertainment than anything else from the whole retrospect; and my depression has nothing whatever to do with that, though I think it is the physical result of the nervous strain of my whole life. All the early excitement, and all the subsequent trouble and sorrow, and all the prolonged exercise of that capacity for superficial emotion—these causes have shaken, I might almost say, shattered, my nervous system to such a degree, that the frequent depression I suffer from seems to me simply the inevitable result of such an existence as mine has been, on such a temperament.* Goethe's poems, long or short, are a poor panacea for mental depression, I should say ; but so far from any want of interest or occupation being the source of my low spirits, I think they are simply the consequence of too much excitement and hard work in former years. I have never, that I can recollect, known my time appear to pass as rapidly as it has done this winter, probably from its extreme unbroken monotony; but certainly the days and weeks devour each other with incredible swiftness.

* One of the dangers of the stage, as a profession, is the habit acting fosters of expressing superficial emotion. That the feeling exhibited is to a certain degree real in people of vivid imagination and quick sensibility only makes it the more objectionable ; for fictitious feeling is destructive of that which is true, and the habitual expression of the one impairs the genuineness of the other, and giving way to superficial emotion weakens the self-control, which ought to govern our feelings. Among Southern people, whose impulse leads them to vehement exhibitions of passion, sensibility is less profound than that of less demonstrative Northern folk ; but their demonstrations, dramatic as they are, are not acted, but perfectly natural. In English people the profession of acting is apt to produce an unnatural manner off the stage, very properly called "theatrical," but the foreign actresses I have known (Pasta, Ristori, and both the Garcias, Malibran and Viardot) have been perfectly simple and natural, though quite as dramatic (*not theatrical*) off the stage as on it. Garrick's French blood made him the incomparable actor he was, and as naturally as artistically so. My own people, the Kembles, who were excellent actors, were not naturally dramatic, being very English, and had a theatrical manner in private life. My mother, who was eminently dramatic and natural, succeeded principally on the stage in parts which might be called original creations, which have never been filled or I believe attempted by any other actress. But my mother was not English, but born in Vienna of French parents.

Twice at least every day (besides many times oftener, many days) I am reminded of and think of you, while I sit cutting with your sharp scissors the holes in the last bit of that embroidery which I used to bring with me to Fitzwilliam Place ; and when I sit at my lonely dinner, turning in my fingers the silver napkin-ring with Dorothy's initials on it, of which I gave you and her a pair at St. Leonard's.   These, however, are only my regular daily thoughts of you, I have many irregular ones besides.

1812, *Rittenhouse Square, Wednesday, February* 18*th,* 1874.

MY BELOVED H———,

Hitherto my coloured servant has continued perfectly sober since he took the pledge, which is now nearly a month ago. I feel much concerned for the man, who was in the war during the Southern secession, with the son of the proprietor of this house.   His master was wounded, and he attended him most faithfully and devotedly all the time he was disabled.   He, my servant, had three brothers killed in the war. Of course, the privations, and exposures, and fatigues of a soldier's life (especially during that war) must have made drinkers if not absolute drunkards of many poor fellows who were not so before.   The brandy-bottle was always at hand, and must often have supplied the place of food, shelter, fire, and rest.   If the accident of his being in my service rescues this poor man from this ruinous propensity, I shall rejoice greatly.   He has a young wife and two little children, for whom it is most important that he should be sober and industrious. He was born a slave in Maryland, cannot write, and can hardly be said to read, so that there is every excuse for him. He tells stories of the war to his fellow-servants, and Ellen told me one of them, how once, when they were half starved for want of food, they lighted upon some small quantity of meal, which he, knowing how to cook (as I believe all coloured people do by nature), made into cakes and scones, for his master and some other officers, without there being enough for him to have a morsel, a scrap, a crumb himself. I should not wonder if he took a good pull at the brandy-flask then.

The general character of the mulattoes in Philadelphia is now precisely what might be expected from people descended from slaves, and in many cases born and bred themselves in slavery : they lie and pilfer, and are dirty and lazy, in spite of which they are rapidly superseding your Irish folk as household servants, and almost all the waiters at the hotels, and men servants in private houses, and coachmen of private carriages are coloured people. As a rule, they are much less addicted to drink than the white population, either native or foreign, here; they are less insolent than the Irish, and less insubordinate than the Americans, and they are (as old President Quincey of Massachusetts said) the only well-bred people now remaining in the country. Their manners are remarkably good, gentle, quiet, and respectful, a result, partly perhaps of slavery, and partly of their indolent Southern blood, in which there is no tendency whatever to habitual harshness, though there may be, on provocation, to sudden violence.

I quite endorse Froude's statement with regard to

the total absence of devotion to public affairs among Americans; that is to say, the best class of Americans. Of course any crisis (as their civil war abundantly demonstrated) brings out with overwhelming force the latent patriotism, which is by no means wanting in Americans; but, except in extraordinary circumstances, the well-educated and refined men decline interesting themselves or taking any part whatever in the management of public affairs. Their own private interests are thoroughly well protected by the laws of the country; their own private concerns absorb all their attention and all their energy. They would have to resign the engrossing pursuit of indefinite wealth, for a settled small stipend as members of congress, if they adopted the government of the country as their business; and they are quite content to give that over to a class of men whose intellectual qualities and general capacity, is at once stamped as of an inferior order, by their being what is technically called " politicians "—a term which in this country not unfrequently means a low, ignorant, unprincipled man, who, being quite unequal to the successful management of his own private affairs, undertakes those of the nation.

The great motive-power of the country, the popular will, upholds this class of representatives as *good enough* for the work they have to do; and the large freedom of the institutions, the absence of all partial or vexatious legislative pressure, upon any portion of the community, the general liberty, and the preponderating general prosperity, satisfy the great mass of the people, who, intelligent as they are, have no special admiration for ability in high places, and would a great

deal rather have their public work done by men
" no better than themselves," in which particular lies
one of the main differences between Americans and
Englishmen.

Our people are essentially aristocratic, and like
gentlemen for leaders ; here, they do not want any
leaders at all, and wish the public service to be discharged by men who are their paid servants, for whom
they have no sort of respect or reverence, but whose
business they conceive it to be so to manage the
" machine " of the government, as to get along without
let, hindrance, or impediment to the private affairs and
interests of the individual citizens.*

There are no men of leisure, the men of wealth are
all money-makers, devoted to that supreme "industry;"
the gentlemen (of whom there is no class) are professional men—lawyers, physicians, bankers, merchants,
with a sufficiently thorough knowledge of their own
peculiar business, and a superficial smattering of
general non-technical education ; and they keep
absolutely aloof from politics and politicians, as they
would keep aloof from dirty work and dirty people.

I cannot tell you what the precise salary paid to
the members of congress is; but it is a fixed sum for
the session (I think a thousand dollars, two hundred
pounds) and their travelling expenses to and from
Washington. There is no such thing as any special

---

* President Lincoln, among whose other admirable qualities
was a great natural fund of humour, wearied out on one occasion
in the midst of his terrible responsibilities during the war by
the impertinent suggestions of an interviewer, at length said,
"Perhaps, sir, you would like to drive this *machine* yourself."

training for a diplomatic career, there is no such thing as a school of diplomacy or a diplomatic career, properly so called. A man is taken from his practice at the bar, or his professorship in a college, or even his practice as a physician (Dr. Rush of Philadelphia was an instance of this), and is sent to represent his country to a foreign court, sometimes without even a knowledge of the French language, the universal language of European diplomacy. I was myself acquainted with a comical instance of the disregard of any such considerations on the part of one of the presidents of the United States. A gentleman having been recommended to Mr. Buchanan as eminently fitted to fill the post of Minister to Spain, because, to all other requisite qualities for the position he added that of understanding and speaking Spanish, the President's sole reply was, "Oh! that is too damned aristocratic!" and another candidate for the office was named, who, it must be supposed, was not disqualified for it by any superfluous acquaintance with the Spanish language.*

I never hear any conversation on politics, and never see any male society, or indeed any society whatever; Dr. W—— comes to see me occasionally of an evening, but by no means frequently, and never mentions public affairs at all. I have only seen him four times in the last past six weeks, and two of those

* I have more than once heard the opinion in the United States that accredited envoys or ministers from them to foreign countries were a superfluous expenditure of the public money, and that all their duties would be quite satisfactorily discharged by the officials of the various American consulates.

were evening visits, when he took tea and played picquet with me. . . . I congratulate Edward [Colonel Taylor, who was Tory Whip of the House] on the success of his party; but hope he will not "whip" himself to death.

1812, *Rittenhouse Square, Saturday, February 28th*, 1874.

It may be as you say, that my intense love of the beauty of nature and passionate enjoyment of it, has been what has preserved for me sweet, and preserved me from bitter, past impressions. At this present hour, the fretwork of brown-red budding branches of the trees in the square where I live, like sprays of coral against the blue sky, every now and then gives me a thrill of ecstatic pleasure, and the clouds at sunset, as I sit watching them evening after evening, fill my eyes with tears and my soul with gratitude to God, that I am allowed to see such sights; and I often exclaim aloud, alone as I am, at the beauty of the heavens.

The friend who gives me the books to read that you have been reading is a lady who, a good many years ago, was seized with a sort of unreasoning and unreasonable admiration for me, which she has contrived to preserve in spite of a very considerable degree of intercourse between us, and her attainment of what should be years of discretion and discernment. I respect and like her very much; she is very intelligent, with a keen active mind, which she stimulates with constant and various reading. 1 once showed you one of her letters, which gave you, I remember, at the time, a very pleasant and favourable impression of her.

My poor black man-servant has hitherto kept his pledge, and I am beginning to rejoice in trembling, with the hope that his coming into my service may have been the means of saving him from ruin in mind, body, and estate.

1812, *Rittenhouse Square, Monday, March 9th*, 1874.

MY DEAREST H———,

. . . I shall make another attempt to get the *Edinburgh* you wish me to read, through the bookseller who, instead of the last *Quarterly*, got the last October number from New York for me, and made me pay for doing so. He is the best agent, nevertheless, for procuring books in the city, and this is the sort of result one may expect from giving him any commission.

You know that I have read Mill's autobiography itself, so that I know what he has chosen to tell of himself, without depending for that knowledge upon the extracts and compressions of reviews. One of the mistakes in his singular moral and mental training appears to me to have been the entire absence of any elevated female influence. . . .

F——— writes in delight of the sunny warmth of the weather in Georgia, of the multitude of singing birds, and the abundance of exquisite flowers now in blossom, and says that in point of climate and soil the place is a perfect paradise. Of the state and prospects of the plantation, I am sorry to say she writes less hopefully and cheerfully.

Two of the men whom they took out with them in the autumn from England have run off, in order to avoid the obligation they bound themselves to of sending their wives half their wages. They can, wherever they choose to go, get the same weekly payment they received from Mr. L——, without any diminution of it for their wives, of whose existence, of course, nobody else with whom they took employment would ever know anything. The men were not Stoneleigh men; but the circumstance has distressed and annoyed Mr. L—— very much. The poor deserted women will, of course, come upon their parish at home for support. I believe Englishmen of the lower classes frequently come over here for the purpose of getting rid of their wives and families, who consequently, fall upon public charity for their maintenance.

F——, in her yesterday's letter, speaks also of a large defection among their negro labourers, under the influence and instigation of two worthless fellows, who had to be dismissed for idleness and insubordination; and who, being rather above the others in quickness and intelligence, have drawn after them a number of the "hands." A neighbouring planter has procured a force of thirty Chinamen—an experiment, the result of which is being watched with extreme anxiety, as unless some method can be found of obtaining supplies of labourers to work the estates, the rapid defection of the negroes, and their preference for a precarious subsistence upon mere jobs of work, to the steady cultivation and industry necessary for the rice crop, will, I should fear, before long compel all the owners and planters of that region to abandon any hope of successfully working their plantations.

For my own part, I am not surprised at this aspect

of the present or prospect for the future. I have never been able to believe in any return of prosperity for any part of the southern country till the whole generation of former planters and slaves had died out. There must be almost a new heaven and a new earth throughout the whole of that land before it can recover from the leprosy in which it has been steeped for nearly a hundred years. Its moral, social, and political condition now is one of such corruption that decay and dissolution must, I believe, do their utmost work of destruction before the first real vital breath of resurrection or renewed life can stir there. Of course I hoped, but never quite believed, in the success of the first experiment of freedom, though all my instinctive and rational faith in God's laws and government was against such expectation. Can you reflect upon the condition of that plantation, as it was within my experience, and think it reasonable to imagine that the sudden abolition of slavery, by the means of the war and the President's proclamation, could cancel the action of all the previous influences that had reigned for a hundred years upon the place and people ?

While I have been writing the last sentence I have seen something that I think worth telling you. A wretched looking girl, evidently a beggar, has just emptied out upon the pavement, by the square railings opposite my window, about a dozen large pieces of bread from a basket, and run off, leaving them there. She is a member no doubt of a whole army of beggars who now infest this city, going from house to house carrying baskets, with piteous stories of starvation, and receiving money and food, bread and meat, from charitable persons.   How little of real starvation exists in their case, or indeed at all, even in the poorest class of the community, is proved by the fact that they constantly throw away the food they have thus received, and nothing is commoner then to see in the gutters and on the pavements great slices of bread and butter and quarter and half loaves of bread.   A small street vagabond has just stopped to examine these fragments of food, and amused himself with kicking them hither and thither, finally stamping upon and grinding several of them to powder.   The birds of the square are already making their profit by them.

My poor coloured man-servant is behaving very steadily and keeping his pledge hitherto unbroken. Of course I lock up every drop of wine and beer with the greatest care, and cannot help hoping that his coming into my service may be the means of rescuing him and his family from the ruin into which his drunkenness would probably have plunged them all; it would be a great delight to me if it should prove so. . . . I am sorry to hear of the destruction of Lord Cadogan's property in the burning of the Pantechnicon. I am afraid my friend Lady Monson had things (pictures and furniture) there.

1812, *Rittenhouse Square, Saturday, March 21st,* 1874.

My dearest H——,

You ask me questions, which I am by no means capable of answering, with regard to the condition of politics here and the government of the country.   Before the war, the Southern slave-holders

were undoubtedly the most influential politicians in
the United States.   Whether as great landowners
their position was more favourable for the formation
of political capacity than that of the hard-working
Northern men of business I do not know; but the
Democratic party, which the war all but annihilated,
was formed in the South, and was led and supported
by Southern statesmen, who controlled the whole
government of the country, with the view of upholding their own peculiar institution of slavery, until the
West and the North threw off their despotism (for it
was that in effect), and the war destroyed, for the
time being, all Southern influence in the councils and
government of the country.   Since its termination,
the South has been politically annihilated; the slave-
holders are gone, and no class of men has come forward
to represent in any way their influence.   A territorial
aristocracy, of course, always has some good elements
out of which to make leaders and governors, and the
power and capacity of the planters (though not their
way of applying them), as efficient political men and
statesmen of ability, are a great loss in the working
of the government.   The freeing the blacks was a
mere *consequence* of the war, and cannot in any way
account for the present low average of the men who
constitute congress, except as the sweeping away of
the Southern slaveholders abolished a class of men
who, for various reasons, were especially adapted to
political life.   The great difficulty here at the north
is, that men of character and ability cannot afford to
sacrifice their personal interests to becoming working
politicians; and those who do the business of the

State are, as a rule, inferior in honesty and capacity
to the great majority of the people whom they represent
(or, I should say, *mis*represent) and rule. It is a most
extraordinary state of things, of which it is difficult
to see the remedy or foresee the result. The scandalous
dishonesty and incapacity of the present men in
power, however, is making the whole country restive
under a sense of disgrace; but, unfortunately (I cannot
say, fortunately), the prosperity of the country is such
that the misgovernment and abuses do not press
sufficiently hard upon any large body of men to make
ardent reformers of them. A pure patriot may lead a
charge against a corrupt government for righteousness' sake; but his followers must be people who
have a grievance and a gain to spur them on. Here
the pure patriot, who could spare the time to lead a
crusade against the government, would be difficult,
and his followers impossible, to find; for the grievances
and the gains do not come home sufficiently to the
business and bosoms of any sufficiently large mass of
people to give rise to any effectual action of reform.
The bulk of the people are too well off to care how
bad their government is. Heavy as the taxation is,
they are able to bear it, and corrupt and degraded as
the present result of the system is, in many respects, it
is always in the immediate power of the people to
make a change when their "machinery" doesn't work
to their satisfaction. Of course the higher-minded
and better-educated people are neither pleased with
nor proud of their government just now; but the
"majority" is not a *nice* creature, and it, apparently,
is contented. With time, things will mend, and the

country, by dint of its material circumstances and its
institutions (mal-administered as they are), is wonderfully prosperous and fortunate in its conditions.

It is not patriotism, but the grossest ignorance and
selfishness, that opposes free trade in America; but by
degrees the advantages of it are beginning to dawn
upon men's minds, though the convincing people of a
future gain, in the face of an immediate loss, is a
difficult process. After all, England was protectionist,
within my recollection; and nothing seems stranger
then the delusions of other people, when they have
ceased to be our own.

I never thought the Southerners *gentlemen* in
contradistinction to the Northerners; they were
aristocrats, men of comparative leisure, by position,
landowners and slaveholders, but certainly not for
any of those reasons necessarily *gentlemen*. I know
nothing whatever of either their condition or that of
their former dependents now. Both, I imagine, are
miserably abiding, and must long continue to abide,
the deplorable results of their former mutually baneful
relation. . . . You ask how I occupy my evenings.
With the same invariable regularity which you know
governs all my habits. I play at Patience from after
dinner till tea-time, that is, for about an hour (I dine
at six at this time of the year), and I knit flannel
shirts for Ellen for next winter, or a shawl like yours
for M——, or a coverlet for F——'s expected baby,
till ten o'clock, when my man-servant, who has a home
and family of his own, comes and puts out the gas,
shuts up the house, and departs, and I go up to my
bedroom, where I read for about an hour before going

to bed. I do not like spending my evenings alone, and hoped I might have secured some society by announcing that I was always at home and glad to see my friends in the evening; but I have had neither many nor frequent visitors. Perhaps I could not expect it. I know little of Philadelphia or its society, and have grown more and more *English* in contradistinction to American as I have grown older.* One of my fellow-residents in the square, a lady, my next-door neighbour, has paid me one morning visit, for which favour I was very grateful to her. She was so handsome, both in face and figure, however, that I found it difficult to answer her amiable commonplaces with propriety, and without breaking out into the Italian couplet—

> "O bella Venere che sola sei
> Piacer degli uomini e degli Dei!"

which I do not think she would have understood. The same effect was always produced on me by a beautiful north-country Englishwoman, whom I never

* My friend Lady Georgiana Gray told me that after the death of her father a similar disappointment attended her mother's and her own efforts to secure a familiar informal evening society. This, with their fine house in Eaton Square, and its political and social traditions and friendly intimacy with all the remarkable and distinguished members of the English society of that day, seems strange; but the intimate, easy, constant intercourse of a French *salon* is not to be obtained in England, the anti-social temper and formal habits of our people being ill adapted to it. Lady Holland and the Misses Berry were the only persons I have ever known who were able to obtain, without special invitation, informal evening gatherings at their houses.

could listen to for looking at. This, however, was
not so inconvenient as the beauty of Mrs. H——,
one of whose admirers assured me that it took his
breath away whenever she came into the room; he
was not in love with her either. . . .

Going out at night here in winter is hardly fit for
elderly people. The carriages you hire do not come
when they are ordered, either to take you or to fetch
you away; they constantly refuse to put you down
or take you up at the house where you spend your
evening, but compel you to walk through pelting
rain and snow, over a foot deep, because they will not
or cannot draw up to the pavement or make proper
room for each other in due succession.

God bless you, dearest H——. I answer all you
ask as well as I can, and am ever, as ever,

FANNY.

1812, *Rittenhouse Square, Good Friday, April 3rd,* 1874.

MY DEAREST H——,

I not only am not likely to prefer Home
Rule in Ireland to Colonel Taylor's Conservatism, but
have a general idea that Irish rule at home, or abroad,
is very nearly synonymous with *no* rule or *misrule.*
Oh! if you could have heard the account given me
this morning by the poor matron of a children's
hospital of her Irish "help"—that is, the eleven
hindrances (maid-servants) under her immediate control (*un*control)—you certainly would have wondered,
as I often do here, whether the Irish alphabet and
multiplication table are the same as those used any-

where else in the world; they seem so incapable of
any but what I think must be called Irish conclusions,
i.e. confusions.

I thought Edward Taylor was secure of his seat,
and was sorry since to hear that he had had to contest
it. I shall be anxious about the result, and anxious,
too, about all the exertion and worry he must go
through. I wish it well over for your sake.

Surely the political progress of England and
Ireland must be very manifest when the speeches of
such a Tory as your nephew remind you of the Whig
speeches of former days. . . .

The plantation is not doing well; the difficulty of
obtaining steady labour—such as the raising of any
crops, but more than any other rice crops, demand—is
becoming so great, as to make it almost doubtful
whether the proprietors of such estates must not give
up the attempt altogether. The negroes are gradually
leaving the estates, buying morsels of land for themselves, where they knock up miserable shanties, and
do a day's work or a job here and there and now or
then, but entirely decline the settled working by contract for the whole agricultural season, which they
have accepted for the last year or two since the war.
One of the planters in the neighbourhood of Butler's
Island is employing Chinese labourers, and F——
writes thus about them: " Mr. B—— has brought his
Chinamen over to thresh out some seed rice at our
mill, and I went down to see them yesterday. They
certainly are not a pretty race, and, to me, are far
more repulsive than the negroes; they have such
low, cunning, ignoble countenances. Nevertheless, I

should not be sorry to see about a hundred of them on this place, working, for work they will, and do.* . . .

The exertion of going out in the evening is a very great one to me. I dread the inclement weather, the extravagant carriage hire, and the intolerable insolence of the drivers, who set you down before a snow-heap, or six yards from the door you are going to in a pouring rain, because some "gentleman" of their fraternity in front of you refuses to move on and let you draw up.

My poor man-servant continues to be quite steady and sober, and I have every reason to rejoice that he does so, as Hancock (a former servant), whose state of health is very miserable, has made up his mind not to risk coming over to this country, and I have no further hopes of his services.

I remember the Mr. Parnell who is now opposing Edward's election coming out to America a great many years ago, with Lord Powerscourt, then a huge big boy, with a pretty girl's face. I recollect, too, hearing soon after of Mr. Parnell's marriage to Com-

---

* Of all the "men of colour" that I have seen, the negroes, in spite of their greatest ugliness, have to me by far the best and least repulsive countenances. They have a kindly, merry, frank, and simple expression of face which answers to their general characteristics ; while the Hindoos, Red Indians, and Chinese that I have seen have had something sinister, ferocious, or base in their countenance which inspired distrust, fear, or disgust. Even the mulattoes, though far less dusky and thick-featured than the negroes, and sometimes indeed eminently handsome, have (morally speaking) worse faces than their full black-blooded kinsfolk.

modore Stewart's daughter (he was a naval, I think, and not a military, officer).

Young Mr. Furness, the son of my dear and venerated spiritual pastor and master, the editor of Shakespeare, comes occasionally with his wife and passes an evening with me. I was so much pleased with the enthusiastic devotion to his laborious task of his Variorum Shakespeare that I gave him the pair of Shakespeare's gloves Cecilia Combe left me in her will, and which had come to her mother, Mrs. Siddons, from Mrs. Garrick. I also gave him a pretty drawing of myself, while I was reading, by the daughter of Richard Lane, the artist, my father's intimate friend.

That precious bequest of Shakespeare's gloves reached me one evening while I was giving a reading in Boston, and occasioned me such an emotion of delight and surprise that one of the few times when I made blunders in my text was when I resumed my reading after finding them in the room to which I retired for rest in the middle of my performance. My Boston audience were my friends; and I think if I had told them the cause of the mistakes I made, when I resumed my seat and my book, they would have sympathized with and pardoned me. Perhaps they would have liked me to show them the gloves, which I never showed to any American that he did not directly put his hand into one of them.

The one exception to this was my dear and reverend Dr. Furness, who hardly seemed to dare to touch them; but "reverence, the angel of this world," had blessed him with its influence. To my great dis-

may, Horace Furness and his wife had a bracelet made
for me after this—from some lines of Shakespeare :

" Bands of straw with ivy buds,
    Fastened with amber and coral studs "

—and sent it me, and I, who, you know, have an
absolute horror of presents, refused it; in spite of
which brutality of mine, they have always been very
good and kind to me, and still come and see me, and
send me vegetables and forced strawberries and mush-
rooms from their hothouses, which I have neither the
heart nor the stomach to refuse.   The other evening,
when they came to see me, they brought me a beautiful salutation lily, which is still perfuming my room
and delighting my eyes.

I have no idea what your prices in Dublin for the
necessaries of life are, but here everything is ex-
orbitant.   We pay thirty-two shillings a ton for the
commonest kind of coal, and three pounds a cord for
wood for the one grate in the house where I burn it—
which is in my dressing-room, and has andirons—in
what is called a Franklin stove.   My tea costs seven
shillings a pound, and that which they drink in the
kitchen four shillings, and so on with every item of
household expenditure ; in spite of which, the wife of
the gardener at Butler Place comes into town and
visits Ellen, with her little girl dressed up in white
Marseilles piqué, all trimmed with needlework, and a
broad sash of rich sky-blue silk, and ribbons in her
hair to match, fit for a duke's daughter.

I hear nothing at all of the Woman's Right question
in this country.   Fanny Cobbe wrote me word, that

the new state of things in England was favourable to
it, and spoke of how many votes they hoped to get in
the new Parliament in favour of woman's suffrage. I
have no doubt that women, both here and in England,
will eventually obtain the right to vote, if they persist
in demanding it; and probably, by slow degrees, what
I covet more for them, a better, perhaps even a
tolerably good, education. Fanny Cobbe always seems
to me to be misled by the very amiable modesty of
supposing that other women are her equals, her intellectual and moral peers; and I believe the women
she talks to are conceited enough to take her at her
word.

I divide my evening between Patience and knitting,
and having done so until ten o'clock, read for about
an hour before going to bed; but I am terribly afraid
of using up my remains of eyesight.

1812, *Rittenhouse Square, Easter Sunday, April 5th,* 1874.

My dearest H——,

You ask me if my man-servant is a thorough-
bred negro or a mulatto, and I find it difficult to say,
because, though his skin is quite black, and his hair
quite woolly, his features are not exactly of the usual
negro type. His face is rather pleasing, both in form
and expression, and his head, though small, is well
shaped and proportioned. The different African tribes,
though resembling each other in the colour of their
skin, and the quality of their hair, differ very much
in figure and features, some of the Abyssinians being
really fine and handsome men, while the more southern
people are hideous, and certainly almost as like

monkeys as men. It seems to me there has been no
lack of endeavour to Christianize the negroes (to some
extent) both on the part of Protestants and Catholics
in the South.   At the same time, as long as slavery
lasted, the planters reserved the right of enlightening
their slaves to themselves, and were extremely jealous
and afraid, naturally enough, of all influence from
without in that respect.   But since the war the slaves
have become voters, and have therefore acquired a
political value as partisans, and an influence over
them may be turned henceforward to account in
all election questions, especially as there are some
portions of the South where they overnumber the
whites, and where they will be a decided power in
the hands of whatever political party acquires power
over them. The Roman Catholic priests perceived
this immediately, and are working, not alone in the
South, but all over the country, to make converts
among them, and to bring them—not only as members
of the Church, Christians, but as members of the
State, voters—under papal dominion ; and if (as they
are labouring to accomplish, and are beginning to
succeed in accomplishing) the race hatred between
the blacks and Irish, gives way under the influence of
the religious bond of a common faith, the Roman
Catholics in this country will have a formidable
political power by-and-by with which to oppose the
native American and imported German Protestant
party.

It is all extremely curious and interesting, especially the action of Roman Catholicism, in this wide
new field of circumstance, and in direct fundamental

opposition to the democratic spirit of the institutions and people of America. *Qui vivra verra!* . . .

I see my friend M——, on an average, about twice a week; she generally comes into town one day on business of some sort or another, and pays me a visit, and I generally go out to Champlost one day in the seven, after breakfast, and stay with her until about four o'clock.

The livery-stable keeper from whom I get my carriage, for the purpose of driving to Champlost, has now raised his price to *two guineas* (the distance is only seven miles), and this will compel me to take to the railroad to visit M——, which involves about half an hour's journey through the streets of Philadelphia, on tramways, in horse-cars, crowded with people standing up in them as well as sitting literally on each others' knees, with men chewing and spitting tobacco round one's petticoats, and every imaginable inconvenience and annoyance.* . . .

I am very glad your nephew has got his seat, which seems to me so properly belonging to him that any attempt to dispute it strikes me as a positive *impertinence.*

* There appears to be no established limit to the number of passengers *accommodated* in these public conveyances. Not only do they sit upon and be sat upon by their fellow-travellers with perfect resignation, but leather straps are fastened all along the top of the "car," as they call the carriages, to support and sustain as many who are *standers* in the vehicle, and protect the *sitters* from being annihilated by their falling on them.

1812, *Rittenhouse Square, Monday, April 20th*, 1874.

MY DEAREST H——,

The agent has just come up from the plantation to visit his family, who reside in Philadelphia.
The account he gives of the prospects of the estate is,
I am sorry to say, not encouraging; and I cannot but
think that another year's experience may convince
the proprietors of the hopelessness of persisting in its
cultivation.   At the same time the property will, I
fear, hang round its owners' necks like a millstone,
for there is no chance at present, at any rate, of their
being able either to sell or to let it. . . .

Your suggestions with regard to my evening
society make me smile; I am much too bad a whist-
player to venture to ask men to come to my house
for the purpose of playing with me.   I have no intimate men friends whom I could so invite, and there
is almost an insuperable difficulty, in that the men
here are all very hard workers, who prefer sitting at
home in their slippers and smoking, when their day's
work is done, to going anywhere to encounter the
inevitable restraints of society.   Another difficulty in
giving invitations for the evening here, is that you
ought to provide hot supper (stewed oysters at least)
and champagne for such of your guests as dine in the
middle of the day, or who, dining later, still keep up
the practice of eating and drinking more than mere
tea and bread and butter by way of final repast.   The
mere cost of living is such, that I avoid the slightest
unnecessary expense in my housekeeping, and the
incompetency and unreliableness of every member of
my household, makes me shun the least additional

demand upon their inefficiency, which is sure to end in annoyance and mortification to myself, and extra trouble, worry, and fatigue to my poor Ellen. But there is no use in contemplating how things might have been otherwise than they have been, and are. I have laboured under a heavy sense of depression the whole winter, and a disinclination to make the slightest exertion, which occasionally makes the ordering of my own meals more trouble than eating is worth, so that I really have not taken any pains to achieve anything different from the life I have led, and which I am therefore not in the least inclined or entitled to complain of.

I am just now obliged to inhabit my dining-room all day long, where I have the disagreeable and, I believe, deleterious company of an anthracite coal fire; the furnace flues are all out of order in the drawing-rooms, and instead of the warm air which they should emit, send forth nothing but smoke, bitter cold blasts, and foul poisonous gases. My landlord must be an insolvent bankrupt, I should think, from the incessant stream of his creditors that has besieged his house ever since I have been in it. The very day of my arrival I found a grim official standing guard over the gas-meter, who, holding forth to me an unpaid bill of Mr. A——'s, told me he was sent by the gas company to obtain payment of the bill or cut off my supply of light. I amused myself, rather wickedly, with urging upon this poor man the universal courtesy of his countrymen towards women, of which I told him I had heard such honourable mention in England, my own country. The poor fellow

looked at his bill, and looked at me, and then desperately exclaiming, "I am an *amployee* (with an *a* and
three *e*'s) of the gas company," rushed frantically from
the premises. The other day a sheriff's notice was
served on the furniture, forbidding the removal of it;
so to ask my landlord to repair his furnace would be
quite hopeless, and I will not touch it myself, partly
for fear of incurring liabilities of all sorts, and partly
because the premises are in such a state of dilapidation that to undertake any repairs would, I should
think, involve the necessity or the risk of pulling the
house down.

We are now having heavy rains, which are giving
everybody violent colds and sore throats, and I am
moreover enjoying sciatic rheumatism, or rheumatic
sciatica, which affects my whole left leg, from the hip-
joint to the heel; it is not *quite* intolerable, but quite
bad enough to be very disagreeable. When the warm
weather comes, I suppose it will go; meantime, I grin
and bear it. . . . I believe women, at present, have no
political rights in the United States, any more than
in England. My impression is, that in very early
times of the republic, the state laws of New Jersey
(you know the several states have all their own
peculiar laws) allowed women to be voters. Whether
the privilege has since been taken from them or not
I do not know; but I never heard of their claiming
the exercise of it. Now, however, I imagine several
of the states may take measures for allowing the
suffrage to women; and I dare say they will obtain
it, if they choose to do so, all over the country, where
certainly the most curious anomalies exist, with regard

to large bodies of (so-called) citizens of the United States.

The negroes are now all exalted to that dignity, and vote accordingly ; moreover, the negroes are at this moment sitting as members of the state legislature of South Carolina : in spite of which, my man-servant, a very decent-looking, respectably dressed individual, was not allowed here to purchase a ticket for any part of the theatre to which I went the other night, and was turned from the door with the announcement that *people of colour* were not admitted even to the gallery there. This man votes, and is to all intents and purposes politically, though not socially, a citizen of the United States.

The present attitude of the government, and aspect of public affairs in this country, is afflicting enough in all conscience to every one interested in it. I am grieved, indignant, and ashamed, at the conduct and character of the present administration, but have not lost my faith in the fundamental principles of right, truth, and justice. The future of this country is an enormous problem for any one to guess at; its condition in many respects, at present, is lamentable and disgraceful.

Good-bye, my dearest H——. I am almost beginning to think of next year, when I hope to return to England and dream of the possibility of seeing you again.

Ever, as ever, yours,
FANNY.

1812, *Rittenhouse Square, Monday, April 27th,* 1874.

MY BELOVED H——,

    . . . I had a letter the day before yesterday from F——, announcing themselves for the eleventh of next month, at which I rejoice greatly; they have left the rice plantation for the seaside on St. Simon's, where salt-water baths and sea air are giving her strength for her journey. . . . Our spring is extremely cold, backward, and ungenial. The winter was unusually mild and fine; but the whole of this month has been stormy and wet, and the vegetation is so backward that there is not a single leaf out yet on the trees in the square before my window. The cold and damp have been such, that a perfect epidemic of influenza has pervaded the city, and measles and scarlet fever have been unusually prevalent. I do not like this sort of codicil tacked on to the winter; but really dread the intense heat of the summer so much more than any degree of cold, that every day that delays the summer is clear gain to me. My dear Ellen, after whom you so kindly ask, has been very unwell indeed, with the same miserable influenza from which I am suffering; but she is the bravest and least selfish creature I ever saw, and has never given way or absolutely laid up, because my whole house depends upon her, and if she is disabled, complete confusion in every department must ensue. She has been, and is, invaluable to me in her courage and affectionate devotion.

My negro man-servant has left me. I am afraid he found it impossible to endure the strain of enforced sobriety any longer. He took an absurd pretext of

offence to give me warning, and has gone off. He has
probably made some arrangement for passing the
summer at the seaside, or at some fashionable watering-place ; where, instead of the seven guineas a month
he got from me, he will be able to get ten, twelve, or
perhaps fourteen ; where he will be comparatively his
own master, and where he can be as idle, drunken,
and worthless as he pleases. More than half the men
and women servants in Philadelphia do this, easily
getting situations with very high wages, in hotels
and boarding-houses at the fashionable summer resorts,
and returning to seek, and find without any difficulty,
situations in the city for the winter. It is a deplorable
system, and destroys everything like steadiness in
service, and the proper relationship of family household life. . . .

Dr. W—— did not accompany S—— in her late
trip to Boston, an arrangement by which I profited,
as he dined frequently with me during her absence,
and took me to the play and opera, and gave me one
or two quiet evenings of piquet playing, which I was
very thankful for, and found very cheerful. I know
nothing whatever about my nephew's marriage; I
have not seen him since he was a schoolboy, and as
his American princess is an entire stranger to me, I
have made no overtures to her royal highness.

I heard yesterday of a New York lady who,
speaking of diminished means and the adjustment of
some family affairs and money disputes among her
relations, said, "she was tolerably well off now, indeed,
she might say quite comfortable; for she could afford
to keep her carriage, and her opera-box, and to give

quiet little dinner-parties (not expensive ones, of course), but that would not cost her more than a thousand dollars—two hundred pounds apiece." What do you think of that by way of diminished means and tolerable comfort? This lady is not a duchess, you know—but plain Mrs. So-and-So, of New York.*

* I have nowhere seen extravagance to compare with that of American women, especially in dress. I knew one woman—I was going to say lady, but I retract that—who, wearing during the summer exquisite linen dresses, made for the American market and light and cool for the heat, never had one washed, but as soon as it had lost its first crisp freshness threw it away. Another lady of the same stamp paid fifteen dollars—three pounds—for the ironing of a flowered dress that was rather tumbled. The head of one of the first lace establishments in Brussels told me that she had received a commission from an American gentleman for a New York lady for a flounce, which was to cost not less per yard than a sum so extravagant, "that," said the great lace-maker, "I did not know how we could contrive to make anything in size, pattern, or fine texture, for which we could honestly demand such a price." The gentleman insisted nevertheless, as that, he said, was the only condition his female friend affixed to the purchase of her flounce, wishing *only that its price should exceed* that of an acquaintance of hers. A New York lady, I am told, has Brussels lace window-curtains in her drawing-room, but whether more expensive than her neighbours, I do not know. On purchasing three yards of lace for the sleeves and body of the dress I wore at my daughter's wedding, and assigning as my reason for not buying more its high price (a guinea a metre), the lady lace-maker said they had sold a whole dressing-gown—peignoir—trimming to a lady recently. "C'était une Americaine," said I. "Oui, madame,' said she.

1812, *Rittenhouse Square, Monday, May 4th*, 1874.

MY BELOVED H——,

I have been anxiously looking for the letter which has just come, bringing me the sad news (which, indeed, I was fully prepared for) of your niece's death. . . . One can hardly help a feeling of regret to think for how brief a space of time she enjoyed her newly found home and its relations, but indeed life might have taken that satisfaction from her, and more painfully than death. Our deplorings and our rejoicings are alike feeble guesses at the significance of events whose real nature is hidden from us. Implicit trust in God's wisdom and goodness, and submissive resignation to His will, are our only rational conditions in this mysterious existence and with our helpless ignorance. . . . I went over, for the first time the other day, the small country house where I am to spend the summer. It is a tiny old Pennsylvania farmhouse, consisting originally of four rooms on each of three storeys, built round one central stack of chimneys, which served all the fireplaces. The stone walls of the house are rough and very thick, the windows narrow and small, and there was formerly neither beauty nor convenience of any sort in the dwelling or any of its surroundings. By dint of alterations and additions, however, a very sufficiently pleasant and commodious residence has now been made out of this original one. The house was built (as all houses of the same date were) as near as possible for convenience to the high-road, a dusty turnpike, formerly the only line of communication between Philadelphia and New York, which divides the Butler Place property in two unequal parts. The situation of the house, in such a position, is the more to be regretted, that at a distance from the highway, further back in the grounds, there is a charming site for a dwelling, looking over sloping fields to the woods of Champlost, and beyond them to a wide expanse of level landscape, where in the purple distance the glimmer of the Delaware may here and there be seen.   My compensation for the proximity to the dusty high-road, which separates me from Butler Place, is that I see, over hedges and through trees, the house where my children were born, my first and only American home.

Though the rooms of the cottage are small, there are enough of them, and all the additions to it—new rooms for the servants, new kitchen, bath-room, etc., are quite comfortable.

The whole, having been newly done up, is bright and clean, and F—— is intent upon putting it all in order for me herself, and deprecates my having anything to do with arranging it, which she wishes to have entirely left to her.   As this is her express desire, I have, of course, acquiesced in it.   She will, I have no doubt, find pleasure in it, will have plenty of help, and not be allowed to over-exert herself.

Our mild winter has been succeeded by a very cold and backward spring.   We have had snow within the last week, heavy chilly rains, and bleak winds, and all vegetation is unusually backward.

York Farm, Branchtown, Philadelphia, Monday,
May 18th, 1874.

This, my dearest H——, is henceforward my
direction. I have not yet removed hither, but I am
leaving this house in the course of this week. F——
and her husband are out at the farm already, in the
midst of as much confusion, preparing to take possession of their house, as I am here preparing to leave
this. It is astonishing what an accumulation of
absurdly useless things civilized human existence
gathers about itself, even in so short a period as six
months, which is all the time I have been here.

I think I must have conveyed to you a worse
impression of this house than it deserved. It is large,
airy, and not ill arranged, terribly out of repair, with
not a sound piece of furniture in all the rooms. Now,
however, that the winter is over, and the misery of
the poisonous smoke from the furnace at an end, the
discomfort is infinitely less, and the advantages of the
position become more apparent. The shade and trees
and grass of the square are pleasant objects from the
front windows, and a magnificient Wisteria Glycene
in full blossom in the back yard is very charming.
The house to which I am going is in some respects an
undesirable summer residence. It stands immediately
upon a dusty road, and has no shade about it; the
rooms are very small and low; and the windows
narrow, admitting but little air. It has one quality
which is good, both for summer and winter—the walls
are very thick. . . . My spirits are the better for the
return of the sweet season of light; and whatever
drawbacks there may be to my present situation, I

am most thankful to be where I am. I am writing to you in the midst of an inconceivable, confused chaos of trunks, boxes, books, pictures, bills, and *bunches of keys*, and feel as if I was incoherent. . . .

A curious circumstance, which only came to my knowledge several years after my residence in this house, in Rittenhouse Square, seems to me to possess sufficiently the qualities of a good ghost story to be worth preserving.

The house was so constructed that a room, half-way between the ground floor and the story immediately above it, commanded the flight of stairs leading to the latter, and the whole landing or passage on which the rooms on that floor opened. These rooms were my bed and dressing-room, the drawing-rooms and dining-room being under them, on the ground floor.

One evening that my maid was sitting in the room from which she could see the whole of the staircase and upper landing, she saw the door of my bedroom open, and an elderly woman in a flannel dressing-gown, with a bonnet on her head, and a candle in her hand, come out, walk the whole length of the passage, and return again into the bedroom, shutting the door after her. My maid knew that I was in the drawing-room below in my usual black velvet evening dress; moreover, the person she had seen bore no resemblance either in figure or face to me, or to any member of my household, which consisted of three young servant women besides herself, and a negro man-servant. My maid was a remarkably courageous and reasonable person, and, though very much startled (for she went directly upstairs and found no one in the rooms), she kept her counsel, and mentioned the circumstance to nobody, though, as she told me afterwards, she was so afraid least I should have a similar visitation, that she was strongly tempted to ask Dr. W——'s advice as to the propriety of mentioning her experience to me. She refrained from doing so, however, and some time after, as she was sitting in the dusk in the same room, the man-servant came in to light the gas and made her start, observing which, he said, "Why, lors, Miss Ellen, you jump as if you had seen a ghost." In spite of her late experience, Ellen very gravely replied, "Non-sense, William, how can you talk such stuff! You don't believe in such things as ghosts, do you?" "Well," he said, "I don't know just so sure what to say to that, seeing it's very well known there was a ghost in this house." "Pshaw!" said Ellen. "Whose ghost?" "Well, poor Mrs. R——'s ghost, it's very well known, walks about this house, and no great wonder either, seeing how miserably she lived and died here." To Ellen's persistent expressions of con-temptuous incredulity, he went on, "Well, Miss Ellen, all I can say is, several girls" (*i.e.* maid-servants) "have left this house on account of it;" and there the con-versation ended. Some days after this, Ellen coming into the drawing-room to speak to me, stopped abruptly at the door, and stood there, having suddenly recognized in a portrait immediately opposite to it, and which was that of the dead mistress of the house, the face of the person she had seen come out of my bedroom. I think this a very tidy ghost story; and

I am bound to add, as a proper commentary on it, that I have never inhabited a house which affected me with a sense of such intolerable melancholy gloominess as this; without any assignable reason whatever, either in its situation or any of its conditions.* My maid, to the present day, persists in every detail (and without the slightest variation) of this experience of hers, absolutely rejecting my explanation of it: that she had heard, without paying any particular attention to it, some talk among the other servants about the ghost in the house, which had remained unconsciously to herself in her memory, and reproduced itself in this morbid nervous effect of her imagination.

York Farm, May 19th, 1874.

MY DEAREST H——,

I am amazed at what you tell me of Harriet Martineau's prolonged literary exertions, I had no idea she was still alive even, much less contributing to the *Daily News.* I had a great admiration for her genius, and during the period of our intercourse we were cordial friends; but it is now many years since I have had any direct communication with her, and indeed do not suppose we could have had any that would have been very satisfactory to me, after her conversion from Christianity to Atkinsonism, which caused me a whole day's bitter crying by the seaside at St. Leonards, for her sake, and that of all those who had believed in her, and still believe in God.

---

* Poor Mrs. R——'s ghost may have been its presiding spirit, without becoming apparent to me, for which I feel very grateful to her.

The return of fine weather is always welcome to me, but you know *darkness* is not an element of the winter here; the brilliant skies that shine over the frozen, snow-covered earth, prevent the cold season from ever being gloomy, however severe it may be; and I remember Dr. Channing, speaking to me of the difference between England and America in this respect, said, "The earth is yours, but the heavens are ours."

My spirits are, I am sorry to say, often depressed, I hope from physical causes; for I should be loth to believe that with so much to be contented with, and thankful for, I was habitually wanting in that cheerfulness which seems to me a natural result of gratitude, and a very decided Christian duty.

York Farm, May 31st, 1874.

My beloved H——,

I am writing to you in a room so darkened that I can hardly see my paper. The terrible summer heat is beginning, and, as in Italy, the only defence against it, or mode of making one's life tolerable, is shutting up the whole house in darkness until the sun sets. Yesterday evening the full moon rose as red as blood, and this morning the whole country was shrouded in dense mist, a sure sign of heavy heat in the day. I wish I was as chilly as you are, how you would enjoy this summer climate!

I left my house in town ten days ago, and spent a week at Champlost, while F—— was fitting and furnishing up this little farmhouse, which she insisted upon getting ready for me instead of my preparing it

for her, which I had been very anxious to do. . . .
Last Thursday, however, the 28th, their birthday,
F—— begged me to come and take up my abode with
her at the farm, and I came over from Champlost
accordingly. The small house is still in much disorder,
but you will readily imagine how happy I was, sitting
down with them both at last, in such perfect peace
and contentment. . . . Although I have been more
than once, in former years, in this small dependency of
Butler Place, I was not familiar with the house, and
find it, though small, convenient and comfortable, and
quite capable of being made a pretty and pleasant
residence.

The house at Butler Place is still full of workmen,
but Dr. W—— and S—— are urging the progress of
matters there as much as they can, and they hope by
the beginning of next month to be able to take
possession. You cannot conceive with what a strange
mixture of feelings (in which, however, satisfaction
and joy and gratitude to God greatly predominated
over all sad memories), I looked at S—— the other
day as she stood on *my* former doorstep, superintending the unloading of cars full of furniture and household goods; it gave me something of the feeling of a
German "Doppel Gänger" to look at her, like an
apparition of my own youth, in that place governing
from the verandah steps the house and domain that
was once my home. . . .

I do not think this house is further from that of
Butler Place than the sides of Fitzwilliam Square
are from each other. The trees I planted along the
low enclosure hedge of Butler Place, thirty years ago,

stretch their branches and throw their shadow half over the road which divides the places—a dusty, much-travelled country road, I am sorry to say, close upon which this house stands, which is the principal dis-advantage of the place. It is a provoking pity that old-fashioned farmer-folk thought only of the con-venience of being as near the highway as possible; for hardly half a quarter of a mile back from where this house stands, is really a charming position for a dwelling, with fine single trees, and very pretty small clumps of wood about it, commanding an extensive distant view, and having in front of it a fine breezy field that slopes to pretty broken ground, and a wooded hollow with a beautiful clear spring at the bottom of it. The large house on the other side, though much too near the road, is not as immediately upon it as this is, but there, too, some charming situa-tions have been neglected, and the dwelling placed in a perfectly uninteresting part of the grounds for the sake of proximity to the turnpike road. . . .

God bless you, dearest H——, think of me here, surrounded indeed with objects full of the associations with my early married life, which I can contemplate at this distance from it with not a taste of bitterness. My existence here just now excites my utmost grati-tude for God's merciful goodness to me; and I can never contrast my past with my present life here without the profoundest thankfulness to the Providence that has permitted such a close to my troubled days. So think of me, my dear friend, and ever, as ever, yours,

FANNY.

York Farm, Tuesday, June 2nd, 1874.

MY DEAREST H——,

I have already written to you one letter from this place, where I took up my abode last week on my children's birthday (you know that they were both born at seven o'clock in the morning on the 28th of May, a striking instance, I think, of my love of system and regularity). We are gradually getting all things to rights in this tiny habitation, which is a small, old-fashioned, but not uncomfortable farm-house, and it begins to look homelike and pretty, with gay chintz furniture and our books and pictures. The rooms are rather undersized for me, who like large ones; but though that is not to my taste, there is quite a sufficient number of them, and when I am alone here, as I shall be through the winter, they will be quite large enough. . . .

America, my dear H——, is a very strange country, and the condition of its coloured population at this moment one of the strangest political pheno-mena. Not only are negroes members of a state legislature in South Carolina, while here in Phila-delphia my coloured man-servant (who is a citizen and has a vote), is turned from the door of the theatre, because he is not white; but at present, in this city, there are coloured men eligible and elected members of the public school boards; while their children are not admitted to the white public schools. This, of course, not by any law, but by the force of custom and prejudice, stronger than any law. Time alone will overcome this; though the removal of all the legal disabilities, which created and prolonged separation between the races, will naturally at first intensify the feeling of repugnance on the part of the whites to any other form of equality between them. The Catholic priests, who are zealously working to obtain influence over the blacks, for the sake of their votes, are doing all in their power to bring them into friendly relations with the Roman Catholic Irish, so as to make one political force of them. Altogether, under Catholic guidance and direction, it is a very curious process to watch.

The President's veto on the Inflation Currency Measure has given immense satisfaction to all (but a few rascals); it has for the time being really saved the nation from enormous disgrace and difficulty.

Last Sunday I went to evening service in the little village church, which is just now without a settled clergyman, and where Mr. L—— has undertaken to officiate while he is here; and reflecting on the merciful Providence which has led me back to this place, under circumstances of so much content and peaceful satisfaction, my heart overflowed with thankfulness.

This morning, dreading the heat after breakfast, I went out at six o'clock, and took a beautiful retriever of Mr. L——'s to swim in a large pond, which is the further boundary of Butler Place. As I walked along the farm road and through the woods to a charming path by the water-side, every step I took reminded me how blessed I was in all my present condition and surroundings, and how infinitely grateful to God I have cause to be.

You would have sympathized with the ecstasy of my companion, a noble beast, with a splendid coat of chestnut hair curling all over him, who leapt from a picturesque piece of rock into fourteen feet of water over and over again, and could hardly be persuaded to come away.

York Farm, Branchtown, Friday, June 14th, 1874.

MY BELOVED H——,

Your letter directed to Philadelphia followed me here, and I think my change of residence has been effected without any interruption to our correspondence. I thought on the arrival of the L——s from the South that he looked thinner, which is probably to be accounted for by hard work—for he has got up early and led a labourer's life upon the plantation, on shorter commons, too, I think, than he has ever been used to—and in the hot southern climate, which even in winter is apt to affect the constitution, and almost always reduces flesh. . . .

The experiment of bringing out English labourers has failed in the instance of all but two of the eight men who, according to the original contract, have worked on the plantation all the winter, and are now engaged in the lumber business in the pine woods near it, till next winter, when they will again return to work on the rice-crop. Two of the men found the life unendurable on the plantation, and ran away, and are still in debt to Mr. L—— for their passage-money, which he had advanced to them. The other four, when he came north, instead of remaining in Georgia cutting timber in the pine woods, insisted upon coming north also, and finding employment here. Of course employment could not be found for them immediately, and the cost of bringing them up from Darien and the cost of maintaining them has been a severe tax upon Mr. L——. Two of them have at length found work with farmers in this neighbourhood, one of them I share the expense of with F——, keeping him to work in this little garden, and do odd jobs here, and one other Dr. W—— is employing temporarily at Butler Place, where there is just now work for a great many hands. But as the wages of common labouring men are from six to eight shillings a day, it is rather an expensive luxury to hire them. . . .

The terms in which this property was settled on me are such that the fact of my having relinquished my whole interest in it avails nothing to enable my children to dispose of it. The entail of the estate is so strict as to make it almost impossible to sell it, and it is one of those legal knots tied originally in the interest of the heirs, for the purpose of securing the property to them, which at present seems to render their dealing with it, for actual purposes, in any way impracticable. . . . The taxes on their landed property here are enormous. . . .

The W——s' are impatiently urging the workmen to conclude the alterations over the way. He comes out from town almost every day, and she once or twice a week; but the house is *not* swept and garnished, and it *is* in possession of many more than seven devils in the shape of carpenters, painters, etc., and I think the most sanguine hope they can entertain is to get possession in a fortnight, and begin furnishing and upholstering after they are in the house. . .

I have the charge of the housekeeping here, or rather Ellen has, who is invaluable, and manages everything for me. F——'s maid is a poor, spiritless, helpless, ailing English girl, who does nothing but cry, and is neither assistance, cheer, comfort, nor company to Ellen. . . . Sometimes I feel a little troubled about my own increased expenditure, and sometimes I am worried overmuch about the details of the housekeeping; for you know, till this winter, I have not kept house for several years, and one loses the habit and faculty for it; oftenest of all, however, I am thankful from the bottom of my heart for the general blessed peace of these, my latter days.

York Farm, Friday, July 4th, 1874.

MY BELOVED H——,

I had a little granddaughter born to me last night in a furious thunderstorm; the "vital spark of heavenly flame," the living soul, came to us between two tremendous flashes of lightning and peals of thunder, and I wonder it was not frightened back into pre-existence. Mother and child are doing well, and, God be praised! we are *all* delivered. . . .

York Farm, Friday, July 10th, 1874.

MY BELOVED H——,

I reproached myself after I had written you despondingly about the southern property, for I am afraid it will have worried you, and I wish I had not written it. I am so very happy in the fortunate issue of my child's confinement and convalescence, and the condition of the fine little baby, that I am less inclined to take gloomy views of other matters than I was when I last wrote to you. . . .

The York Farm, where I am now living, is a small part of the property on the other side of the road, between forty or fifty acres, I think; it is let at a low rent to the man who farms it, and is burdened with an enormous land tax. It would prove, however, very valuable if it were cut up and sold in building lots, for small villa residences, such as are springing up on all sides in this neighbourhood.

F—— and her child are going on admirably well, and everything is prosperous with them, God be thanked, and all is better with me than I could ever have dreamed it possible to be. . . .

My poor little half-witted English cook has been disabled now for nearly three weeks with a felon in her finger. For one week we hired a half savage Irishwoman, at *two guineas a week;* but she, who is the only charwoman to be obtained in this neighbourhood for love or money, prefers drinking by the day and night together, locked up in her cabin, to working, even at the rate of two guineas a week, and so latterly we have done without any additional help, and Ellen has done the greater part of the cooking. We have not, thanks to her admirable energy and management, any great difficulty with our double household; and it is most fortunate that, in spite of her delicate health, she has a decided gift and a decided liking for controlling and managing. In the week presided over by our Irish char lady we had *fifty-three quarts of milk* and *seven quarts of cream,* for which economy I paid her two guineas a week. I cannot afford either piano or carriage, but hire most grudgingly, at a guinea a drive, a job carriage to return my neighbours' visits : in spite of which small annoyances I am most thankful to be here, and as happy as I can be, and infinitely happier than I ever hoped to be. . . .

Our heat is very dreadful—ninety-six and a hundred and one occasionally ; on an average ninety in the day, and as much as eighty-four at ten o'clock at night, three hours after sunset. We had drought nearly the whole month of June, now we are having furious thunderstorms, and heavy rain, but no mitigation of the heat.

York Farm, August 2nd, 1874.

My dearest H——,

I quite agree with you that a woman's nursing her own infant is the right thing both for mother and child, whatever modern theorists may say to the contrary ; indeed, I am by no means charmed with modern theories in these matters, and moreover, for my own part, am of opinion that the year in which a mother holds her baby at her breast and sees it looking up into her eyes is a sufficient compensation even for the most miserable marriage. . . . I am now told, with regard to the scrupulous care with which a woman's diet was formerly regulated, with a view to its effect upon her child, that that is a mere nonsensical superstition, an exploded old woman's fanatical fallacy ; that whatever agrees with the mother is sure to agree with the child, and that a baby is to become inured by experience from the very first to the effect of every variety in its nurse's diet,—to which I can only reply, "it may be so," it was different in my time. Mais nous avons changé tout cela.

I have not been able to afford either a pianoforte or a carriage, so both at home and abroad am rather curtailed of my usual recreations, but mere living here is inordinately expensive. . . .

The season, upon the whole, has not been one of excessive heat—a circumstance for which I cannot be too thankful, for I had looked forward with dismay to the sort of atmosphere I remember enduring here in former years, when during some nights of intolerable heat I walked about the gravel paths of the garden at Butler Place barefooted and in my nightgown, like another Jane Shore; and failing to find anything tolerably cool to put on my bed, I laid upon it a piece of oil-cloth on which I lay down. This house is small, with small rooms and low ceilings, and little narrow windows, of the old-fashioned farmhouse kind. It stands immediately on the road, from which it is entirely unsheltered, receiving all day long the clouds of dust that a six weeks' drought and a dry soil have made all but suffocating. Under these circumstances, I have been thankful enough that the thermometer has not *averaged* higher than ninety.

I am very fairly well, though never free from sciatic rheumatism, either by night or day. Ellen is a good deal worn out, and I shall be glad when her cares and labours and responsibilities become lighter by the reduction of the family. . . .

God bless you, dear H——. If we both live a year longer, I may have the great happiness of seeing you once more, and you will rejoice to hear my voice again, though you will not see me.

Ever, as ever, yours,

FANNY.

York Farm, August 16th, 1874.

MY DEAREST H——,

It may yet be permitted to me to embrace you once more. If I live, I expect to return to England next year, and may perhaps be in Dublin a year from next October. *Keep yourself* for me till then, dear H——. Perhaps, as you say, there are things that one does forget; age has some privileges, together with its many privations, and sorrow loses some of its bitter savour, to the dulled palate that has almost lost the taste of sweetness.

Our baby is to be christened to-day, by her father, in our tiny village church, where he has been kindly doing duty since he came north, in the absence of a regular incumbent, which, for some reason or other, there is not at present. It is only just eight o'clock in the morning, and we have already received, in honour of the occasion, beautiful flowers enough to make a *hay* cock (Irishly speaking).

Thus far, my dearest H——, I wrote before breakfast. An old and attached friend of my children, who was to be the baby's godfather, came out to breakfast with us, so there I stopped. S—— sent her sister a magnificent china bowl full of splendid flowers, all gathered from Butler Place and arranged by herself. The day was a very trying one to me, recalling with acute vividness memories of former days, and render-

ing the church service of my little grandchild's chris-
tening full of conflicting emotions; recollections of
past sorrows, combined with heartfelt thankfulness for
all my present blessings, as I saw the dear father with
his baby in his arms at the font, with its mother kneel-
ing before him, the whole thing was so indescribably
touching to me that I was greatly overcome by it,
I had to entertain a large party at lunch, and was glad
when it was all over, for I was very much worn out.

American women are like French women in several
respects, and do not generally nurse their children.
F——, I am happy to say, does nurse her own baby.

You ask me if I continue to read my *Spectator*,
and what I think of English affairs generally? which
would be a serious question for any one who did
occupy their minds in any such wide field of speculation. I think little or nothing about them, and though
I do read the *Spectator* regularly, I have been much
more interested by the articles on Dr. Carpenter's
psychological work than those which discuss the Tory
Government and Whig opposition proceedings in
Parliament. I have felt interested and sorry for the
predicament in which the poor Labourers Union
terminated. Certain important and radical changes
in the condition of England, such as the disestablish-
ment of the Church and the absolute alteration of the
present system of land proprietorship, I look forward
to as inevitable, sooner or later. I watch the political
movements and measures which affect the present
position of the Church and of the tenure of land, with
as much curiosity and interest as are compatible with
an unswerving conviction of certain unavoidable

results. The separation of Church and State appears to me more imminent than any great immediate change in the system of landownership; but both appear to me infallibly *ordained*. The thing that interests me most in England now is the religious condition of the country, or rather the state of thinking people's minds upon religious subjects. I very often think of this, and am moved even to tears and to prayer by the spiritual distress and mental difficulties and dismay that must cause anguish to many conscientious souls in these days of disturbed faith.

We are followed everywhere by the *Times*, and the *Guardian*, and *Punch*, and the *Illustrated London News*, and innumerable county papers, so that we have piles upon piles of newspapers in every room, and if I am not acquainted with what goes on in my own country, it is certainly not for want of the means of information. . . .

I go on at a steady jog trot pace with my Memoirs, and have arrived at the period of my marriage and the first letters I wrote to you from Butler Place; and it is strange enough to raise my eyes from that record and look across the road to the trees and grass and garden-walks, at the back of that house, opposite to the windows of the room where I am now writing. . . .

Perhaps modern notions may be wiser than the mere animal instincts of a she creature towards her young; especially when these have become partially impaired by civilization, yet I doubt it.

"Great nature is more wise than we."

York Farm, Sunday, September 20th, 1874.

My dearest H——,

My little granddaughter was christened Alice Dudley Leigh. The name of Alice Dudley was agreeable to her father, because it was the name of a certain Alice Leigh of the seventeenth century, who, marrying Robert Dudley, the illegitimate son of Queen Elizabeth's worthless favourite, the Earl of Leicester, was abandoned by her worthless husband, and created Duchess Dudley in her own right, as a sort of acknowledgment of her virtues and charities and manifold good works, among which was the endowing to the vicarage of Stoneleigh with certain benefices, upon the condition that every Whitsunday a commemorative sermon should be preached in her honour by the vicar in Stoneleigh Church. So after this worthy Alice, Duchess Dudley, our baby was christened.

Dr. W—— told F—— that a great many notions upon the subject of nursing were exploded fallacies and old wife's traditions; that whatever agreed with the nurse could not injure her milk or disagree with her baby, and I am bound to confess that this appears agreeable to common sense. . . .

The blackberries in this country are cultivated into almost as good and large garden-fruit as fine mulberries, of which last I have never seen any at all here. . . .

Poor S—— has had a cook for the last three days. How long she will be able to keep her it is impossible to guess, and I live in daily terror of hearing that she is again without a creature to cook a meal for her. I heard the other day of an unfortunate woman who

had had *twenty-three* cooks in ten months. Our friend
Dr. M——, told me that he was lately sent for, by
a female patient of his, whom he found in a miserable
condition of nervous prostration, and asking her what
was the matter, received for reply, " Oh, doctor, *cook's
fever.*" . . .

Oh, my dearest H——, when you ask if M——
could come and stay with me, how little idea you have
or indeed can have of the way in which I live. M——
could and would come and stay with me, no doubt,
if there were any necessity for it; but I should no
more think of asking her to do so than I should
think of asking her unnecessarily to do anything else
perfectly inconvenient and uncomfortable. She has
an ample income—would be a rich woman even in
England—and is able to live upon it in what we
should call, in England, decent comfort and propriety ;
and has a well-kept and comfortable establishment.
To ask her to my small house would be simply to ask
her to inconvenience and discomfort of every sort,
compared with her own establishment. I see her two
or three times every week, and she has begged me,
since my family left me, to go and stay at Champlost ;
but I dare not leave this house in the charge of the
perfectly incompetent and unreliable servants who,
with the exception of Ellen, make up my household ;
and she, being my personal attendant, would of course
go with me to Champlost, if I went there.

[The servants I should have left in my cottage in
America would certainly all have gone out of it, all at
the same time, if it suited them, and all as often as it
suited them, leaving every door, from the cellar to the

garret, the door of the house included, unfastened and
very likely wide open; they would possibly have set fire
to the house by accident, and possibly by accident have
deluged it by turning on the water-pipes and forgetting
to turn them off; they might have committed, from
carelessness, recklessness, and thoughtlessness, any of
the feats of "Clever Alice" in Grimm's charming
story of that name. But they would not have done
what two servants I left in my house in England, one
summer when I went abroad, did, who had let men
into it, during my absence, and were both candidates
for the lying-in hospital. Or two others (one of
whom had lived with me four years), who received
and entertained, during my three months' stay abroad,
gentlemen friends of theirs, who opened my closets
with false keys, and stole and pawned my valuable
miniatures of my father and uncle.

Considerations of compassion, and a desire to
shield from disgrace, and perhaps ruin, some of the
parties implicated in this affair, induced me to refuse
to bring them into court or institute a prosecution,
without which, however, I was warned that I should
not be able to recover my property ; so I sorrowfully
made up my mind to the loss of my miniatures.

Circumstances, however, served me better than
I could have anticipated. A dog's collar was found
among "the things that were found in the drawer of
the cook," belonging to the honest gentleman, her friend,
and which he confessed to have removed from the neck
of a dog that he had stolen and sold. Rather impru-
dently, I think, this honest gentleman had left his
address, to which a legal functionary was despatched,

dog collar in hand. Upon charging the honest gentleman with his breach of the law and the eighth com-
mandment in my house, he denied having ever been
there, or opened a closet, or stolen a miniature; where-
upon the legal functionary, producing the dog collar,
threatened to give him into immediate custody with a
policeman, whom he would instantly call in. The honest
gentleman then altered his story. He *had* slept in my
house, he *had* opened my closet, he *had* stolen my
miniatures, and had pawned them at a certain shop, the
address of which he gave, and whence I rescued them at
a cost of twelve guineas.]

One cannot ask people to live with one when one
is never sure of one's supply of food. Sometimes the
butcher does not come till too late to be of any avail,
sometimes he comes and does not bring what was
ordered; sometimes he comes and instead of what was
ordered brings what suits himself, or what he finds
convenient to bring. About a week ago, in consequence
of such a performance, I had *nothing* for dinner, and
Ellen sent out to an Irishwoman, from whom we sometimes get poultry, and procured a pair of ducks whose
carcases (literally skin and bone) were my whole
supply for two entire days. M—— is a very rich
woman, and sends into town for all her marketing,
having servants to spare for such duty; but under
such liabilities as these of mine, and they are frequent,
one cannot invite one's friends to come and stay
with one. . . .

I shall certainly not get a pianoforte yet; for I am
still under promise to pay two hundred guineas for
my daughters' pictures, which I expect to do, towards

the end of next month, when the portrait which S——
sat for in Boston for her sister will be finished, and
when I shall give S—— one hundred pounds to have
F——'s likeness taken by the same artist, if she wishes
to do so.

The question of a pianoforte is rather a troublesome
one, as my room is too small to hold any but a cottage
piano, and cottage pianos are not to be *hired,* for some
reason or other, but can only be *bought,* and that for
not less than two hundred pounds, and it really does
not seem worth while to go to such a heavy expense in
such a matter. I do miss my poor daily music, but not
enough to make the exertion of going over to S——'s
piano when I want a quarter of an hour's strumming.

York Farm, Branchtown, Philadelphia,
Sunday, October 25th, 1874.

My dearest H——,

You ask how my Memoirs get on. Why, I
creep along with them, and have arrived at our return
to America, after my first visit home with S——. It
amuses and interests me, and gives me an occupation
for part of my time daily, without trying my eyes as
much as the same amount of reading would, or be as
tedious as constant needlework might be.

I believe I told you I had been reading a treatise
by Bossuet, a famous one, on the nature and knowledge
of God and the human soul. I am now reading a
treatise by his rival ecclesiastic, Fenelon, upon the
existence of God. Mr. L—— left these books behind
him here, and as fine samples of French style I find
much pleasure in reading them.

Fanny Cobbe has sent me a *Theological Review* with an article of hers on evangelical religion which I have not yet read, but am about to do so.

Carlyle's "Sartor Resartus" was the first of his books I ever read. I read it when I was a girl of sixteen, at my mother's Weybridge cottage, at the instigation of my brother John, and under the influence of his admiration for it, and was enthusiastic in my approbation of it and knew it almost by heart. Since then I do not think I have read a word of it. It was his first work of any importance, and his first specimen of the curious Anglo-German style which he afterwards adopted almost entirely, and which, being stranger even than the thoughts he expressed in it, increased the general impression of great originality produced by his books. His "French Revolution," seems to me his finest book, but I always regret the mannerism of his style.

I do not speculate much about the condition of the United States. It is in many respects (chiefly that of political morality) very degraded and disgraceful certainly; but Anglo-Saxon people are not apt to endure their abuses beyond remediable point, and, though I am very sorry for, and thoroughly disgusted with, the present condition of things, I neither think it likely to last long or to get much worse.

The antagonism between the blacks and the whites at the South, or rather the "outrages" supposed to be caused by it, are being extremely exaggerated for electioneering purposes, and with a view to bringing General Grant in for a third term of the Presidency, which I sincerely hope will not be accomplished.

Good-bye, my dear. God bless you, my dearest
H——.

Ever, as ever, yours,
FANNY.

York Farm, November 8th, 1874.

MY DEAREST H——,

You ask me if *all* Americans are anxious to
leave the United States. Not *all*, probably, but a
considerable portion of them certainly; and it is not
very surprising that it should be so, considering what
the difficulty of existence is here. To artisans, and
working people of almost any and every description,
the country holds out great advantages; to persons of
fortune, or good settled income, absolutely none whatever. Wealth does less for the comfort and enjoyment
of its possessor here than in any other part of the
world; and merely to be released from the incessant
struggle and torment of housekeeping is a consideration that may well weigh with every woman whose
means will give her freedom from it by going to
Europe. The American women not only find amuse-
ments and enjoyments abroad which they have not at
home, but exemption from intolerable worry which
they have here.

Living in America is so expensive that people
literally save a portion of their income by going out
of this country, so that there is every inducement to
do so. Americans *now* never go to service. When
first I married, in this country they did; but they
have gradually withdrawn before the influx of the
Irish, who have perfectly flooded the United States,

and who alone now supply the domestic service of the
cities, or have done so for many years past. Quite
recently the large German emigration to America has
afforded some little variety of choice; but in the case
of both German and Irish, it appears to be only the
lowest, the most ignorant, and the most incapable
who come to supply the domestic market here. . . .
The cold of last winter did not try us very much; but
it was an exceptionally mild season, and the house I
inhabited, though not thoroughly warmed by its own
furnace, was so in some degree by those of the adjoining houses. York Farm stands high and unsheltered,
and has always been thought a very cold house. This
winter, however, it will have the advantage of a
furnace in the part of the building which has been
added to the old tenement, and I hope we shall not
suffer much from this winter's cold.

I have had no talk with Horace Furness about
"Who wrote Shakespeare?" His labour of love in the
fine Variorum Edition of the Plays he is working at
leaves him no leisure for discussing or considering
that nonsensical question. Indeed, I have had but
little conversation with him, even upon the more
serious aspects of the important task he has undertaken and is fulfilling with such devoted industry.
While I was in town last winter, he came occasionally
to spend an evening with me; but when the warm
weather began, he and his family went out of town,
and, though they are now again in Philadelphia, there
is very little probability of my seeing anything of
him, as the same circumstances that seem to impede
all one's social conditions here militate against one's

keeping up any comfortable intercourse with one's friends, even at this inconsiderable distance from town.

I have no dog, and am in deep mourning for a charming animal which belongs to Mr. L——, and which has been staying with me ever since August, and was sent off to the plantation yesterday with the two Englishmen who have been working here all the summer. He was a large Irish retriever, one of the handsomest beasts I ever saw, with hair curling all over his body, and passing off towards gold on his ears. His eyes are like human eyes, and he was the most sweet-tempered, docile, gentle creature that ever wore the shape of a brute. He has been my inseparable companion ever since his master's departure for the South, and I miss his quiet, affectionate, but most intelligent fellowship extremely, especially as he does not talk.

We have a beautiful cat of half Persian blood, given to me when I last left Lacock Abbey; but she is peculiar and not amiable in her disposition, and, so far from being companionable to me, will never stay in the room with me, if she can possibly get away. She is devoted to Ellen, whom she follows about like a dog, and from whom she will never be separated; but, except the pleasure of admiring her splendid bushy tail, I derive no great satisfaction from her. . . .

Long years ago, without calling human beings "Trinities," I had an idea that they consisted of three different elements—body, mind, and soul—and in my Journal and my letters to you, I constantly speak of these as the *different* component parts of a human being. I have now no such notion. My own nature and that of my fellow-creatures occurs to me only as an inscrutable mystery; but the body seems to me so infinitely the predominant power here, that I think our principal cares, thoughts, attention, and speculation should be directed to understanding (as far as it is possible) that, and the laws of its health and good government. It is all important *here*, for it is through its agency that we think and feel, and no study appears to me comparable in importance to the study of our bodies through the wonderful machinery of which our processes of thought (and therefore of *belief*) are carried on; and the longer I live, the more I am convinced that no subject of investigation is of such vital value to us as that of our physical organization, the difficulty being made so enormous by the non-material results of the material action. I cannot begin to write upon this subject—it is inexhaustible, and my sense of my own dark ignorance too profound —but I have ceased to divide the human creature into three parts. It is *here* a body of *matter*, to which most mysteriously belongs the power of thinking and feeling on *immaterial* subjects. Of more than this I know nothing, and (as you know) never speculate.

York Farm, November 15th, 1874.

Thank you, my dearest H——, for the *Times* containing the notice of Charles Greville's Memoirs. Nothing is more striking to me than the impression of bitterness and cynical ill-nature produced by the book upon all who did not know the author. The article upon it in the *Spectator* spoke with positive authority of his contemptuous dislike of our Royal

Family, and also of his own class, the English aristocracy ; and I find the impression here made by the
book is, that it must have been written by a very ill-
natured man. Now, Charles Greville's character of
universal, social referee, of course could only have
belonged to a person willing, as well as able, to advise
others. Making all allowance for his greed of gossip,
and his morbid curiosity about the personal private
details of everybody's life, concerns, and circumstances,
his readiness to serve and take trouble for people, was
almost proverbial, and though he certainly had not
an exalted opinion of the men and women of his own
world (or any world), I think he was neither a bitter
nor ill-natured person.*

S—— says that if anybody were to set down,
as Charles Greville did, every day all he heard and
knew about people in his own society, the result
would inevitably be such a record of what was base
and bad, and silly and mad, so much inevitably evil
speaking about evil doing in short, as necessarily to
give an impression of ill-nature on the part of the
chronicler.

Henry Reeve, the editor of the *Edinburgh Review*,
who was his very intimate friend, edited the Journal,
and, though I dare say he has exercised some discretion in selecting what he has published from what he
has suppressed, and that, moreover, the present instal-

* But an accurate perception and description of general
humanity is very apt to be characterized, by those who neither
perceive nor describe, as unjustly harsh by those who do ; and
I have heard Thackeray condemned repeatedly as cynical, hard,
bitter—and know that he was one of the tenderest-hearted,
compassionate souls that ever lived.

ment of the record comes no further than 1838, I
have no doubt plenty of people will be hurt, and still
more frightened, by its publication.

[I was well acquainted with Lady Charlotte
Greville, Mr. Charles Greville's mother, and his sister,
Lady Ellesmere, and his brother Henry, long before I
knew him. After having made our acquaintance, he
became one of mine and my sister's most intimate
friends, though never to the same degree as his
brother, to whom he was superior in intellectual, but
inferior in moral, qualities. He was more worldly-
wise than most people, and a clear-sighted and excellent judge of all worldly matters and social relations,
whose opinion and advice was valuable in all questions
relating to them; beyond or above that particular
sphere, perhaps not so good.

He lived for the last years of his life, and died, in
the house of Lord Granville, to which he was often
confined by acute attacks of gout, during which his
friends, male and female, used to visit him there;
sometimes, when his hands were painfully disabled,
writing for him, in which office of amanuensis I one
morning found a very gay and grand duchess employed.
He was very well read, a person of highly cultivated
taste, and a most agreeable and entertaining talker,
especially to those who, like himself, were interested
in personal gossip, which I am not. On my telling
him one day when I had had an inordinate dose of it
from him, that I did not care for it, he exclaimed with
unfeigned amazement, "Good gracious! what do you
care for then?"

On one occasion that I went to see him, when

he was shut up with the gout in his hands and feet, he asked me to open a closet under a book-case, where an immense number of books, evidently manuscripts, were arranged. He told me they were his Memoirs, and upon my asking him if they were to be published, replied, "Not till fifty years after my death; too many people are alive who are mentioned in them to make any earlier publication of them possible." Perhaps Mr. Greville referred only to the entire mass of his Diaries, or he changed his mind, and allowed Mr. Reeve to publish the first volume of them, which appeared but a very few years after his death. He several times discussed the question of the properest person to whom their editorship should be confided, and repeatedly mentioned Mr. Reeve (which seemed to me strange, if he intended the publication to be postponed for fifty years). I suggested his niece's husband, Lord Enfield, but he said he was too young.

Mr. Greville gave me several of the first volumes of his manuscript Diary to read, and I was very much amused to find certain strictures upon the ugliness of my hands and feet, and an indifferent opinion of my merit as an actress, among the earliest entries in his Journal. Moreover, a record of a Sunday dinner at Lansdowne House, where he went expecting to meet my father and myself, his notice of which was, "Charles Kemble came, but not his daughter, Miss Fanny not approving of Sunday society. Methodism behind the scenes!" His having given me these observations upon myself did not surprise me: when he wrote them he did not know

me, and when he knew me he knew how perfectly
indifferent they would be to me. But in the same
volume of his manuscript was an incident of such
atrocious Irish barbarity, that I did not think he
ought to have let me read it, and I was curious to
know if he had done so consciously. I did not like,
however, to challenge him directly upon the subject,
but asked him if he remembered the contents of the
book, and the very uncomplimentary things he had
said of my personal and professional defects? He
seemed quite surprised and very much amused, and
laughed a great deal, saying at the same time that he
had entirely forgotten what he had given me to read,
and adding repeatedly that he must look the whole
Diary over again. Whether he did so or not I do not
know, but some discretionary power was certainly
exercised in the matter by somebody, for neither the
strictures upon my extremities, my acting, nor my
sabbath-keeping appeared in the book, nor the horrible
incident of Irish brutality either.

Mr. Greville gave me his Italian Journal to read,
which I thought pleasant and interesting, though that
he should have hung up a votive silver horseshoe at
one of the famous shrines of the Madonna rather surprised me, as I do not think he believed much in her,
though probably in horseshoes (not silver) more or
less. Whether the offering was for the sake of future
or past successes on the turf, I forget. Upon my
complaining, when I returned his manuscripts to him,
that the people of whom he wrote seemed to me
neither very amiable or respectable, he gave me a
charming pen and ink portrait of that most charming

woman, his friend, Lady Wharncliffe, and another of
Sir James Mackintosh, both of which were warmly
eulogistic and extremely well written.]

The servants in Philadelphia are of the lowest
class of ignorant Irish, having never, before they came
to America, seen the inside of any more civilized house
than their own mud hovels; and immediately find
situations as cooks, or housemaids, or nursemaids (for
all of which they are as well qualified as for coachmen, grooms, or gardeners) at ten shillings a week
(the lowest wages given), and quite as often at fifteen
and twenty. A great many Germans (also of the
lowest class) come; but they have to encounter the
difficulty of not speaking or understanding English,
which of course gives the Irish an advantage over
them. The influx of this sturdy, robust European
flesh and blood tells advantageously on the third
generation of the feebler and less physically healthy
Americans, with whom they intermarry.

[American is the direct descendant of Irish beauty;
the lovely hair, teeth, eyes, and complexion of Erin's
daughters, transplanted across the Atlantic, derive, in
the second or third generation, from change of climate
and diet, and various other favourable influences a
character of refinement (as well as intermarriage with
Americans), which is not Irish; the features become
sharper, the figure lighter, the hands and feet smaller,
and the whole result is that delicate and brilliant
beauty, remarkable alike for elegance of form and
vividness of colour, by which the American women
are distinguished.]

I do not know whether the coloured people are

those you allude to when you ask if a race of half-castes will ever be of any use to themselves or others. There is a very large body of mulattoes employed as servants in Philadelphia, but the difficulty with them is that your whole household must be composed of negroes, if you have any, as the Irish will not live with them; and a poor young coloured lad, who was brought from the South by F——, came over from Butler Place crying, and almost white with indignation, at the insults he had had to endure from S——'s Irish kitchen and housemaids. He was made to *eat by himself*, and not one of the women would make his bed for him.

I am not aware that the whisky *war* has resulted in any permanent good anywhere. In Germantown (our small neighbouring country town), a short time ago, the whole population came to the determination to suppress the greater number of drinking-houses; and it was done by *general consent*, much to the benefit, undoubtedly, of the place and neighbourhood; and this appears to me a pattern for all reforms. . . . My friend M——'s servants (except when in immediate attendance upon her) do pretty much what they please, and nothing else. She pays higher wages than anybody else in this neighbourhood, or in Philadelphia, and yet I have known her for months unable to get a cook that suited her, and for weeks unable to find a decent man-servant. . . .

York Farm, November 29th, 1874.

MY DEAREST H——,

The reckless, unprincipled carelessness prevalent here, about everything, adds to one's anxiety in all matters connected with health. When first Ellen became almost blind, which she did about two months or six weeks ago, she took a quantity of belladonna by the doctor's orders. Some time after that, having sent to the apothecary for a repetition of a certain prescription, she perceived a difference in the taste of it, and upon reference to Dr. W——, who tasted it, he said the apothecary had put more syrup to the quantity of strychnine than he ought in his preparation of the medicine. The phial was taken back to the shop, and returned with a modification that from sweet made the dose bitter, and caused Ellen every morning the most violent retching and intolerable headache for the rest of the day, so possibly the quantity of strychnia may this time have been increased, according to the same apothecary's assistant's judgment by which the previous dose had been modified. . . .

S—— was as fond of her baby as I think she could be of any creature too nearly resembling a mere animal to excite her intellectual interest, which is pretty much the only interest in infants or adults that she seems to me to have. . . .

M——'s is the only establishment, that I know, where some of the servants (her own maid and her maid's sister, who is her housemaid) are Americans. . . .

I do not think the frequent change of President would signify one way or other, if the theory had not grown into a custom, strong as law, that when the

President goes out of office every creature nominated by him, down to village constables and postmasters, goes out of office too. The employments in the President's gifts count by *thousands* throughout the whole country, and of course a new President means so many thousand people struggling to retain, and so many thousand people struggling to obtain office, *i.e.* emolument, that is to me one of the worst features of the whole system, and one of the most fruitful of mischief and political degradation. . . .

The gradual pacification and reorganization of the Southern states questions of internal policy now pressing on the nation, and requiring the utmost wisdom in the head of the government, would tax the capacity of the greatest statesman that ever lived; and the terrible financial disorder by which the whole mercantile and commercial processes of business are affected and disturbed, would prove a labour of almost insuperable difficulty for the greatest financier. General Grant is accused of being indifferent as to the quality of common honesty in the persons he appoints to offices of high importance and responsibility. Being an honest man himself, he probably believes in the honesty of his friends, and supports them with a certain pertinacity which is a characteristic quality of his, better perhaps in the conqueror of the South than the president of the nation. . . .

York Farm, Sunday, December 6th, 1874.

MY DEAREST H——,

  . . . It is not possible for me to feel the slightest interest in the sort of literary feat which I consider writing upon "who wrote Shakespeare ?" to be. I was very intimate with Harness, Milman, Dyce, Collier—all Shakespearian editors, commentators, and scholars—and this absurd theory about Bacon, which was first broached a good many years ago, never obtained credit for a moment with them; nor did they ever entertain for an instant a doubt that the plays attributed to William Shakespeare of Stratford-on-Avon were really written by him. Now I am intimately acquainted and in frequent communication with William Donne, Edward Fitzgerald, and James Spedding, all thorough Shakespeare scholars, and the latter a man who has just published a work upon Bacon, which has been really the labour of his life; none of these men, competent judges of the matter, ever mentions the question of "Who wrote Shakespeare ?" except as a ludicrous thing to be laughed at, and I think they may be trusted to decide whether it is or is not so.

I have a slight feeling of disgust at the attack made thus on the personality of my greatest mental benefactor; and consider the whole thing a misapplication, not to say waste, of time and ingenuity that might be better employed. As I regard the memory of Shakespeare with love, veneration, and gratitude, and am proud and happy to be his countrywoman, considering it among the privileges of my English birth, I resent the endeavour to prove that he deserved none of these feelings, but was a mere literary impostor. I wonder the question had any interest for you, for I should not have supposed you imagined Shakespeare had not written his own plays, Irish though you be. Do you remember the servant's joke in the farce of "High Life Below Stairs," where the cook asks, "Who wrote Shakespeare?" and one of the others answers, with, at any rate, partial plausibility, "Oh! why, Colley Cibber, to be sure!"

I have read Fanny Cobbe's paper in the *Theological Review*, and am in the middle of her preface concerning Mill's posthumous works. The paper on what she calls "Heteropathy" I have also read, and like the essay better than I had expected I should, from a sort of sketch she gave me of its scope and purpose in talking of it one evening before it was written.

The lady you mention as of *Dutch* extraction, would, I imagine, resent any such alteration of her descent, which was that of granddaughter to Alexander Hamilton, the most interesting and remarkable of Washington's contemporaries, one of the really great men of the American Revolution. She was a Miss Mary Hamilton of New York, and married Mr. Schuyler, who *was* of distinguished Dutch extraction. She has been earnest and efficient in much admirable philanthropic work; besides being prominent, not to say predominant, in the successful women's effort for the purchase of Washington's estate and house on the Potomac as a national monument and possession. . . .

The small church of our small village is supplied with an officiating deacon, a gentleman not yet in full orders, who has been appointed to the duty by the bishop of the diocese, and whose ministrations I attend, without however deriving any peculiar benefit, that I am aware of, from his particular share of the service. There really is not a sufficient Episcopalian population here to support a church of that denomination, most of the people residing in the neighbourhood being Quakers, Methodists, or Baptists; and I, who do not belong to either of those religious brotherhoods, but, nevertheless, give a pound towards the maintenance of the church each time I attend service, was more amused than edified at hearing our present worthy "clergyman" class Unitarians and Atheists together in his discourse. . . . Mr. Henry Ward Beecher is so far from suffering any diminution of his popularity as a preacher or lecturer from the defamatory accusations brought against him, that he is now paid double what he formerly received for either preaching or lecturing—the great attraction of his eloquence being enhanced in public estimation by his position as a martyr to an infamous slander, or the hero of a scandalous intrigue. I have been assured that he will be supported and maintained in spite of everything in his own church, as a mere matter of money interest. The church was built upon speculation by a body of gentlemen, who engaged Mr. Beecher to preach there, expecting an immense sale of their pews at a very high price, as the result of his popularity as a preacher. Hitherto their speculation has answered admirably, and the present scandal has added to their profits by cramming the church fuller than ever, and in the interest of their pew-rents they will contrive to keep their preacher's popularity undiminished with the public, as I am assured. The whole thing exhibits a moral tone in the community where it is taking place so incredibly degraded and so vulgarly vicious, that I think the lapse from virtue imputed to one individual, clergyman though he be, far less shocking and revolting than the whole religious tone and condition of his congregation and the society of which they form a part. A regular lawsuit upon the subject is now just being instituted by some of the parties concerned, and the whole disgusting and deplorable affair is again to be dragged before the public from beginning to end.*

I have seen nothing of Charles Greville's Journal but the few extracts in the *Times* and *Spectator*. Comparatively few people here care for it.

You say you wonder how I shall get on with my Memoirs when I reach the more troubled part of my life. Why, I shall either stop writing them altogether, or confine my notes to mere memorada of the places I went to and the people I met.

* I had a very slight acquaintance with the Rev. Henry Ward Beecher; but was greatly struck once with his description of his praying with and preaching to a body of emigrants from the Eastern to the then far Western States, and of their camp—their church as it then seemed, far in the wide wilderness—with their waggons and cattle loaded with their necessaries of life, by way of protecting fortification round them; his powerful preaching must have been doubly striking in such a temple. On another occasion when I met Mr. Beecher, he gave an animated description of an old woman he had passed in the street, who he said he should put into his next sermon. "Oh," said a clergyman of the Unitarian profession, one of the most eloquent preachers I ever heard, "if you take your sermons so out of the street, no wonder they are popular." Mr. Beecher replied, "Our Saviour took His so," and this mode of preaching, which he drove to the verge of familiarity, was probably the reason of what a young man said to a friend of his who told him he was going one Sunday to hear Mr. Beecher preach, "What on a Sunday!" exclaimed his friend.

Hitherto we have no winter, but lovely warmth and sunshine, and total absence of frost and snow; it is really most extraordinary, and resembles the winter climate that people fly to Italy in search of.

York Farm, December 9th, 1874.

MY DEAREST H——,

. . . Fanny Cobbe's paper in the *Theological Review* that she sent me, the " Fauna of Fancy," was not upon a subject that interested me much, though her treatment of it at the beginning of the article was interesting. I thought towards the end it rather degenerated into a mere catalogue of imaginary creatures. I did not care for the subject itself, but only because she had written it. I have not yet finished reading her preface or rather article upon Mill. As far as I have read it, I like it extremely, and it is a comfort and consolation to me to have my own vital and *indispensable* belief confirmed by the eloquent expression of a faith and hope like hers. But, alas! in my opinion faith and hope are *incommunicable*, and though she may *confirm* those who already think like her, she will not, I fear, with all her noble eloquence and religious fervour, *convert* those who do not. But I rejoice that she is inspired to write such things, and think them her proper and peculiar work. Her article on "Heteropathy," as she calls it, she told me about, and talked to me of it in London, before she had finished it; I then thought it a little fanciful, but found more plausibility in it when I read the article itself, and felt inclined to agree with her in thinking the development of the element of sympathy in the human character, a product of gradual civilization—civilization under the influence of Christianity, for it seems to me part of the slow dawning and gradual growth and spread of Christian love.

The worst of this kind of writing (I mean this essay and article writing) appears to me, that from the peculiar exigencies and limitations of that species of literature, it inclines writers to lay hold of some *one* side, some portion or aspect only, of subjects which have a very large and wide scope ; and induces them to write out that mere fragmentary truth, as if it covered much more ground than it really does.   For if the truth itself, as we comprehend it (as may very well be the case), is merely fragmentary, the article must nevertheless be a finished and complete whole, and I think that merely valuable suggestions and partial perceptions of considerable interest are injured by being extended into systems of philosophy, and made the subjects of much more extensive deductions than belong properly to them, and to account for many more phenomena than they really reach.*

That children undoubtedly do exercise cruelty, and (according to their intelligence) the refined moral cruelty of endeavouring to play upon and hurt the feelings of others, seems to me to belong more to the love of power and the love of excitement than to the pleasure of inflicting pain.

---

* One consequence of all this periodical literature, is that our reading has become chiefly monthly, and if good writing has increased, good reading has diminished with us. We read reviews of books instead of the books themselves, and articles instead of volumes.

[Two comical instances of this occurred to me in my experience of teaching young children to read : the one was a fine robust boy of between three and four years old, who, in the middle of a reading lesson, of which he had apparently had as much as he liked, began suddenly to *roar*—I can use no other term for the extraordinary and terrific noise he uttered—when, turning to look at him and expecting to see him as much convulsed with the sound as I was with hearing it, I encountered his angelic face, without a trace of emotion upon it, his sweet blue eyes only less wide open than his rosy mouth, while giving vent to this hideous bellowing, which he continued until he perceived that they merely produced in me a stare of silent surprise, when he *snapped* his mouth to, took up his book and resumed his reading in a perfectly subdued and habitual tone.

The other occasion of the same sort was when I was teaching my eldest daughter, a child of about the same age, to read. Upon her beginning to utter a series of horrible howls, while remaining at the same time perfectly dry-eyed, I turned to some writing, about which I was occupied, when presently, finding that I paid no attention to the hideous noise she was making, she said in her sweetest voice, "Don't I interrupt you, mother ?" and upon my answering, "Not in the least, my dear," the roaring ceased instantaneously, and was succeeded by a perfectly placid resumption of the reading.]

I think Fanny Cobbe is quite right in her statement of the hatred of children for the appearance of suffering, and their instinctive shrinking from ugliness, infirmity, distortion, and the grotesque side (a very powerful one), of physical anguish. In this respect poets are very like children. As for animals, as a rule, I believe, they persecute and destroy the ailing and infirm among them; but there are very curious exceptions to this, both among domesticated and savage animals, who have been known to succour and assist each other's infirmities with wonderful tenderness. I think it is Edwards, the Scotch shoemaker-naturalist, who mentions having wounded a bird among the rocks on the seashore,.two of whose companions lifted it by its wings, and twice carried it beyond his reach. I am at this moment assured, by the lady who witnessed it, that she had seen one cow *pump* for another, raising the pump-handle between her horns, while her companion drank.*

* Cats are not supposed to be peculiarly tender hearted, or demonstrative beasts. We had one once which, without any assignable reason, had such an affection for my father, that she used to watch for him and join him the moment she saw him, invariably following him like a dog in his daily walk in the garden, rubbing his legs and purring with satisfaction, and constantly running before him to prostrate herself on the gravel path in front of him. I had a fine white cat which brought four kittens into the world, three of them were white like herself, one was perfectly black, for which anomalous infant of hers she displayed the most decided preference. One day she and her kittens were brought in their basket to pay me a visit in the drawing-room, where I was also occasionally visited by a very large Newfoundland dog. The cat and he had met before, and always with apparent good-natured toleration of each other. On the occasion, however, when the cat came with her family to see me, she exhibited the most unequivocal signs of disquiet and annoyance, standing up in her basket mewing piteously, looking all round the room, and gazing at the door with evident

A dog which spent the summer here with me was one of the most lovable brutes I ever saw; he was a retriever of great size and strength, with the most aristocratic character any animal ever possessed. He never fought, or acknowledged the petty insults of low-bred curs, or the squabbles of the ignoble street dogs (*canaille*), otherwise than by a low grave growl of disapprobation, but an old companion of his, who was indeed his father (not that he knew that) being once attacked by another dog, he flew to his assistance and all but annihilated his assailant. I think, however, that that favourite dog of mine was really a brother of his master, who for some reason or other (as in the

apprehension. At length she made up her cat's mind what to do, and taking her precious black child in her mouth, jumped out of her basket, and inviting her other babies to follow her with a tender call (not purring or mewing, but very like a pigeon's coo-coo) she made her way to the lowest piece of furniture in the room, a sofa under which it was impossible that the big Newfoundland dog should thrust himself, and there established herself in great apparent content, till she and her little ones were replaced in their basket and carried back to their kitchen quarters. I have seen an expression of unmistakable tenderness in this beast's countenance while gazing at her black child. Another comical exhibition of intelligence, prompted by affection, was that given by a cat who had the most devoted love for a dog who lived in the same house with her, and from whom she could never bear to be separated. On one occasion when she was shut out of the room where he was, after scratching and mewing in vain for admission, she stood up on her hind legs, and with one of her front paws powerfully and rapidly turned the handle of the door till she opened it and gained admission. This clever device of their cat amused her owners so much, that they used to divert themselves and their visitors with its exhibition.

Arabian Nights) had been turned into a beautiful gentle and noble animal, with a fine forehead, Grecian nose and profile, like the Neapolitan Psyche; with the advantage over the goddess of beautiful clear brown eyes of the most pathetic human tenderness.

I see that at the end of her preface on Mill, Fanny Cobbe herself says a few words upon the inadequacy of an article in a periodical to treat at all fully the subject which she has called "Heteropathy." It is a misfortune to our literature, and goes even deeper than that, I think, that so many of our best thinkers are perpetually on the look out for mere "article-subjects." Certainly the periodical literature of the day is wonderfully serious, profound, and interesting; but it still offers the temptation of writing not only *bits*, but upon what are in truth only *bits* of subjects, and this must be peculiarly the case with people who are obliged to write for money. . . .

Now farewell, my dearest friend, may God bless you, living or dying, for ever.

Yours, with all the grateful love I am capable of,

FANNY.

York Farm, December 23rd, 1874.

MY DEAREST H——,

Whatever you may be suffering from, cold and snow and your present atmospheric condition in Ireland, I defy them to be as trying to health and comfort as the extraordinary vicissitudes of this climate. Three days ago the cold was intense, the thermometer twenty-five degrees below freezing—that is, you know, within a few degrees of zero. Yesterday and to-day it has been up to sixty, and in my little greenhouse, where the sun shines, it has been between seventy and eighty. Just conceive the effect of such a sudden variation of temperature on one's whole constitution! The fires in the rooms have been intolerable; and I have been sitting in my drawing-room with open doors and windows, and am now writing to you in my dressing-room without any gown on, because of the *heat*. To-morrow we shall perhaps be freezing.

I am very glad that a peerage has been offered to your nephew, and I hope he will accept it. It seems to me a very proper honour to be bestowed upon a gentleman who has been so honest, so faithful, and so useful a political partisan. Without any sympathy for his particular views, I have always greatly admired his entire devotion to them, and the disinterested sacrifice of time and labour which he—a pleasure and ease-loving man—has always been ready to make for the sake of his party and his convictions. I think it is a proper and just reward for his services, and that his son may be proud of inheriting it. I hope they will give him a pretty title, and shall be anxious to know if it is Lord Ardgillan. How delighted his warm-hearted, excellent mother would have been! I am sure his sisters will be pleased, and sympathize most cordially with their pleasure. [Colonel Taylor, I believe, refused the peerage.]

I have been much interested by our purchase of the Suez Canal. It seems to me one of those political events that appear to open great vistas into the future, vistas of progress and improvement, and changes of

deep and beneficial importance to the world. I think
the whole question of the existence of Turkey and
Egypt and the Danubian provinces and their future
conditions intensely interesting. . . .

I had a charming account of my dear little granddaughter in her mother's last letter from the plantation. She says the rick-yard is sunny and dry and
warm, and the little woman is carried down there of
a morning, and thence *surveys* the rice-planting, and
the orange-gathering, and all the agricultural opera-
tions with extreme excitement, and holds her little
court, being idolized by all the negroes, who, in spite
of their newly obtained freedom, perpetuate on her the
title of "Little Missis," and are all her very devoted
slaves. The number and variety of the farm-yard
animals please and divert her extremely, and she is
well, happy, and merry.

The account of everything is very prosperous; their
orange harvest alone has proved very valuable, and it
is such a beautiful crop that it must be a perfect
delight to gather it. The trees had been so loaded
with fruit as to be obliged to be propped up, and
F—— says that on dull or rainy days the profusion
of golden oranges makes a perfect sunshine of its
own.

My beloved H——, I long inexpressibly to see you
once more. Perhaps God will grant me that great
happiness before another year goes by.

Ever, as ever, yours,
FANNY.

York Farm, December 31st, 1874.

My dearest H——,

I think American women deficient in softness—sensibility—at least they do not exhibit much;
but they are less demonstrative than women generally
are, and this may make them appear less tender.
They undoubtedly love their husbands and children,
and fathers and mothers, and brothers and sisters,
and uncles and aunts, and "all their good friends
and relations;" but there is a dryness of manner
in their habitual intercourse which seems to me a
national feminine peculiarity, and which makes the
women of this country unlike any others I have
ever seen. The animal nature is feeble and ill-
developed in them. Their physical organization is
apt to be weak and poor and sickly, and the intellectual element predominates over the emotional
and sensual to a degree that makes them apparently
deficient in softness and sensibility, and deprives their
manner of a good deal of feminine charm and attrac-
tiveness, and very often gives it a character singularly
at variance in its sharp abruptness with the delicate,
refined order of beauty for which they are remarkable.
I attribute their dry cold manner in great measure to
physiological causes in both men and women; but in
the latter the desperate spoiling in their training, and
their unreasoning and unreasonable tyranny over the
"softer sex," (as Lady Morley used to call the men)
has a good deal to do with this ungraceful ungracious-
ness.*

* In travelling I have repeatedly seen ladies take possession
of seats in railroad carriages, which were vacated by men

Everything overworks everybody here, and Christmas is a season of such infinite *labour*, as well as expense in the shopping and present-making line, that almost every woman I know is good for nothing in purse and person for a month afterwards, done up physically, and broken down financially.

The cold has suddenly become intense. The sun is shining brilliantly, and I ran over the way to see S—— for five minutes, wrapped in a fur cloak, but felt as if I should be frozen even in crossing the road and the garden, and this is since yesterday, when it was quite *mild*. Such alternations are terribly trying to people's health.

I hear a great deal about Charles Greville's book, but have not yet seen it. M—— has sent out to Hatchard's for it, the first importing bookseller in New York telling her he could not procure it for her under six weeks, and, had she applied to any bookseller in Philadelphia, they would very likely have

immediately on their appearance, without so much as a word, a look, or a bow of acknowledgment, the gentlemen thus unseated finding seats if they could, or standing if they could not. I have often thought that if I had been one of them I should have said to the lady to whom I gave up my place, "You pretty creature, say 'Thank you!'" But then, I am an Englishwoman, not *inured* to such courtesies ; and, by-the-by, I heard a very *national* anecdote of some Englishmen travelling in this country the other day. They were sitting in the smoking compartment full of men, each, like themselves, with a cigar in their mouths. Suddenly the door opened, and two ladies, who apparently had not found or chosen to take seats elsewhere, came in ; immediately every cigar was thrown out of the window, except those of the two Englishmen, who insisted on, and persisted in, their right to smoke in the "smoking car."

kept her waiting twice that time for it. It seems to be creating a great sensation in England, and the report here is that the Queen has dismissed Mr. Henry Reeve from his post in the Privy Council Office for having published it.

It is the last day of the year, and, thank God, I can again hope and believe that I may once more embrace you.

Ever, as ever, yours,
FANNY.

York Farm, January 4th, 1875.

MY BELOVED H——,

My servants are having a party, and, though the walls of this small house are, like those of most old buildings, very thick, and the laughter and merriment which I suppose and hope are going on do not reach my sitting-room, the whole house every now and then gives a shake which bears witness to some ponderous feats of agility, and distinctly testifies that the guests in my kitchen are not fairies. I went in just now to bid them welcome, and give them the "Happy New Year," and found them apparently in high good humour and enjoyment. Meantime the two cats, which are our only pets, have been brought to me in the drawing-room, because the sight of so much strange company in their own quarters scares them, and they are having a most outrageous game of "New Year's romps" all over and under and round my furniture, to their unbounded satisfaction and my no small amusement. Each of my servants asked some of their friends and relations, and the people from

over the way, and our farmer's family and some of
H——'s folk, make up a party of neighbourly acquaintance, all intimate and friendly with each other,
and I give Ellen funds for the entertainment, which
she orders and directs, I hope, to the general satisfaction. . . .

S—— rides without a servant, entirely alone, and
after dark. The roads in every direction are infested
with tramps and footpads, and the papers are full of
outrages and robberies committed by the vagrants,
who have lately become quite a feature in this whole
neighbourhood; you may judge, therefore, that these
prolonged solitary twilight rides of S——'s cause me
no small anxiety. . . .

When you ask me if people on this side of the
water care about the Suez Canal and the Prince of
Wales's Indian progress, I can only answer for myself.
I see nobody, and never hear anything about anything. I am profoundly interested by our new position
in Egypt. Our influential position there appears to
me a circumstance which may involve the most
important consequences, and, as it were, the opening
of a new chapter in the history of that country and
Turkey in Europe.

There has been an extraordinarily heavy fall of
snow, within the last few days, in the north-eastern
states, and our weather has undergone a sudden
change from oppressively hot to fine, bracing, temperate cold, for which I am most thankful. The
thermometer at seventy at Christmas is neither
pleasant nor wholesome. I suppose now we shall
presently be smothered in snow here; but that, at

least, will be seasonable, which the great heat of the last week has not been, and I confess I would rather have winter in January than in April, which was the case with us last year, the two heaviest snowstorms of the whole season occurring in the middle of April. They say that there will be no fruit at all this year, owing to the present advanced state of the buds on all the trees, which must infallibly be killed by the first severe frost.

We are just now rejoicing in a houseful of oranges, magnificent fruit, sent from the plantation, a barrel apiece, containing about thirty dozen each, to me, to S——, and to M——. Of course a considerable proportion reach us in an unsound condition, but twenty dozen and a half of my barrelful were perfect. I sent off this morning a supply to our neighbouring hospital, and have distributed in every direction to my friends and neighbours, so that our golden abundance diminishes rapidly.

I have seen to-day a letter from Fanny Cobbe, in which, I am sorry to say, I think she takes rather a desponding tone with regard to things in general in England. As she has always seemed to me hopeful in her temper and views, I regret this on her own account.

York Farm, January 10th, 1875.

MY BELOVED H——,
    You ask me if I am coinciding more entirely than I have been hitherto with Fanny Cobbe's opinions. I do not know precisely to which of her opinions you allude, whether to her theological or political and

social views. Of course, ignorant as I am, it is quite impossible for me to form positive opinions upon the dogmas generally received by Christians, and about which I have for a great many years had a doubt that amounts very nearly to disbelief. But Fanny Cobbe and I never discussed such subjects. I have not the requisite information, and I suppose (not believing that order of opinion *vital*) am tolerably content to remain in my present frame of mind—that is, undetermined, not having the means of arriving at any determination. I suppose I heartily agree with all her *religious beliefs*, but not so heartily with her *theological disbeliefs*. With regard to her other opinions, those more especially that refer to the position of women in civilized countries, I am again not sufficiently well-informed, nor have I thought enough upon the subject, to be entitled to an opinion. I know that I am quite willing that women should be allowed to do whatever they *can*—I mean, be politicians, members of Parliament, doctors, divines, lawyers, *soldiers, if they can*, and vote by all means, if they like. My own earnest ambition and desire for them is a better, more thorough education, and a higher estimate of their own great natural calling of wives and mothers, and a more intelligent apprehension of their duties in both capacities.

[The most eloquent and energetic advocate of Woman's Rights in America was Margaret Fuller, a remarkable person, who left a vivid impression of her individuality on the minds of all those who knew her. She was an uncommonly good classical scholar, and the intimate friend of the most distinguished young

men, who were her contemporaries in Boston and
Harvard, over whose mental development and character
she exercised a very considerable influence.* After
protesting vehemently against the subordinate position
of married women, she married an Italian gentleman
of the name of Ossoli, and, returning with him from
Europe, they were drowned together off the American
coast. I saw a letter of hers after her marriage, in
which she spoke of her husband in a tone of affectionate
protection and conscious superiority, such as a mother
might have used towards a son. Her death by drown-
ing may have suggested that of Zenobia in Hawthorne's
novel of the Blithedale Romance—both Margaret Fuller
and Emerson having been members of that singular
society, the Concord Philanstery; and Zenobia, it is
said, was intended by Hawthorne as a portrait of her
in his book. One of her great friends and admirers
said Margaret Fuller, in spite of her claim to absolute
equality with men, on the part of women, was extremely exacting with regard to the small courtesies
which men never show each other, but never omit
towards the feebler sex. She expected her fallen
glove or handkerchief to be presented to her, her
shawl placed on her shoulders, the door of the room
opened for her; and, on the occasion of showing her
these civilities, her friend would a little sarcastically
remark, quoting her own words, "Let them" (women)
" be sea captains, colonels of regiments, etc."

She was good enough to send me her book,
"Women in the Nineteenth Century," and to express

* Emerson, who admired her greatly, introduced her to
Carlyle, whom she bored very nearly to death.

more than once her desire to become acquainted with
me.   We never did meet, however, and I am not sorry
that we did not, as I am afraid I should have incurred
her contempt for my small sympathy with her views
respecting the emancipation of women, as I have
reason to fear I did that of her most intimate friend
and fellow disciple, who came to see me once, almost
on the part of Margaret Fuller, to explain and urge
my acceptance of them.   This lady was a Trojan,
i.e. inhabited the city of Troy, where she conducted,
with great efficiency and high reputation, a numerously
attended school for young ladies.   After in vain
urging upon me the claims of the " women's cause,"
and expressing her unfeigned surprise that I was not
among its advocates and willing to join them on their
" platform," I suppose I sank myself for ever in her
opinion, by quoting to her Mary Stewart's opinion
with regard to some of her *superior* sister Elizabeth's
gallantries, " Parceque dans ces affaires là, la plus
sage de nous toutes, n'est qu'un peu moins sotte que
les autres," and representing to her that as she had a
perpetual stream of young womanhood passing through
her hands and under her influence, if she contrived to
prevent her pupils from becoming desperately in love
with, and desperately afraid of, very contemptible
men, she would do more for the emancipation of
women than all the speeches, pamphlets, and " plat-
forms " in the world.

On one occasion my dear and admirable friend,
Charles Sedgwick, reporting to me some newly passed
enactment of the Massachusetts Legislature in favour
of woman's rights, with regard to their independent

possession and disposal of their own property, expressed his surprise at the apparent indifference with which I received this intelligence of the improved legal condition of my sex, saying, that of all women, I ought most to have sympathized with it; to which I could only reply, "Oh, I do rejoice greatly at it. Legislate, make laws for justice to women, in all such matters you cannot do too much, for you will never do enough to counteract the natural law, by which women are constituted and constitute themselves the *subjects* of men."

My friend, Frederica Bremer, that very amiable woman and charming writer, was apt to become vehement on the subject of "the women's cause," and exclaiming once, in a frenzy of assertion, that they had a right to be soldiers, if they pleased, saying, "Why shall they not fight?" with her little hand (she was a *very* small woman) clenched in her warlike ardour. I took hold of it (it was like a little crumpled bird's claw). "Because of this," said I. "If fisticuffs are to decide the matter, the weakest man's fist is stronger than the strongest woman's, 'et la raison du plus fort est toujours la meilleure.'" I wish to record here a compliment paid to me by Miss Bremer, not only because she paid it me, but because, for a stranger, speaking a foreign language, "it was as ingenious as graceful." Calling upon her one day, when she was not very well, I expressed a fear lest the exertion of receiving me should be too much for her. "Oh no, no!" she cordially exclaimed; and then laughingly added, "And yet I do not know that I ought to see *so many people as you are.*"]

Fanny Cobbe and I take different views with regard to our sex, for I think she rather despises what I consider a woman's natural calling, and believes she may find or make a better business for herself, with which opinion I do not at all agree. I greatly admire whatever she writes upon religious subjects, for her convictions and fervour in expressing them seem to me excellent, and always comfort and invigorate me spiritually.

I did not see the sermon of Dr. Martineau's that you refer to in answer to Professor Tyndall, but notices of and extracts from it, by which I judged that it must have been very powerful and eloquent.

Our winter is upon us now with bitter and intense cold, the windows remain clouded, thick with frost, even in the rooms where there is a large fire burning. I came down this morning to find a favourite plant that Mr. L—— had put in a fine china pot, given me by M——, frozen, I am afraid, to death, standing on one of the library window-seats. There is a huge fire in the room all day, but in spite of shutters and curtains, the night had done the mischief, and I do not think the poor creature can recover.

The number of people out of employment just now is very terrible, and in the cities, I imagine, there is very cruel suffering and distress. We, here in the country, however, are in no way the better for this affluence of poor unemployed artisans and working-men. They are not farm or garden labourers, and to such a man on this little place of mine I pay forty dollars—or eight guineas a month (a guinea a week wages, and a guinea a week for his board), and these are the only terms upon which I can hire the very commonest Irish handler of a spade in this neighbourhood. Our household servants still receive their most inordinate wages—my own man-servant, a sort of cross between a butler and a footman, seven guineas a month (of course he boards and lodges at my expense) and the women of the household in proportion. So this sad number of unemployed hands does nothing towards diminishing the cost and difficulty of our housekeeping.

The affairs of the plantation are going on well and steadily; the crop of magnificent oranges is becoming quite a valuable item of the profits, and is a harvest very unlike the rice crop, for it costs nothing, and raises itself.

York Farm, January 20th, 1875.

MY DEAREST H——,

Dr. W——'s injecting morphine under the skin of my arm merely relieved me from pain, but was no remedy in itself for the disease that caused the pain. . . . Some years ago, Mr. de Mussy made me take quantities of Vichy water, and I continued to do so habitually, till my sister told me I was incurring the risk of some very serious disorder in my system, after which I only took it occasionally, until Dr. W—— forbade it altogether. I remember a very clever Swiss physician, the first medical man of Lausanne, telling me that the first year people went to Vichy the effect of the waters was generally so favourable that they returned again a second season, hoping for the same benefit, but that the result was invariably far less beneficial; a third course of the waters, he said, was just as likely to kill them as not, and I have since thought that the dreadfully depressed state of my nerves, and low condition of my whole system, from which I suffered the whole time I was at Widmore, was a result of this ignorant use of this medicinal water.

Our winter here has been the most extraordinary I ever experienced. The variations of temperature have been so extreme and so rapid that they alone would have been sufficient to make any one ill, who was not very young or very strong. Yesterday the heavy heat of the atmosphere was so oppressive, that it was almost intolerable, and at two o'clock in the afternoon such thick darkness overspread the sky (not fog, but dense blackness), that it prevented me from seeing to read, and the effect was almost that of an eclipse or an imminent thunderstorm of the heaviest kind. In the evening, for about an hour, we had a hurricane of wind and furious rain, such as one reads of in the tropical tempests; it subsided as suddenly as it rose, and in the night the weather became quite cold, and to-day we have a clear brilliant frost. It requires a constitution of iron, or rather gutta-percha, to stand such atmospheric vicissitudes.

I do not agree with your admiration of French manners—at any rate of the manners of Frenchmen. A Frenchman always thinks that he does and says the right thing, and is unpleasantly self-assured; an Englishman never thinks that he does or says the right thing, and is unpleasantly self-diffident; a simple person never thinks the one or the other, and is agreeable in consequence of self-forgetfulness. Simplicity is a great element of good breeding.

York Farm, February 2nd, 1875.

MY DEAREST H——,

I have begun to fear that the exertion of dictating might become irksome to you, and I was therefore not surprised when I found from E——'s letter, which I received this morning, that this was just now the case. It has been surprising to me that you were ever able to dictate with any comfort to yourself, and I have often thought that I should have found it easier to master any method of writing, devised for the blind, than to dictate what I had to say in a letter. . . .

S——'s domestic difficulties do not diminish, for, having been left by a housemaid, who might be called an *old family servant*, having lived with her a *few months*, she engaged another, who came yesterday and went away this morning, leaving her without a housemaid.* She seemed, however, to be taking her misery philosophically, when I went over to see her this

---

* The practice of engaging servants upon the terms of so much per week, which prevails in America, facilitates the immediate throwing up of their situations upon the slightest pretext. Forfeiting a week's wages is a small consideration, compared with the month's salary which must be forfeited in England, if a servant does not give or receive that length of warning. I think in some respects the weekly payment of wages, like that of all tradespeople's bills, advantageous ; and have always practised it, even in England, where I find the members of my household prefer it to receiving their due at monthly intervals.

morning, and has gone into town this evening to console herself by seeing the ballad of the "Mistletoe Bough," acted in pantomime, by a parcel of very pretty girls, who are to gesticulate and attitudinize through the whole, while the ballad is sung or declaimed by somebody, after the fashion of the Greek chorus. She amused me very much by telling me that in the ball scene, with which the story opens, these Philadelphia beauties had determined to dance a minuet, which performance they supposed to consist of merely walking about in a stately fashion and curtseying to each other. . . .

I received to-day a letter from my dear old friend William Donne, giving a miserable account of the winter weather in London. I cannot at present complain of the winter here. Thus far it has not seemed to me extraordinarily cold, though the thermometer has marked several degrees below zero once or twice; but we have had very little damp or dark weather, and with the pure brilliant skies and vivid sunshine, with which we are favoured the greater part of the time, I find the cold itself quite endurable. Walking is not easy; and in going to the house over the way, a distance of about half a quarter of a mile, I am in constant dread of falling and breaking my limbs. The middle of the road is like a sea beach of *snow sand*, from the trampling of horses and passing of vehicles; on each side of this is a broad strip of ice macadam—that is, lumps of ice, instead of fresh broken stones, in short, the ice *shingle* to the aforesaid *snow sand*; beyond this, and stretching to the frozen ditches on each side of the road, is a clear sheet of treacherous ice as smooth as a looking-glass, upon which it would be impossible to set one's feet without falling.

The story that you read in the *Times* of the case of kidnapping, from the neighbourhood of Germantown, is a very true and sad incident indeed. The little boy carried off was playing in the road, close to his parents' house, who are wealthy people, residing in quite a populous place. There is not much romance about it, for it is supposed to be merely a crime committed for the purpose of extorting money; but the condition of the unfortunate father and mother is something too dreadful to think of. Not long ago two burglars were shot in an attempt upon a house in the neighbourhood of New York, and one of them confessed that they had been concerned in stealing the child, who, however, had passed out of their hands. Of course, this excited the most sanguine hope that the child would be traced, but this apparent clue has hitherto led to no result. It is a very strange and dreadful incident, and the perpetrators of the cruel villainy are at present undiscovered, and apparently undiscoverable.

I have just finished reading Charles Greville's Memoirs, and am amazed at the indifference to decency and propriety which the publication of such notices of the Queen's family exhibits. The book has rather raised my estimate of the author's ability, but greatly lowered my opinion of his character. Nor can I imagine how it could be thought by anybody fitting to publish such records of George and William IV., while their niece, the Queen of England is alive. The slur cast upon that excellent woman, Queen Adelaide, is abominable; and the constant mention of persons, whom the writer was meeting on apparently cordially friendly terms in society, as the "bastards," and the "bastardy," is disgusting.   I think the whole tone of the book painfully unworthy of a gentleman.   You know how much I liked Charles Greville, in spite of my not very exalted opinion of his morality; but though once or twice, in the course of my long and intimate acquaintance with him, I had a slight misgiving about his *other* character (I mean that of a gentleman), I confess this book has been a very painful surprise to me.   I am thankful his sister and poor dear Henry are gone; I am sure it would have shocked and grieved them very much.

The last news from the plantation were good.

York Farm, February 8th, 1875.

MY DEAREST H——,

I did not tell you that I had no *convictions*, or that they did not suffice to me.   I told you, when you asked me if I had embraced all Fanny Cobbe's opinions, that I had very few *opinions*, which appear to me to be mental results, arrived at by intellectual processes, which I am not naturally capable of, and for which, even if my reasoning powers were better, I have not the requisite information.   There has been no change or diminution in my *convictions* on matters theological, political, or social, that I am aware of.

When I said that I considered it a woman's vocation to have children, I said (or meant to say) that I considered it her vocation to *train* children, quite as

much as to bear them, and it is for that most important
avocation that I wish women were better fitted by a
better education.

"What is 'Truth'?" say you. Why, you are as bad
as Pilate! And before and since his time how often
those words have been uttered in mental and spiritual
anguish. Scientific facts, and arithmetical calculations,
and geometrical demonstrations, are tru*ths*, but tru*ths*
are plenty and *truth* is scarce. The truest thing in
the world, I believe, is the desire and intention to be
true of an upright soul, and yet how often they fail to
reach the result they seek is lamentable. The truth
is habitually spoken by honest people unconsciously
and unintentionally; the moment they *tell* the truth,
with an intention or an endeavour, they generally
fail to do so. The attempt at absolute accuracy makes
its achievement so difficult, that falsehood or misrepre-
sentation, inaccuracy, at any rate, is almost always
its result. They frequently find the truth who do not
seek it, they who do, frequently lose it.

F—— wrote me a good account of herself and her
baby the other day, and told me she had been planting
a hundred orange trees. I think that lovely and
delicious fruit will come to be an important item in
the return of the plantation. Certainly it was the
golden fruit of the Hesperides, and worthy of a dragon's
guard; and if Eve had lost Paradise for a fruit of such
a savour, flavour, colour, and odour, I could have for-
given her better than I can her apple of knowledge. If
oranges were less plentiful and cheaper, people would
know better how good they are. . . .

We are having intense cold now, and last night all

the plants in my little greenhouse were more or less frozen.

York Farm, Branchtown, February 10th.

MY DEAREST H——,

The last letters from the plantation were every way cheerful and pleasant. They had no overseer, and Mr. L—— was looking after the work of the estate himself, and so industriously and efficiently, that they were in a state of greater forwardness with all their spring processes of planting than they had been for years before so early in the season; and are in this respect better off than any of the neighbouring planters. F—— herself had been planting a hundred orange trees, a most admirable outlay of labour, for besides the lovely flowers and fruit for their own enjoyment, the oranges are worth three guineas a barrel, here at the north, and are becoming quite a valuable crop.

My dearest H——, many years must pass before the United States become over-populated. There is just now considerable distress in the Atlantic cities, proceeding from the money difficulties and bad financial administration of the government, and the impediments and restrictions put upon trade and commerce by the foolish tariff duties—a system of recruiting the revenue really almost ludicrous in the inefficiency of the result, compared with the enormous abuses it has given rise to. A number of temporary influences combining together are just now depressing trade and manufactures in the northern and eastern states, and many people are out of work in the cities; but as for this vast country being already over-peopled, the bare idea makes one smile, when one thinks of its immense extent and incalculable resources. . . .

For the last ten days, ever since the beginning of this month, we have had awfully severe weather, the bitter intensity of the cold rendered more intolerable by furious winds. The short distance between the opposite house and mine is really a perilous passage, from the sheets of smooth ice which in some places completely coat the gravel walks through the grounds. I have dust and ashes strewed over my half of the way, but across the lawn, on the other side, I really walk in terror of life and limb.

I went to pay S—— a visit this morning, to carry her some charming hot-house flowers, that a friend had brought me yesterday. She is at home always all day on Wednesday, in order that people who drive or rail the six miles from town to see her may be sure of finding her on one day of the week. So she was sitting at the receipt of custom, very becomingly dressed, and looking very handsome, and we discussed the arrangement of the furniture in *my* old drawing-room, in *my* old home; and as I find myself thus once again all but inhabiting this my former "house of woe," I am occasionally seized with a bewildering sense of surprise, and, overwhelmed, with a sudden flood of reminiscence and association, feel almost inclined to doubt my own indentity.

York Farm, February 12th, 1875.

My dearest H——,

I have nothing to tell you, for my life affords no incident and has no variety, except, indeed the event of my having bought myself a piano, a less expensive process here than hiring one, and, indeed, from some peculiar notion upon the subject of hiring instruments, which prevails here, a cottage piano, which is the only sized one my small drawing-room can contain, is not to be hired at all. They can only be had by out-and-out purchase, and the most moderate price for which one can be obtained is a hundred and fifteen pounds, for which sum, I believe, in London or Paris a grand piano may be bought; but this is according to the exaggerated value of everything in this country.

I have just been making up my yearly account, summing up my expenses for the past twelvemonth, a thing I have done for a good many years past, and I find that I have spent four hundred pounds more than I did during my last year's housekeeping at St. Leonards, where I had (I was going to say) the same number of servants; but I keep a gardener here, who costs me ninety-six pounds a year in wages. But my household in England was composed of the same number of people, and I had a larger house. I travelled for three months abroad in the summer, and bought myself an outfit of new clothes in Paris; whereas, during the past year, I have not stirred from this place, and one winter bonnet (an old one that I bought from F——) and three pair of gloves are the only articles of dress I have bought since I have been in America, and yet I have spent four hundred pounds more this year than I did in England. Such is the cost of living in this country now.

Having a piano once more is a great resource to

me, and I have resumed my old habit of practising
after breakfast for an hour daily. I take up the old
music that I love (Handel's "Sampson" was what I
played and sang to-day), and it carries me for the
time into a world of pleasant thoughts, and delightful
memories, and dear associations. In the evening, after
dinner, by firelight, I play from memory all sorts of
things, and always begin with a pretty little air that
dear Dorothy used to play, and that you were very
fond of, and which I caught by ear. On Sunday I
never open my piano, not from any religious scruples
of my own, but out of respect for those of others, and
therefore on Saturday evening always wind up my
musical reminiscences like a good Englishwoman, with
" God save the Queen," which, indeed, was the first
thing I played in token of respectful rejoicing as soon
as I got my piano.

At about noon I walk every day that the weather
permits. I went out to-day, though the cold was
intense, the earth frozen deep down, and as hard as
iron, and sheeted everywhere with a perfect floor of
smooth ice, just covered deep enough with snow to
make it doubly treacherous. I walk in the middle of
the high-road, where the horses' hoofs and the cart
and carriage runners have ploughed the surface and
made it safer to tread upon. I take my alpenstock
with me, and have for companion a very nice little
Pomeranian Spitz dog, that M—— gave me on my
birthday, whose society is a very agreeable addition
to my solitary exercise. When I return home I read.
Charles Greville's Memoirs is the last new book I
have had; but I constantly fall back upon the old ones

—Goethe's life of himself in the German, Macaulay's essays, the *Spectator* (not Addison's, but the newspaper), and a good American weekly paper called the *Nation*. I always have some coarse needlework on hand that does not try my eyes, and am now doing a border for a table-cover for Mr. L—— of the Zingari colours and pattern on wide canvas. In the evening I knit fine little Shetland wool shirts or socks for baby, and play Patience. I do my writing in my dressing-room, after I leave the rooms downstairs, which I do at ten o'clock. I find writing by candle-light tries my eyes less than either reading or needle-work, and so it is in the couple of hours before I go to bed that I write my letters and go on with my Memoirs, and so the hours go by, and so I spend my days.

The last letters from the plantation were very satisfactory. The baby was well and "very jolly," and the business of the rice planting was going on prosperously, and both Mr. L—— and F—— write cheerfully about the condition of the estate. I fear I shall not come back this year, and God knows if I shall ever see you again.

I confess I am a little surprised at what you tell me about E——, though it is rather unreasonable to be at *all* surprised at anything anybody does. The individuals whom we know best and have been longest most intimate with will at some time or other of our intercourse with them do that which we should least have expected of them, or leave undone what we should most certainly have looked for. The whole *gamut* of good and evil is in every human being, certain notes, from stronger original quality or most frequent use, appearing to form the whole character ; but they are only the tones most often heard. The whole scale is in every soul, and the notes most seldom heard will on rare occasions make themselves audible. No exhibition of human character is surprising ; it may be unusual, but is not unnatural. *Everything* is in *everybody* more or less. *More* is what we are familiar with, and do not expect or suspect the *less*, which is there, however.

York Farm, Branchtown, February 16th, 1875.

MY DEAREST H——,

I received a letter from Fanny Cobbe the other day, in which she said that you had sent her back a book she had sent you, thinking it would interest you. Are you no longer read to ? or are you no longer interested in metaphysical works ? Fanny Cobbe doubtless has told you of all the worry they have had about their house, and that they have taken one in Cheyne Walk. I do not know exactly where that is, but I think somewhere in Chelsea. I have called upon Carlyle and his wife there, I think ; and if so, Fanny Cobbe will have, at any rate, one neighbour who is good company, or *was*, for people alter with age in this as in many other respects.

Dr. W—— has just been sent for, on account of a serious accident which has occurred to some young people of his acquaintance, who were amusing themselves with what is called " coasting."

There is a long and steep hill on one of the cross-roads between here and Germantown, which at this moment is one smooth sheet of ice. The young people profit by this to get upon what they call "sleds," which are simply flat boards of a certain length and width, with runners under them, upon which they slide with immense velocity down this icy hill (a sort of montagne Russe of a primitive kind).

One of these sleds, with some young men and women, all friends of Dr. W——'s, was ill-*steered* by the gentleman who undertook to steer it down the hill, and the whole party were dashed violently against a wooden paling at the bottom, and though no one was killed (which they all might have been), they are all of them more or less seriously hurt and injured. One very pretty girl has had her face all cut open, and may remain disfigured for life.

The most extraordinary part of this dangerous pastime is that it is pursued in the middle of the public high-road ; and that if you are driving up one of these hills (you being in a sleigh, of course, for wheels cannot travel in this weather), you are liable to encounter a whole train of these maniacs shooting down by you, and it depends entirely upon the dexterity with which they are steered whether they do not come flying down straight between your horse's legs. In any other country in the world such perilous diversions would be illegal, and punishable by "fine or imprisonment," and the police would interfere to prevent them ; but here nobody thinks of preventing anybody from doing anything, and in Boston a street, in one of the most populous parts of the city, being a steep incline, is entirely given up to the boys and their sledding.

The weather here has been terribly severe since the beginning of this month; and I, having turned off the hot air in my little greenhouse, carelessly forgot to turn it on again, and a whole quantity of thriving geraniums, many of them in bloom, were frozen black in a few hours. My grandson wrote from his school, which is in one of the New England states, that the thermometer has marked *thirty-seven degrees below freezing;* that is tremendous cold. It is nothing near as cold as that here; but still it is bitterly hard, though the sun shines, and the sky is exquisitely bright and clear, and the sunsets are magnificent. My little house is very sufficiently warm and comfortable, and I continue my practice of sleeping in a room where there never is any fire, and .with the door opening into one where there is a fire only in the day, and where the window is open all night.

Tell me, if you do not care to be read to any more.

Though I do not admire the manners of Frenchmen as much as you do, there is a point of their morals which I have always admired (in the sense of wondered at) very much. Frenchmen are the most respectful, obedient, and devoted sons to their mothers. Frenchmen are entire disbelievers in the virtue of women. Does every Frenchman consider his own mother as the single exception to the rule of the general female depravity?

York Farm, March 1st, 1875.

Yes, my dear H——, I am surprised that you still have energy and activity of mind, and concentration of thought enough to dictate letters such as I receive

from you; but you know, from the earliest beginning
of your inability to write, your power of dictating
surprised me, and I thought I should have found it
easier to acquire any of the mechanical processes of
writing devised for the blind than to dictate my
letters. I wish I could have dictated anything I
wrote from my spoken words. Those in which I think
are infinitely better *style* than what I elaborate from
them in the process of writing.

You speak of the "estimation" in which I held
Charles Greville, and, if that word is an equivalent
for "esteem," it does not at all suit the character of
my feeling for him. I liked him extremely, and often
wondered how I could like so much a person whom I
did not esteem more. I thought him thoroughly
worldly, and in some respects unprincipled; but he
was one of the most agreeable persons of my acquaintance, and I liked him, without any better reason than
that. His book exhibits more ability than I gave
him credit for, and more latent sensibility to beauty,
and feeling for goodness, so that in reading it I sometimes felt that in some respects I had hardly done
him justice; while, on the other hand, the coarse
indecency and ill-nature of his scandalous notices of
Queen Adelaide, and his perpetual offensive reference
to the illegitimacy of persons, whom he was meeting
every day on terms of apparent cordiality, made me
feel that he was not as much of a gentleman as I had
imagined him to be. The political part of this book
and the sketches of our great statesmen interested me
very much.

You ask me why I have removed my money from

St. Louis. I have not removed it yet, but I am about to be compelled to do so, and place it with the rest of my small fortune in Boston, where the lower rate of interest, which is the utmost that I can receive for it there, will lessen my income by something between two and three hundred pounds, a serious diminution of my revenue to me, situated as I am. About six years ago the two gentlemen who had charge of my funds in St. Louis quarrelled upon politics, and one of them refused to act any longer with the other as my trustee. The consequence has been that ever since that I have had virtually but one person responsible for my investments there, an unsafe condition which has given me some anxiety. Now, however, the sole remaining trustee desires to give up his charge of my property, on the score of failing health and a desire to relieve himself from care and anxiety; * and, as I know nobody in St. Louis to whom

* These gentlemen undertook voluntarily and gratuitously the care of my property, and discharged their trust, as long as they retained it, with the most disinterested zeal. When the republicans came into power, and that paper money (" green-backs," as they were called) were pronounced legal tender by the government, a payment due to me was proffered in that form. One of my friendly trustees, a fiery democrat, refused it, and said he would dispute its legality in a law court. He was himself a lawyer, but in this instance lost his temper for my sake, and in his political abhorrence of the republican party. My other friend, his co-trustee, a staunch republican, warned him that he would lose his suit, which indeed he did, and most generously made good to me the loss I had sustained by it. My funds, which were bringing me three per cent. in England, returned ten in St. Louis. The " green-backs," pronounced legal tender by the republican government, were of course unequal

I can transfer the trust, I am obliged to remove my money, and, instead of ten per cent., must be thankful if I can get six, which is more than doubtful. I wish this had happened when I was still able to read and earn money; but it is too late for work now. . . .

Yes, dearest H——, I sleep well for an old woman and I rejoice to hear that you are able to do so; but I do what you never did—sleep " by day more than the wild cat." I do not mean of *malice prepense;* but if I undertake to read the most interesting book in the world, I am pretty sure at the end of half an hour to find myself not awake but *waking*. . . .

I was at church last Sunday, and, oh, how I wished that, while altering the English Book of Common Prayer to suit themselves, they had eliminated from the Psalms of David (if David's they are) the execrations, and imprecations, and maledictions which occur in those sublime utterances of a religious spirit—the prayers and praises which we read in our daily devotions and recite in our weekly worship. Doesn't it seem strange that, if David invoked those curses on the head of his adversary, he should twice have spared the life of Saul (his bitter enemy and relentless persecutor, who in one of his frenzies had attempted to murder him) and satisfied himself with mere verbal vengeance. In all history I know nothing so tragical as the life of David. The traditionary legends of Greece, the family of the Atridæ, the house

in real value to specie payments, and I lost very considerably on the payment in paper of a sum of money I had lent to a friend, whose executors after his death so returned what I had given in gold.

of Œdipus, with all their horrors, are fabulous; but the Hebrew chronicle of that ancient Eastern king is as trustworthy as its remoteness of date and place permits; and we have, with every detail of love, and friendship, and hate, and personal crime, and filial iniquity, and revolt, the whole story; from the triumphant blaze of the youth's first victories, to the dust and ashes of the miserable old man's affliction and humiliation.*

.*York Farm, March 13th,* 1875.

MY DEAREST H——,

In one of my last letters I explained to you how it was that I found myself obliged to withdraw my funds from St. Louis, my sole trustee there having declined any further administration of my affairs, upon the plea of failing health and increasing age. My other trustee struck work about six years ago, and I have been rather nervous ever since at having my property in the sole charge of one guardian, to whom, if anything happened, I did not know what would become of it. This is the one circumstance which reconciles me to the removal of my small semi-fortune from where it brings me ten per cent. to

---

* A very admirable preacher and profound Hebrew scholar holds that by the divisions into chapters and verses of the ancient text, the translation which we use is often made quite unfaithful to the original. Thus, he says that in the Hebrew text the maledictions which we read as David's are undoubtedly those intended to be separated, as invoked upon him by his enemies. The very frequent transition from these dire curses to expressions of prayer, praise, and thanksgiving, give plausibility to this explanation.

where at the utmost I can only obtain six for it—
a change which at once diminishes my yearly income very considerably, and, now that I am quite
past work, that makes me rather unhappy, as at
present I live up to my income, and, not without some
carefulness and the foregoing of unnecessary expenses
such as keeping a carriage or making journeys, etc. It
cannot be helped, however, and must be accepted. . . .

Arnold was the name of the person who opened
the English opera house, and sued the great theatres
on account of their patents, and was Mr. Beazley's
great friend.

I am sorry that your brother's death and your
nephew's desire for the details of the earlier circumstances of his father's life should be taking you back
to all the sorrowful memories of those times. How
little those who come after us can imagine the
dreariness of such retrospects !

I go on very leisurely indeed with my Memoirs,
and have got beyond the year 1839, the period of our
return from Georgia. Yesterday I was looking over a
number of Emily Fitzhugh's notes to you, written while
I was staying at Banisters, after I came back from
Italy, when I was obliged to resume my profession for
a maintenance. They contained many details of my
distressful bargainings with the London managers,
about terms for my reappearance on the stage. Heaven
knows, all that portion of my history is desolate and
dreary enough and not worth preserving, for it can
interest and amuse no one, and will never become
interesting and amusing to me.*

* When first I went upon the stage my salary was fixed at

We have had, since I last wrote to you, the heaviest snowstorm of the winter, and that is now being washed away by a sweeping spring rain. The frost, which had contracted the fibres of the earth at least two feet deep, is gradually coming out of the ground, and is here just that depth of mud, and the roads are utterly impassable for human feet and very nearly so for wheels and horses' legs. This is a terrible time of year here, and will last nearly a month, at least it will probably be as long as that before walking will be possible, let alone pleasurable.

My experience would induce me to say, trust, *and* try your friends; my observation, trust, but do *not* try them. You, my dearest, will not misunderstand this, though with such friends as God has blessed me with it might sound ungratefully cynical.

thirty pounds a week, the highest weekly wages my Aunt Siddons received in the middle of her theatrical career. When in middle life I resumed my profession, Mr. Knowles, of Manchester, offered me the highest terms I could then obtain, forty pounds a night, with which very liberal remuneration I was more than satisfied. After that, the natural decrease of my attraction and popularity made any such terms quite hopeless for me ; and I was very glad to obtain from Mr. Madox, of the Prince's Theatre, a salary of fifteen pounds a week, the highest I got during the last year of my theatrical career, to which succeeded, to my inexpressible relief, my most fortunately successful attempt of public reading, which I never hated as I did acting, but often enjoyed more I am sure than those who heard me, and thought I ought not to be paid at all for what gave me so much pleasure.

York Farm, March 16*th*, 1875.

DEAREST H——,

I get on very slowly with my Memoirs, and
have only crept hitherto as far as the year 1839 and
our return from the plantation. The copying of my
letters (from which of course I wish to omit very
considerable portions) is very tiresome, and so I am
lazy about it; but I have no other occupation to
demand my time and attention, and so I go plodding
on sleepily but steadily at it, and almost wonder if I
had done with it what else I should do.

After a succession of merely ephemeral clergymen,
borrowed from one place and another, for a succession
of Sundays, we have at length a resident incumbent
for this tiny church; but the fact is that there is really
and truly no congregation to fill an Episcopal church
here, and no call for any such ministration. The
church itself, the most diminutive of fanes, was principally built and got up by a very rich Philadelphia
banker, who lived in this neighbourhood, and had a
fancy for an Episcopal place of worship. He and
F—— were really the foundation stones and upholding
pillars of this small sacred edifice. The banker in
question has been obliged to sell his great country
house and disappear from the surface of things,
having swindled, cheated, fleeced, and robbed the
United States in general, and every individual citizen
in them in particular. Miss F—— B—— (as she then
was, in the days of her former residence here) lives
here no more, and is no more Miss F—— B——, as
you know, and has no longer any personal desire or
necessity for an Episcopal place of worship in this

immediate neighbourhood. All our well-to-do and *genteel* neighbours are Quakers born and bred, and the small village shopkeepers and mechanics are bred and born Dissenters of some shape or other, only coming to this church because it is nearer than any place of worship of their own, and also because latterly Episcopalianism has been the fashion and Dissent has not. S—— does not go to the church frequently, and is, I suspect, an indifferent Episcopalian; and I, who go as regularly as I can, but am not even an indifferent Episcopalian, am, I verily believe, at present the principal stay and support of the small establishment, to the maintenance of which I have subscribed, ever since I came here, at the rate of three guineas a month.

The clergyman, having, I suppose, the most infinitesimal salary that ever vicar had, has thought fit to take to himself a helpmate, to assist him in spending it, and brought his small young girl of a wife here the other evening to pay me a visit. She came from the village of Sing Sing, on the Hudson, and bemoaned to me the dreary dulness of this her present residence at Branchtown, the total absence of all social and intellectual resources here, as compared to the "world" from which she had come. Certainly such matters are comparative, but I could hardly help smiling as I assured her that I quite appreciate the dearth of social resources, recreations, and excitements of Branchtown. The young clergyman studied abroad, in Germany, and there increased a natural taste, which he appears to have, for art and its beautiful creations; and was quite enthusiastic in his admiration of my collection of Greek coins. I feel very sorry for them both, poor

children, in this barren banishment of theirs, where I
do not think they will have the consolation of achieving
much spiritual good for their very queerly composed
parish.

My intercourse with my opposite neighbours has
been more seriously interrupted by the thaw than it
had been by the previous hard weather. The mud is
inconceivable and indescribable; the ground, which
has been frozen at least two feet deep, is now thawing
to the same measure; a heavy fall of snow, the heaviest
we have hitherto had, is melting at the same time;
violent rain is pouring steadily from the sky, and the
condition of the road between the two houses and of
the gravel-walks and grass to be traversed before we
reach each other's door must be seen to be believed.
I generally spend one evening a week with them (and
as many more as I am *desired*), but for the last fortnight it would have been impossible to go the half
quarter of a mile, if a conveyance had not been sent
for me.

I dare say you do not remember "in the abstract,"
as you say, the pretty air which I caught from
Dorothy, and now play regularly every evening by
firelight *in memoriam* of you both. It was a simple
graceful dance tune, with rather a sentimental vein in
its gaiety. I cannot tell you when I learned it, but
it was one of the many times when I was with you
both and she played it, and as it was very simple I
caught it easily by ear.

When Fanny Cobbe wrote me word of their proposed change of residence, she said they had taken a
house in Cheyne Walk, which I think is beyond the

Houses of Parliament and down towards Chelsea. I remember it as a row of quaint old-fashioned looking houses, in a street adjacent to which I used to call on the Carlyles, regretting always, as I did so, their immense distance from my part of town. Carlyle, you know, was one of my early idols, and has remained so always. His genius has influenced our time more than that of any other man, though he was a Scotch peasant (perhaps because), and that foundation underlies his whole mental and moral edifice.* . . .

God bless you, my dearest H——. I throw the arms of my heart round you, and am ever, as ever, yours,

FANNY.

* I do not know whether I am singular in not endorsing very heartily the enthusiastic admiration of his wife's genius bestowed upon her after her death by Carlyle. In my personal intercourse with her, she seemed to me a bright, clever, intelligent woman, but as to any comparison between her mental powers and those of the two great geniuses of our day, George Sand and George Eliot, it was really absurdly inadmissible. She either had caught from Carlyle or was naturally endowed with a fine general contempt for the intellects of her acquaintance ; and in her letters I think displays an *effort* at brilliancy and point quite destructive of its effect. A very small instance of this, with reference to myself, will illustrate this tendency. "Mrs. Butler paid me a visit," said she, "with a riding whip, I suppose to keep her hand in." I was dressed in my habit, and just going out on horseback, and necessarily carried my riding whip, which I am not aware of ever practising (keeping my hand in the use of) with any creature but my horse. The desire to write something *smart*, such as this observation of hers exhibits, seems to me unpleasant, and unsuccessfully and frequently apparent in Mrs. Carlyle's letters. I wish clever people had a higher and juster respect for simple stupidity.

P.S.—I am so rejoiced that you have Miss Lambert and her nieces near you. It must be an immense resource to E——, and all their uncommon Danish and Norwegian experiences must give them much material for interesting and amusing talk with you.

York Farm, March 22nd, 1875.

My dearest H——,

At present we seem to be really further from spring than a month ago. Since March came in, which it certainly did in old proverbial fashion, "like a lion," we have had a second edition of winter. Two evenings ago I started to go over the way, and was obliged to turn back before I reached my own gate, the bitter blinding sleet beat like a furious storm of pins and needles so sharply in my face, and the ground was so covered with a smooth coating of ice that I was in danger of falling at every step. Yesterday evening, by keeping quite in the middle of the public road, which had been broken up and roughened by the passing of horses and vehicles, I contrived to walk to church, about a quarter of a mile from here. I had been prevented by the weather and the impracticable condition of the roads from getting to church for nearly a month, and yesterday was the first Sunday since the middle of February, when it seemed possible to do so; and I do not know when I have seen anything more wonderful and beautiful than the radiant full moon shining on the trees literally coated from top to bottom with clear ice, their branches hanging downwards with the crystal weight, and the dark blue sky and resplendent stars seen through their glittering boughs. In spite of the cold, I stopped repeatedly in the road to exclaim aloud (though I was alone), and wonder at the strange and beautiful spectacle. This morning the cold is still severe, though the sun shines brilliantly and the trees retain their silver covering, even to the topmost twigs, and are so bright one can hardly look at them. In no other part of the world have I ever seen a winter pageant comparable to this splendid show. . . .

The last letters from F—— were written in good spirits, and spoke favourably of the general condition of things on the plantation.

I must leave this letter for an hour while I try and get my first walk for nearly three weeks. If I do not get out before the sun has become more powerful, the middle of the road, where I am obliged to walk, there being no safe footing in any other part of it, will have become a mere alternation of broad puddles and deep mud-holes, while the sides of the road will be one smooth surface of ice impossible to stand or step upon. Certainly the bright sky that I rejoice in so much over one's head here has a heavy *per contra* in the conditions of the earth under one's feet.

My dearest H——, I have just come back from a *struggle* of half a mile up the road, which, with the half mile back, has taken me nearly an hour to achieve, with one foot sticking in mud, while the other was sliding on ice, and a fierce March sun and wind alternately scorching and piercing one.

Since I have come in, S—— has just called, and you may imagine the state of the roads, her feet were so loaded with mud, and her petticoats so dripping with wet, that she would not even come into the house, but stood at the hall door, while she gave me a letter she had just had from F——, describing one of those terrible freshets or inundations to which they are liable down there. She says, " Pray that you may never witness a freshet, even where no human life is in danger, and only poor chickens and rabbits go floating by your window. Up to the last we hoped it would not 'top' the banks [the dyked banks of the river], but last night we saw it slowly creeping in, and this morning, as far as eye could see, was nothing but a sea of muddy water. The tips of my poor roses are just above it, but I fear neither they nor any of the rest of my flowers will survive." Further on she says her husband and a friend, who is paying them a visit, had just gone off in a boat over fields and banks to the upper end of the island, to see if they could rescue some of the poor sheep that have got caught up there by the flood. "The rest of the animals," she says, "are all huddled together on a mound in the rick-yard, and have to be sent off as fast as possible to St. Simon's [the cotton plantation fifteen miles down the river]. The poor chickens fare worst of all, for if they stay on the trees they starve, and if they come down they drown. There are more than a dozen floating about the garden now, besides hen-coops, boxes, bottles, oranges, and all manner of household articles, including a slop-pail. Inside the house we are devoured by mosquitoes, brought by the water, and overrun by rats and mice, which have taken refuge from it." Is not that a picture of an agreeable condition? They were of course going to leave the plantation immediately, and betake themselves to Florida. Their being able to return at all to the Rice Island, before coming back to the North, would depend upon the length of time this deluge lasted.

I had been looking with some anxiety for news from them, for I heard yesterday that there had been a violent tornado in the interior of Georgia, which, though at a considerable distance from them and limited in its area, had done a great deal of mischief, and destroyed both life and property, so that I hope the freshet, bad as it is, may be their only share of these elemental disturbances.

York Farm, March 24th, 1875.

MY DEAREST H——,

I have no means of ascertaining what becomes of my letters, when once my own gardener, who is a trustworthy, careful fellow, has carried them to the post-office, which he does (or rather goes thither for that purpose or to fetch my letters thence) twice a day. I am afraid if my letter of the 15th of last month has not reached you yet, there is very little chance of its ever doing so. I do not know that our village post-master is exceptionally inattentive to his functions, but there is a careless, reckless, easy-go-lucky kind of way of doing business in this country which suits the *hasty* existence of the natives themselves, and the character and disposition of their Irish fellow-citizens, but which is gall and wormwood to English residents of my stamp.

I ventured out yesterday for the first *walk* I have taken for ever so long; but though the sky was bright and clear, the progress I made was small and slow, and consisted chiefly of sticking fast in the mud with one foot, while the other was sliding rapidly and ungovernably over a smooth surface of ice, a species of gymnastic more curiously grotesque than graceful or agreeable at sixty-five years old, and at which I laughed as if I could see myself. By-the-by, pray am I sixty-five, or how many years old? I think you know better than I do, but you know young women understate their age from vanity, and old women overstate theirs from the same motive.

To-day we are having a heavy snowstorm, and shall have to undergo all that dreadful melting process again, by far the most odious of our winter experiences. Hitherto the winter has not been at all unpleasant to me, though everybody has complained of its extreme severity, I have really not suffered from the intense cold, and have enjoyed the remarkable clear brilliancy of sky and sunshine, by which it has been accompanied. But ever since the beginning of this month the sky has been dark and the weather dismal, and I am now almost as tired of the prolonged and inclement winter as everybody else is.

My poor frozen geraniums were not killed, I am happy to say, though they certainly had all the appearance of not being likely to recover. They are all putting out young leaves, however, and appear likely to live. The accident occurred in consequence of my having let a canary bird, which my grandson gave me at Chistmas, fly in the greenhouse, where, fearing he might accidentally get into the hot air-vent, which has only a widish grating over it, I turned off the heat, and after the bird was safe in his cage forgot for several hours to open the flue again, during which time my poor plants were chilled within an inch of their lives.

The news of Mitchell's death, the ticket-*of-no-leave* member of Parliament, has just reached me. I suppose this termination of his election question will be a real convenience to everybody concerned, himself as well as everybody else.

York Farm, Branchtown, April 12th, 1875.

MY BELOVED H——,

I enclose you an obituary notice of a friend and neighbour of mine lately dead, a Quaker lady, who lived less than half a mile from here, whose parents were among my first acquaintance when I came to live at Branchtown, after my marriage. I was very intimate with her, and I liked and respected her very much ; but why she should have been made the subject of a newspaper obituary notice puzzles me a little. She was a middle-aged single woman of high principle, fine character, great good sense, and very simple manners, but without any quality whatever, or any peculiarity of position, to render her liable to newspaper illustration and commendation. I do not know whether it is a peculiar custom among the Quakers so to celebrate the quietest members of their peculiarly quiet sect, or only the general American taste for notoriety. To me, a newspaper notice of such a private gentlewoman appears entirely inappropriate and slightly offensive. I thought it was only *such as*

I who *incurred* that sort of compliment.* Her house, a pleasant, old-fashioned residence, something between farmhouse and country seat, is at present shut up and uninhabited, none of the remaining members of her family being so circumstanced as to be able to live there; and this throws a gloom over the whole neighbourhood, for during my friend's life her house was a hospitable, cheerful centre of reunion for all the members of two very large families, all the relations and connections of which looked upon Wakefield (the name of the house) as a sort of general meeting-place for their two clans. . . .

I do not see the *Times*, but read (I think in the *Spectator*) an account of Garibaldi's zealous purpose and endeavour to have the course of the Tiber altered, in order, if possible, to prevent the terrible frequent inundations of Rome by it. An American engineer explained to me how costly and difficult (though not of course impossible) any process that could accomplish such a result would be, because there was no fall whatever in the land between Rome and the mouth of the Tiber at Ostia, and that the consequence was, when the river was at all full, either from heavy rains or the melting of the mountain snows, and that the

* I have since seen so many newspaper notices, and even pamphlet records of perfectly unobtrusive, unnotorious private individuals, male and female, which could have no possible interest beyond the circle of their immediate personal friends, that I think this sort of *celebration* of individual character and conduct must be looked upon here as a tribute of affectionate respect. To me, who think notoriety anything but a privilege, it seems *dis*respectful, especially towards women, of whom the ancients held that the *best* were those *least heard of.*

sirocco of Africa drove the Mediterranean upon the Italian shore, the water coming down the Tiber was met by the sirocco-driven sea and pushed back, causing it to inundate Rome and all the level campagna round it, to where the last slope of the subsiding Apennines prevents the upward progress of the water, and sends it back again upon the Roman plain. These natural ·causes are of course both difficult and costly to counteract or contend against.

I had heard through the newspapers of Garibaldi's refusal of the pension of four thousand a year which the government or people had offered to settle on him. Miss Storey, who lives with her parents in Rome, wrote my daughter an account of Garibaldi, which was simply that he was "living with his contadina wife and children" near the walls of the city (riddled with his cannon shot) in some villa, the name of which I forget, "keeping himself quiet and giving no trouble," which rather contemptuous notice of the heroic Italian patriot did not surprise me on the young lady's part, as I imagine she and her family have small sympathy with his character or career. . . .

Surely, dear H——, a life of great *unhappiness* is compatible with immense and intense *enjoyment*. The first belongs to the moral and mental nature, the last to the physical organization.

York Farm, April 18th, 1875.

MY DEAREST H——,

I write to you under two depressing influences —a bad bilious attack and a heavy snowstorm, the second we have had within this week ; and as we have had more than enough of bitter winter, and that we are now in the middle of April, to see the whole earth covered with this wintry white is rather discouraging.

I had a letter from my sister the other day. She had had H—— staying with her at Warsash, and spoke very favourably of him. She said he was doing well in his profession, earning a good weekly salary, and becoming known and valued for his steady application to his work A—— also said that he was a very nice fellow, well-bred, with quiet unassuming manners. . . .

There is a strong prejudice in this country in favour of nursing babies through their second summer, on account of the heat of the season and their teething, which combination of adversities is supposed to try the children less if they are still kept at the breast. I am not, however, a convert to this opinion, and weaned both my children when they were between nine and ten months old quite successfully.

F—— wrote in her last letter that Mr. L—— was extremely busy preparing a number of the young negro men on the island for confirmation. The bishop was paying them a visit, and they were feeling very much interested in their young people and their religious education. She has not mentioned any damage done to the crops by the inundation, and so I suppose there was none, which is very fortunate. They were going down to St. Simon's, the cotton plantation on the sea, at the mouth of the river, for the month of May, and then were to come here to me in June.

York Farm, Saturday, May 1st, 1875.

May day and the sky scowls, and we have barely
a sign of spring about us, though some *audacious*
violets have been caught in the woods, and the wild
anemones are beginning to show their white stars in
sheltered nooks; but the season is unusually cold and
backward, and the raw chilly air feels as if winter
was only just round the corner, as indeed he is, for we
had heavy snow a short time ago, and it still freezes
every night. This will sound comfortless to you, my
dearest H———, to whom warmth is such a necessary
of life; but for my own individual comfort the longer
the summer *keeps off* the more thankful I am, though
I confess, if I could see a few leaves and blossoms, I
should think the world prettier and pleasanter. . . .

I wish I could hear of another good Transatlantic
tenant for the house at Widmore. The Americans
seem to be the only people who live what upholsterers
and *such* call " regardless of expense."

My Southerners will not be here for a month yet,
and indeed I do not expect them before the second
week in June, for they are to come north direct by
sea, and will go to Newport to secure a house or
lodging for the very hot months, July and August,
before they come here, when they expect to spend the
month of June with me.

I wrote you word of the failure of their Savannah
agents, with a thousand pounds worth of their rice in
their hands. We have not yet heard what arrangement the firm make with its creditors, or how much
of the value of the rice can be rescued, if anything.
What with the uncertain nature, climate, and crop,

and the more than uncertain principle and practice of
the Southern men of business, a rice plantation in
Georgia seems to me the least desirable of all properties.
Certainly excitement is never wanting in connection
with it, but it is unfortunately almost always of a
disastrous or disagreeable kind.

There *is* furious party feeling in America between
the politicians, *i.e.* the men who make a trade and
speculation of the government of the country, the
greatest riff-raff of low rascals, I suppose, to be found in
any world, old or new.   But the old-fashioned, *respectable* political parties of the earlier days of the American
Republic, when both the members of the government
and the opposition were still in character, feeling, and
principle, *English gentlemen,* are dead and buried
long ago, and would certainly not acknowledge their
present representatives as such.   Party politics (and
there now are none others) simply consist of a desperate
conflict between the blackguards who are in, and the
blackguards who are out of office.   I think, however,
public affairs are assuming a more hopeful aspect in
this country, inasmuch as an opinion appears to be
gradually dawning in the national mind of the United
States that a decently honest people (which they undoubtedly are) had better not be represented or
governed by a pack of shameless sharpers, which
they also undoubtedly are. . . . .

Of course there is quite as much vanity in self-
accusation as in self-justification.   Simple people, I
fancy, are as little given to the one as to the other.
The latter is rather pride, and the former vanity; but
excessive pride occasionally assumes an appearance of

humility. Self-examination may be a good thing, but self-forgetfulness is a better. And spiritual health is no more indicated by constant introspection than physical health would be by perpetually examining one's tongue and feeling one's pulse. St. Paul, in one of his letters to his Christian converts, says that it is a very little thing for him to be judged by them, and that indeed he "judged not his own self."

God bless you, my dearest H——. You ask after my health, and it is good enough to be thankful for at my age; and, in spite of fifty years added to it since first you knew me, I am still ever, *as* ever, yours,

FANNY.

York Farm, May 4th, 1875.

MY DEAREST H——,

In going over the immense mass of letters you returned to me, I am astonished at the minute and abundant details of the events of my life which the all but daily history of it, in my correspondence, conveyed to you. You have known pretty much everything that has ever interested or concerned me, and I find in these incessant communications a degree of detail of much that I experienced that I now think I should have done far more wisely not to record. . . .

I do not expect my children till the second week in June. I am now anxiously looking for some detail with regard to the amount of loss they have sustained through the failure of the agent who has had the selling of their rice crop partially entrusted to him. We hope they may recover something of a thousand pounds worth of their rice in the hands of the firm at the time of the failure.

I can hardly say that we are yet rejoicing in the departure of winter, for snow and ice have been with us until quite lately. Still the spring is on her way, though apparently very reluctantly, and to-day, under a still steady rain, the leaves appear to be visibly sprouting. Yesterday I counted about twenty small spikes piercing the asparagus bed, and after this tardy progress, I suppose the whole vegetable development of the season will come upon us with a rush, and the spring will carry the world by storm. . . .

M—— desires me to tell you not to be anxious on the score of the diminution of my income, as any deficit in my means must be amply made up by the vast sums I win from her at ecarté and picquet, when we play together on the evening of our weekly meetings, our "Soirées du Lundi," as we call them.

York Farm, May 10*th,* 1875.

My beloved H——,

I have seen no swallows yet about us here, the rapid, darting creature who is always associated (as is the first bee, I see) with you in my thoughts. Our spring-appearing birds hitherto have been the bluebird, a very beautiful creature, I think related to the jay, which is one of the early spring birds in England.

> " When through green holts new flushed with may
> Ring sudden laughters of the jay."

There have come almost together the cat-bird, which is in fact the northern mocking-bird, and has a magnificent and various note, besides the harsh sort

of scream to which he owes his vulgar appellation of
the cat-bird, several thrushes, the American robin red-
breast, a truculent feathered biped as big as our black-
bird, with a splendid scarlet velvet waistcoat coming
half-way down his thighs, like a beau of George II.'s
time, or Mr. Garrick in the character of Macbeth.
Besides him we have a bird called the wood robin,
whose note is precisely like the sound of a flageolet,
reedy, soft, and more mournfully melancholy than that
of any bird whose voice I ever heard, and as I sat
listening to it yesterday at sunset, it recalled the days
of my former life over the way, when I sat heavy-
hearted, looking down the avenue and listening to
this prolonged sweet plaintive note among the branches
touched with the departing light. . . .

At present these are all the birds that the spring
has brought back to us, but I have seen none of your
swallows yet, though they must have come some time
ago, for we have already had oppressively warm
weather and thunder, and are dried up and parched
for want of rain.

My exercise has dwindled to almost nothing, and
has become very irregular, partly on account of the
(till quite lately) unfavourable weather and impracticable roads, and partly because of my own greatly
diminished desire and capacity for it. I find now
that a moderate walk of a couple of miles in the
morning takes so much out of me that I am hardly
fit to spend the evening over the way, I am so much
tried by it. To-day I am going to dine at Champlost,
and have not walked, for fear of being overtired this
evening; still, I do walk frequently, though no longer

regularly every day. A moderate stroll of between two and three miles, once or twice a week, is pretty much all I am good for, and after that I am glad to lie on the sofa and rest. I think the desire for exercise in a naturally active person is a fair measure of their need of, and capacity for it, and I find myself now little inclined for the daily *tramp*, which I took very regularly till the last winter, when the weather interrupted it, and disinclination has now supervened with the loss of habit, and when I come back now from my *crawl*, I feel not younger, but considerably older, than I was a few months ago.

The spring is always relaxing, and here the heat comes so suddenly and is so oppressive, that it is doubly trying; we have close sultry days already, with thunder in the air, and consequent headaches and languor. It is a most trying climate.

I am going to tell you something curious, which I do not believe you would believe if anybody else told it you. I think I have mentioned that the farmer's house, with adjacent barn-yard, hay-yard, and poultry-yard, is behind this cottage. Some time ago I perceived that a solitary hen was frequenting the lawn in front of it, and had apparently withdrawn from the society of her fellow fowls at the back. Whether she *boarded* at home, returning to the poultry-yard for her meals, or contented herself with foraging in the flowerbeds and grass of the garden, I do not know, but she certainly had shaken the dust of her former residence from her claws completely at other times.

One day I perceived an unusual commotion and

agitation in a handsome pine tree, whose branches sweep the lawn, and to my amazement beheld one of our cats, engaged with this hen in the liveliest game of hide-and-seek; running in and out under the tree after each other, the cat crouching, wriggling, and darting beneath the branches, and the bird occasionally hopping up on one of them, whither the beast pursued her. At first I thought it was war, sudden death, and murder; but presently perceived it was peace, and the pursuit of innocent amusement with the friendliest good understanding. After this I watched them, and to my infinite amusement saw this game repeated over and over again. Then these curious companions took to walking sedately side by side (almost what you might call arm-in-arm) round the gravel walk, and finally settled amicably down together, on the nice hot glass frame of one of the vegetable pits, in the kitchen garden. Here I have seen them sitting, winking and blinking in the sun, apparently perfectly happy in mind and body, until suddenly the hen would turn sharply round and give a vicious peck at the cat's face or breast (what it had said to shock or offend her I did not hear), upon which the four-footed feline creature (hurt, no doubt, in all its feelings) slid down and made off rather shamefacedly, the biped, the feathered fowl, remaining in undivided possession, though apparently in ruffled dignity, of the comfortable hot glass. Now, isn't all this strange? If I had not seen I should not have believed it. I wish I knew what that cat said to that hen; it must have been something highly improper.

[I have since heard of a similar curious companion-

ship in an English farmyard, and seen a remarkable
instance of it while staying in Paris, at the Hôtel du
Rhin, in the Place Vendôme, where a magnificent white
warlike-looking cockatoo and splendid white Persian
cat used to walk up and down the sunny courtyard of
the hotel half the morning together. Both the animals
were of unusual size and strength, and any dispute
between them would have been a terrible spectacle; but
I would have backed the cockatoo against the cat.] . . .

I do not myself know any American Alcocks, but
believe there are Bostonians of that name. All the
colonists in the north-eastern and midland states of
the Union were originally English, or, at any rate
British, and there can hardly be a family here whose
parent stock is not on the other side of the water, and
probably the relation between the branches, which
have spread on either side of the Atlantic, would be
easily traced in most instances. . . .

My dearest ·H——, it is my dear M—— who
ministers to *me*, not I to *her* in our constant intercourse. No day passes without my receiving from
Champlost some token of affectionate remembrance,
from the flowers and fruit, that come to me in beautiful and bountiful profusion from her garden and
hothouse, to the pleasant drives she fetches me to take
with her, and which are so great a refreshment and
pleasure to me, though so little, I am sorry to say, to
her, suffering as she does incessantly from nervous
apprehension of accidents, of one sort or another, by
which her drives are converted into absolute penances,
from which I should think it impossible that she could
derive any benefit, either to her health or spirits.

Almost all the country roads in this pretty neighbour-hood are traversed by railroads, and it is difficult to take a drive in any direction which avoids them. The park itself is free from these iron interruptions, with their hissing and screaming teams, but between Champlost and the park several would have to be crossed, besides the almost equally disagreeable impediments of the suburban tramways. These latter nuisances are so absolutely in possession of all the principal streets in the city, that it is running the risk of dislocating one's whole carriage and all one's own bones to undertake a morning's shopping.

York Farm, May 14th, 1875.

My DEAREST H——,

The L——s are now down at St. Simon's, a pleasant and healthy place on the sea, at the mouth of the Altamaha river, far better for them all than the rice plantation ; but then they are at a much greater distance from the little town of Darien and all the amenities of civilization, medical assistance included, which of course is a disadvantage. I shall be thankful when they are all safe here, which I hope now will be in about three weeks.

The winter, I suppose, is really finally gone, though the gardener still postpones bedding out the green-house plants, saying that the nights are frosty still. The whole process of the spring here is so sudden, that the leafing of the trees and blossoming of the early shrubs comes really, as with the waving of some fairy's wand, in less than a week ; the whole aspect of the woods and fields changes from barren

bareness to vivid grass and foliage, thick enough to
make a shade, the sunshine is oppressive, and the
dust in the road, between the house over the way and
mine, all but ankle-deep already. The whole of last
year this region suffered from constant drought, and
the spring has hitherto brought no rain, so that people
are beginning to be very anxious about the failing of
the water supply and the injury to the agriculture.

I am very sorry for your account of Fanny Cobbe's
overworking herself. I suppose at the rate at which
the world moves now it is almost impossible for any
one who wishes to do anything not to do too much.
When I was in London she appeared to me to be
overtasking herself; her eyes were beginning to fail,
and she was threatened with loss of power in her
right hand from too constant use of it in writing. I
should think her nerves might be shaken with the
painful nature of the interests in which she was exert-
ing herself, with so much zeal and sympathy. Any
ridicule that she might incur by her advocacy of the
" rights of animals " would be quite indifferent to her,
I am sure; but the details of cruelty with which she
has been obliged to become acquainted must have
tried her kind and loving nature severely. I have
been afraid that she would injure herself seriously by
her exertions in this cause. However, a person who is
forwarding works of humanity and benevolence, and
measures of progress and enlightenment, by which
others are to benefit, can hardly be said to be *throwing*, though they may be *giving* their life away.
Nobody is a judge of duty for another. Anxiety for
those we love, and uncertainty in our judgments about

them, is the stuff half one's life is made of, for who
is wise ? and who is reasonable ? and who governs
their existence just as they should do ? And assuredly
the people who kill themselves by labouring for
others are not the majority.

York Farm, May 31st, 1875.

MY DEAREST H——,

I am, of course, deeply interested in the
condition of the country I am living in, and am quite
hopeful about its future, in spite of all that is disgraceful in its present. The political and financial rascality
are astounding just now, no doubt; but the nation is
vastly better than its politicians or financiers, and by
degrees the people, who are beginning to be ashamed
of their rulers and government, will reform the abuses
which are bringing such discredit upon the whole
country. The great *misfortune* is its real general
prosperity, and the consequent little interest which
any but professional politicians take in public affairs.
Private prosperity here seems really to destroy patriotism, and unfortunately any private business *pays better*
than the business of the State, *i.e.* serving the country
in any capacity, and so the public servants, or the
servants of the republic, are the least respectable individuals to be found in it. Our own political honesty,
even among men of the highest rank, dates no further
back than late in George III.'s time, so I am not
without hope that the American government may
before long cease to be the dirty jobbery that it is
now. I think it is curious that at the time when a
miserably low standard of honour and morality pre-

vailed among our politicians, public men, and statesmen, the commercial conscience of our people, the
integrity, honesty, and character, of our English merchants and men of business, was decidedly higher and
better than it is at the present day.   The influence
and example of America has been unfavourable to us
in this respect ; their speculating mania and rage for
rapid money-making has infected our slow and sure
and steady-going mercantile community.   The plodding
thrift and scrupulous integrity and long-winded patient
industry of our business men of the last century are
out of fashion in these " giddy-paced " times, and
England is forgetting that those who make haste to
be rich can hardly avoid much temptation and some
sin.

York Farm, June 8th, 1875.

My dearest H——,

I think I must have told you that my money
affairs have now become settled again, in so far that
my property is reinvested, but it is at a diminution
of interest of nearly three hundred pounds a year.   Of
course, as I spend every penny of my income, this has
caused me both vexation and anxiety, and being quite
unable to betake myself again to my former industry,
or open my mouth to fill my pocket, I have very
glady accepted a most liberal offer, made to me by the
publisher of the *Atlantic Monthly Magazine*, one of
the principal American periodicals, who wrote me
word from Boston some time ago that he would be
glad of any article I would send to him.   This, of
course, is an immense relief to me for the present, and

I am going to publish my manuscripts in his magazine. I do not, however, trust the manuscript I read to you out of my own hands, and am therefore obliged to copy it all over again, a heavy job of writing, which will give me steady pen-work for many a day to come, and which just at starting has kept me so occupied as to delay my answer to your last two letters. I am now, however, fairly beforehand with my publisher, and shall have leisure for a month to come to resume my usual rate of correspondence. It has been a great satisfaction to me to find I had still in my power the means of self-help.

I am really thankful for this renewed supply of means just now, because, what with the enormous price of living in this country, and the increase of my family, for one or two months of the year, the loss of two or three hundred pounds annually made me feel very uncomfortable. I know myself to be quite incapable of any such changes in my mode of life as a lesser income would necessitate, for though I spend nothing in *superfluities*, the general comfort in which I live is in itself expensive. I do not keep a carriage, but I have four servants, and am obliged to keep a gardener at eight pounds a month, and so spend much in keeping the place in order.

I am expecting my dear Mr. L—— to-day. He only comes on from New York to fetch some clothes he left here, and then returns immediately to sail for England, where he expects to spend the next two months, the dreadful hot months of July and August. How I wish I was going with him! F—— remains in New York till after he has sailed, and then comes here with her baby and three servants, a considerable addition to my small household. The length of her stay is quite uncertain, but will depend upon how the child endures the heat ; she is remarkably backward with her teething, and this, of course, will make the oppressive summer weather additionally trying to her, and she will be taken away to the seaside, at Newport, during the great heat. S—— also expects to go away during the summer to the seaside, and talks of taking her boy to Niagara, a pleasure I greatly envy her, or rather rejoice in for her. I cannot afford travelling, which, like everything else, is inordinately expensive here, but shall be kept in countenance by M——, who is not well enough to leave home and encounter the infinite and *unwholesome* discomfort of American hotel living.

I have been reading Coleridge lately (his prose works). Why does he say the Italians are, as a nation, witty, but not humorous ? I wonder what he makes of that whole family of Italians, harlequin, pantaloon, Punch, and that representative Folksman the Turinese Gian Duca ? Abekeu told me that the Bergamasque Arlechino was an Italian popular version of the German Erlkönig, the sudden appearances and disappearances, and dark invisible face, being common characteristics of both ; but I don't believe it, though it is very difficult to tell, whether certain popular beliefs and superstitions originated in the north or the south, or sprang up simultaneously (or at any rate independently) in various parts of the world, the East, apparently, being one of their earliest cradles.

York Farm, June 9th, 1875.

MY DEAREST H——,

Your memory, of which you complain as failing, often seems to me more retentive of events, and even minute details than mine. I have no recollection that it was on Trinity Sunday that you and I had gone up to Fairlight church, though I remember very well that we did go thither, and I think more than once together. I admired that beautiful height and the view from it greatly, and thought the buried there must be *"dided very dead"* (as S—— said, when she was three years old, of the poor chicken she had squeezed to death in her love of it) not every now and then to sit up and look about them. I do not think hearing J—— Y—— preach would have been any great satisfaction to either of us, he always seemed to me rather the wrong man in the wrong place, being essentially and by nature an actor, which I do not think an advantage to a clergyman, though there is no doubt that the two professions have some elements and some temptations in common. The personal presence, the effect (if *effects*, so much the worse) of the countenance, voice, deportment, and gesture, tells for so much in the pulpit, especially with the female part of a congregation, that simplicity and self-forgetfulness are difficult virtues in a "fashionable" clergyman. [I remember my friend herself coming home one day from hearing Bishop Wilberforce preach a very eloquent sermon, of which she expressed her admiration, adding, however, at the same time, "the worst of it is—the impossibility of telling if he is not only a first-rate actor."]

I have no doubt a consciousness of this had something to do with Frederick Robertson's little delight
in his Brighton pulpit popularity, and the dislike .
bordering on disgust which he once expressed at an
engraving which reproduced a rather sentimental
version of his face and figure while preaching. The
fact is, there is shrewd danger of the popular preacher
being dramatic, either in expression or in the *inten-
tional absence* of it; as in the actor's case, the man
himself is part of his work, an immense difficulty in
that highest and holiest of callings—that of a priest.

M—— and I and a neighbour and friend of ours went
last week to a famous sea-shore watering-place, four
hours by railroad from here, in hopes that the change
of air and scene might do all of us, but especially
M——, good. But the execrable food, sour bread,
tough meat, and general miserable discomfort of our
quarters at the principal hotel in the place (a huge
wooden barrack) compelled us to return after only one
day's experience of the delights of Longbranch. Certainly no one whose house is as comfortable as M——'s
ought to go anywhere else in this country, unless for
such positive beneficial result as is worth the sacrifice
of every decency and every convenience of civilized
life.

We have just got through the tremendous process
to which the extreme variations of this climate compel
all housekeepers here. Every carpet has been taken
up, and every curtain taken down, and together with
every woollen table cover, rug, blanket, fur, or similar
object of furniture or apparel packed in rolls with
pepper and camphor, in receptacles lined with cedar-

wood, having been previously sewn up in linen covers, judge of the *sneezing* throughout the whole household when they are unpacked in the autumn; but without all these precautions they would then have become, not "food for worms, brave Percy," but for moths, the mothers of worms.

Our floors are covered with matting, our windows with plain white muslin draperies, our furniture with brown holland, and every picture, looking-glass, and engraving, with coarse leno gauze, to protect them from the swarms of flies; all which, of course, gives an appearance of coolness, and really adds to what little can be obtained, by keeping the shutters shut and the rooms darkened all day.

You say you do not ever doze in the day, which surprises me, as I never take up a book for a quarter of an hour, at any hour of the day, without going to sleep. Of course I cannot do this while writing or working with my needle; but reading is an infallible soporific. I am very sleepy now, for I had a night of much pain, and got up at half-past six to see that my dear Mr. L—— had an early breakfast before starting. As soon as I lay down my pen, and take up the *Spectator*, I shall be in the blessed condition of the "little boy blue under his haystack fast asleep."

York Farm, June 10th, 1875.

My dearest H——,

I was just sitting down to write to you, when an amiable young lady called. She had come from town to see S——, but found her gone into Philadelphia, so she came and bestowed her tediousness

upon me for an hour; and, expressing her intention of
going on to see M——, I was so glad to get rid of her
that I offered to go with her by the "Lady's Walk,"
across the fields and through the woods, the nearest
way to Champlost. I have come back in a hot bath
with walking in the sun, and thoroughly uncomfortable for the rest of the day, and so I wish the amiable
young lady had not come to see me.

Mr. L—— left me yesterday, after a visit of a
night. He sails for England on Saturday, and on the
same day F—— and her baby, and her maid, and the
child's nurse, and a little black servant of the baby's
will arrive. Mr L—— left behind him yesterday, as
an instalment of the rest, a beautiful Irish retriever of
his, who passed last summer with me—a very fine,
large, intelligent dog, of which I am very fond, and,
which lies now panting at my feet, after his run across
the farm in the midday heat, which, in spite of his
being shorn as close as possible of all his fine brown
locks, seems to distress him as much as it does me.
Mr. L—— says his little girl looks delicate, because
she has a very white, colourless complexion; but that
she is large and muscularly strong, very gay and
lively, and hardly ever cries at all, which is certainly
a sign of physical well-being. I am very anxious to
see the little creature again, the thing that troubles
me about her is that she has got no teeth, and this at
eleven months old is being very backward, and I fear
very much the effect of the summer heat upon her
during that trying process, which I suppose must take
place presently.

I envied Mr. L—— going home to England and to

his family, and escaping the horrible heat of this climate, though only for a short time. He talks of returning at the end of July, with his nephew, Lord L——'s eldest son, who has been intending for some time past to visit the United States.

F—— now says that they never intended to spend less than three winters in Georgia, as less than that was an insufficient experiment with regard to the plantation. Certainly, when I came to America, I understood that we were to return this summer to England. Of course I have given up all such idea now, as I could not be happy on the other side of the Atlantic with both my children here; but it is a severe disappointment, and in every way trying and distressing to me. My remaining here is an advantage to F——, because she not only gets her rent for the house, but the place and property are taken care of as they would not be likely to be by any other tenant. Naturally I am glad enough to be of use to her in any way, but I should have rejoiced to return to England this summer. . . .

S—— is just now going through one of the miserable household crises which so perpetually afflict her, her lady's-maid is leaving her, and she is without a cook; but when this thing becomes chronic, as I really think it may be called in her case, I suppose, like the eels with the skinning, people get used to it.

Our hot weather has kept off hitherto mercifully, but it will not forbear us much longer, and I am invoking patience and courage for the endurance of it.

York Farm, June 25th, 1875.

My dearest H——,

I have now had F—— and her baby with me for upwards of a week. The little girl is the most delicate-looking creature I ever saw. She is so thin that one can see and feel all her little bones. She is as white as ivory, with dark shadows under her eyes, and has not a single tooth yet, in spite of all which she never cries or frets, and is habitually bright and lively and animated, so that I hope, as time goes on, she will acquire more vigour and get more nourishment out of her food. She takes as nearly as possible two quarts of milk in the four-and-twenty hours, and has had with them as much as six tea-spoonsfuls of brandy, which seems to me quite enormous for an infant; but is in accordance with the medical treatment of the present day, the fashion of which appears to be to give as much stimulant as possible.

Poor F—— is herself apparently well, but she feels depressed naturally, when she sees two of the farm people's babies, born just within a month of her poor little girl, rosy and plump, and with four teeth apiece.

Certainly this is the most trying climate in the world. It is not a week since it was so *cold* that we were obliged to have fires; and this morning, walking in the shade at seven o'clock, before breakfast, the perspiration ran down my face like rain. I shall be inexpressibly thankful when the summer is over, for I cannot afford to leave this place, and have to look forward to three months of physical misery, compared to which the cold of the winter was nothing.

Our whole neighbourhood just now is infested

with a horrible insect, which they vulgarly call the
potatoe bug, and which has come all the way from the
wild lands of Colorado. The farmer who cultivates
the forty acres of this small estate has a potatoe field,
where twice a day he collects two great milking pans
full of them, and in our potatoe patch, here in our
small kitchen garden, my Irish labourer showed me a
dozen of them on the first two or three potatoe plants.
I said I hoped they would not get over to Ireland,
'Och, murther!" cried he, "that would be the end of
the wurrld!"

You ask me if American men are like English men?
No; American gentlemen are a cross between English
and French men, and yet really altogether like neither.
They are more refined and modest than Frenchmen,
and less manly, shy, and rough, than Englishmen,
Their brains are finer and flimsier, their bodies less
robust and vigorous than ours. We are the finer
animals, and they the subtler spirits. Their intellectual
tendency is to excitement and insanity, and ours to
stagnation and stupidity.

Dearest H——, the heat is so oppressive that I can
hardly sit up to write. F—— in the next room has
closed all the shutters, undressed, and laid herself
down, and I must go and take a bath.

York Farm, June 26th, 1875.

DEAREST H——,
    . . . I wrote you yesterday what I had to
say about F—— and her baby. The little creature is
the most delicate child I ever saw; and now that the
awful heat has come upon us, she really looks as if

she might melt away, like a little wax model of an
infant. . . . I think American women are generally
rather deficient in animal instinct, and have little of
the excessive maternal feeling which derives from
it. . . .

Poor dear M—— and I profited but little by our
excursion to the seaside. We went, intending to stay
two whole days, and return on the fourth from our
departure. The place is one of the most fashionable
seaside resorts in the country, where the President has
a summer residence, and where, in the season, all the
gay Philadelphia world flocks in crowds. We went
to the best big hotel there, and such was the miserable
discomfort of our accommodation, that after enduring
it for one day, we all agreed with common consent to
return home, and having been obliged to have a fire,
and being chilled through with the bitter sea blast, we
travelled back to Philadelphia in broiling scorching
heat, and were thankful at any price to be in our own
houses again. M—— was none the worse happily for
the exertion; but unless the mere change of air com-
pensated for starvation, dirt, and every other detestable discomfort, she certainly was none the better.

You write me that you have had your hair cut
short, and yesterday I made Ellen cut off the whole of
mine, which she did very unwillingly. The intolerable
heat of a mass of hair on one's head and neck, in such
weather as we are now having, the impossibility of
keeping it dry and free from perspiration, and the
tendency to erysiplas, which I thought quite likely to
be the consequence of the rusting of the hair pins used
in putting it up, determined me to this shearing; and

my hair is now short, a grizzled crop all round my head, and very dreadfully frightful indeed I look in that condition; but the relief is immense, and I only wish I could be shaved and go about bald, with only my skin for skull cap, as Sydney Smith wished he could throw off his flesh and sit in his bones in hot weather.

I was enchanted with the idea of those out-of-door Shakespeare readings. I wished I could have given mine so. I choose to believe, you know, that "As You Like It," was written in the deer park at Stoneleigh. He did not steal his venison there, but at Charlecote, as it is said, which I don't choose to believe.

Dearest H——, I must stop writing to you and set to work copying for the devil, *i.e.* printer; so for the present, good-bye, and God bless you, ever, as ever, yours,

FANNY.

York Farm, July 1st, 1875.

MY DEAREST H——

I am quite aware how necessary it is for me, under my present circumstances, to be prudent and economical as far as I can. The very liberal terms offered me by the American editor for my Memoirs, has, of course, relieved my immediate anxiety. It is not, however, a subject that I think much about, or care to let my mind dwell upon; certainly, at my age, it is quite unnecessary to be over anxious about any such matter.

I have already reported to you the unsatisfactory physical condition of my poor little granddaughter, and it seems to me very singular that so puny and sickly a little creature should be so invariably good-tempered, quiet, gay, and contented. She was weighed yesterday, and weighed only seventeen pounds, which for a baby a year old (to-morrow is her birthday) is a miserable weight. She is unusually tall, long limbed, and long bodied, with arms and legs as thin as yours, and she is as white as wax. She has, however, uncommon muscular strength, and the most serene uncomplaining disposition I ever saw in a poor little baby. She has not yet a single tooth, and has been covered with nettle-rash, from the frightful heat, from which we have all been suffering, more or less, but nothing seems to make her irritable or fractious. She has sweet dark blue eyes, and pretty golden brown hair. If she lives, I should think she will be a pretty and very tall woman. She is bright and intelligent, and exceedingly fond of music.

I wrote to Fanny Cobbe, as in duty bound, as soon as I entered into this arrangement for printing any portion of the Memoir, because, before I availed myself of these Records, to stop the gap in my income, I had obtained her permission to leave all my papers to her, a charge which she had most kindly and considerately accepted, and which might have involved some trouble and responsibility; and so I wrote to her to tell her what I am about to do, and so relieve her of the charge she had accepted.

I do not wonder at her pursuing, with all the devotion of her affectionate, warm-hearted nature, the cause she has undertaken in behalf of the poor animal brutes whom the brutes of men are torturing with so little shame or pity. She is, at any rate, beginning an excellent work, and has enlisted so much public opinion and sympathy in its favour, that I do not suppose the subject will be lost sight of again till some abatement of the wicked cruelty has been obtained.

I did not think my dear Mr. L—— looked well when he came up from the South, and he has lost weight by at least a stone, which does not perhaps much signify, for he will soon recover more than that in England. He did not say much about his longing to see England again; but that may have been a little qualified, as he was leaving my child and his child behind him.

F—— takes very little interest in the coming Centenary Exhibition. You know she is by way of being Southern in all her views and sentiments, and the South is too much depressed to join in any national rejoicing.

S——, I think, regrets that any appeal whatever has been made to other nations to join in what she considers a strictly American jubilee; but as the thing has been embarked in, she hopes and wishes that it may be successful. I look upon the whole thing as a mere bit of jobbery and State speculation, and, with the moral and financial credit of the country at its present low ebb, I think the challenge sent forth to the world to come and witness its progress and prosperity not especially well timed. The American gentlemen of a hundred years ago, with Washington at their head, would probably have thought the *progress* in some directions questionable.

Good-bye. God bless you, my dearest friend. This summer has brought me one bitter disappointment, in not seeing you again; but of that it is not wise or well to speak.

Ever, as ever, yours,
FANNY.

York Farm, July 2nd, 1875.

This is our little baby's birthday. This day she came to us in a terrific thunderstorm, that we heard without heeding, and that raged with the utmost fury during the hour that preceded her birth, and now we have to thank God for the child sent safely to bless us. I have already written to you more than once of their being with me, and to-morrow they go away to Newport for fresh air and sea breezes, and I am anxious to have them gone, though I shall miss them sorely.

As for the trip to the sea, which I undertook with M—— and Mrs. T——, there never was so miserable a failure. We went intending to spend two days, and were back at the end of the first, utterly disgusted with the odious discomfort of everything—the weather so cold and cheerless that we were obliged to have a fire, and the only room in the hotel (which in the season accommodates hundreds of people) where there was a fireplace was a huge barn of a public sitting-room, with four doors and six windows. The food was dirty and detestable, and everything disgusting. So we came back as quickly as possible, and could only rejoice that if M—— was not the better for the expedition she was not much the worse for the fatigue.

The fact is that the wretched discomfort of these watering-place hotels and the life people lead in them can only be endured by any one accustomed to the common decencies of existence for some most important benefit to health, and I should think would go far to neutralize all possible advantages of sea air and bathing, and change of scene and atmosphere. . . .

As for archery being merely a youthful pastime, I think almost all the members of the club are at least middle-aged, and my grave literary friend, James Spedding, who must be near seventy, while I was last at Widmore, was still an ardent toxophilite; and at St. Leonard's the old maiden lady who was the queen of the archery-ground was over sixty, and still "shot a fine shoot," as Justice Shallow says.

Our weather now is moderate, and I am really thanking Heaven for the relief from the horrible heat, of which we have just had an uninterrupted week. The week before that we had *fires*; yesterday night it was so cold that we had to ask for *blankets*; and three nights before one could hardly sleep for the heat, though lying on the outside on one's bed with only one's nightdress on. I do not believe such another climate is to be found anywhere else in the world.

I never heard of Messrs. Moody and Sankey in this country. My first information respecting them was what you wrote to me of their popular religious assemblies in Dublin.

You say you hope that S—— has got over her domestic troubles; but it was only this morning that F—— and I agreed that *hopeless* was the only word

to be applied to them. She is now without housekeeper, lady's-maid, or cook, and in all this dire heat
has been going in and out of town almost daily in
search of the wretched servants, whom she engages
one day, who come out to her the next, and leave her
house again on the third, proving utterly incompetent
to the duties they undertake, and in every way intolerable.   I sometimes really fear S—— will be
worried out of her senses by the life she is compelled
to lead, and do not think it will be possible for them
to endure it if this thing continues as it is at present.
I see nothing for it but their leaving their house
and going to live either at an hotel or some boarding-
house.

Ever, as ever, yours,
FANNY.

York Farm, July 5th, 1875.

MY DEAREST H——,

I have written you all I have to tell about
my child and her child. They were with me nearly
three weeks, and left me the day before yesterday for
the seaside.   I miss F—— very much, she is a very
cheerful, pleasant companion ; and I miss the dear
little, pale-faced, quiet baby.   The departure of three
servants and a very noisy little pet dog from such a
small house as mine makes a wonderful silence, still-
ness, and *sadness* at first.

S—— is going to New York for entire change, and
also to see if she cannot there obtain a better class of
servants than are to be found in Philadelphia. I am
told, by those who have some knowledge of the sub-

ject, that there is a demand and supply there of a better sort of person than the ignorant, incapable wasteful, insolent, low Irish women, who form the material here from which people recruit their household. A housekeeper is an extremely difficult person to find here, and servants, who will be subject to a housekeeper, still more difficult to find, so that the case, I am sorry to say, is a very hopeless one.

You ask me if the union of the three primary colours, which united constitute light, ever represents to me the idea we form of the Trinity. You say " we form," but I form no idea of any sort upon that subject, which entirely transcends my powers of thinking, and never presents any conclusion to my mind when by rare chance it considers that dogma of the Church. Of course, the object you mention is a very good physical illustration of the Trinity, and so are the three stems of trees, growing, as I have seen them, into one, and so are the three petals of the clover ; but to multiply material types of the Trinity is in no way to make its immaterial metaphysical existence evident, as a spiritual fact, and therefore does not, I think, afford any assistance towards conceiving the mystery accepted by most Christians under that name.

Dante has made three gyrating wheels of the three colours, the symbol of the highest celestial glory, but to me that culminating splendour of heaven in the " Paradiso " never suggested anything but a gigantic tricolour cockade, the emblem of the French motto of Liberty, Fraternity, and Equality, which the gendarmes in the Paris streets wear as their warrant of authority.

" Nella profonda e chiara sussistenza
    Del alto lume parvemi tre giri,
    Di tre colori e d'una contenenza."
                                        Il Paradiso.

I prefer Milton's pure white splendour—

"For God is light,
    And never but in unapproached light
    Dwelt from the first ; dwelt then in thee,
    Bright effluence of bright essence increate."

I rejoice to say that in the conversations I have
had with F——, while she has been here, she does
not seem to contemplate her husband settling in this
country, but, on the contrary, his returning to his
home next summer. Still, all their plans must depend
in some measure upon what becomes of their property
here. I think he might have had one of the largest
churches in Birmingham, had he been in England last
year. I think they would be glad to part with their
Southern property, and I wish they could succeed in
letting, if they do not sell it, and that Mr. L—— could
return to his own country and profession.

Darien is inhabited by three men, who are all from
the British Islands, English or Scotch, uneducated,
intelligent, enterprising, energetic men, who have made,
or are still making, fortunes in the timber trade. The
rest of the inhabitants are the mere dregs of the
southern planter population of the district, adventurous
northern workmen and artisans, and a large majority
of free negroes, of every conceivable shade of colour,
and for the most part idle and worthless ; in short,
you can imagine what the lees of slavery are likely
to be. The place, however, has some special advan-

tages for its principal trade, which is the lumber of the great southern pine forests, and is becoming more and more a resort for foreign vessels engaged in that business. Houses and land in the small straggling town are rising in value, and I suppose that its being a place of considerable commercial importance and prosperity is only a question of time.

I do not think there is any strong movement upon the subject of altering the wretched commercial and financial system (currency, customs, etc.) which the present government has maintained, and which has as nearly ruined this poor country, in fact at home and in credit abroad, as it is possible. The world has certainly never yet seen such an illustration of the truth, that moral elements are indispensable for public as well as private prosperity, as this extraordinary nation presents. Wealth, enormous positive wealth, energy, activity, intelligence, unbounded space and unlimited freedom in the use of all these advantages, but for want of common sense and common honesty in the government, the country, just now, is in a state of absolute prostration, an incredible collapse of all its energies alike, without means of using its own immense resources, and cruelly dishonoured and discredited abroad. It will come out of the slough by degrees and be more prosperous, more powerful, and, I doubt not, more wise ; but in the meantime universal suffrage does not appear to produce the most perfect results here just now.

Ever, as ever, yours,
FANNY.

York Farm, July 20th, 1875.

MY DEAREST H——,

I had a letter from Newport yesterday, saying that the poor little baby had got one tooth through and would probably put forth one or two more in a day or two. Now that half the summer is over, that her teeth are come, and she is in a mild temperate climate by the sea, I trust, poor little spark of vitality (very vivid vitality, too), she will gather strength and hold on to this existence, in which she has hitherto done little else but battle bravely for leave to live. Upon the whole, I am inclined to be hopeful about the little creature, when I remember S——'s boy, and his most miserable beginning of existence, and see him now—a tall, broad, healthy lad—speriamo!

He came home from school for his holidays, the very next day after the departure of F—— and her baby, and came to see me yesterday and told me that I reminded him of "Mariana in the moated grange," which rather surprised me, because, though an old woman is not generally the liveliest companion for a lad of fifteen, there is a profound depth of melancholy, not to say despair, about Tennyson's Mariana that made me wonder at my suggesting it to him. We all treat him not so much as a young man, as a boy and a gentleman, a very pleasant combination, and very much what he is. . . . I do not know anything of Mr. Arthur Arnold, but do not think he is a son of the person you mention, the former proprietor of the English opera-house. I imagined he was that son of Dr. Arnold who went to India, and wrote a book called, I think, "Oakwood," and at one time had charge of Ralph King.

The heat we had in June was all but intolerable to me. I was copying hard for the press, and sat in my bedroom in only one garment, no shoes and no stockings, with a wet pocket handkerchief over my head (of which all the hair has been cut off) to protect my face and shoulders from the plague of flies with which we are tormented—me voyez-vous? and in this plight I sat and scribbled, with the perspiration rolling off me in great drops, while F——, in a similar (absence of) costume, lay in her bedroom *trying* to read. Thank Heaven, the weather has moderated; yesterday it was positively cold in the evening, and to-day it is damp and chilly. On Sunday we had a furious sort of tornado. Certainly my enduring this climate is a proof of my affection for my children.

I have not been much interested by the poor old Duke de Sermoneta's marriage. I was attached to his last wife, whose sister was my intimate friend; but this lady I have only met once or twice. He ought to have a wife to take care of him, for his daughter and daughter-in-law have husbands and children of their own, and cannot devote themselves continually to his blind helplessness. I do not think it very strange that English women should have been willing to marry the Gaetani. Sermoneta's first wife was a Polish woman. He married his second (my friend's sister) partly because he was really attached to her, partly for her fortune, and partly to have a lady whom he respected and trusted to look after his daughter, by his Polish wife. He is now marrying for a nurse; and the title and position of Duchess of Sermoneta is worth the while of a short nurseship to the lady he marries. . . . The young Princess Teano was a lovely beauty, but she had no fortune, and could not have married anything like such rank and social position in her own country.

York Farm, July 28th, 1875.

My dearest H——,

. . . You ask me if I think all classes of women in the United States are deficient in maternal sentiment. I speak of the deficiency as comparative rather than positive, and of course there are plenty of individual exceptions; but the men and women of the United States are upon the whole the least animal race of human beings that I have ever seen. The men have no backs to their heads, and the women no backs to their bodies, and their animal nature appears to me weaker than that of either English, French, Italian, or German people.* The

---

* The brain development in this country is earlier, and its action more rapid than elsewhere, and the *mental* processes of the Americans quicker and more vivid than those of any other people. Their intellect is subtler than that of the English, and there is a tendency to insanity with them which does not exist with us. They want our heavy, sound, material ballast to qualify their higher and finer brain. The Americans, as a rule, are wanting in animal spirits, properly so called, because they are generally the result of vigorous animal health, and abound in the young, in whom the animal vital element preponderates. The Americans know nothing of the nursery life of English children, that existence so carefully devoted to physical habits of the wholesomest simplicity and regularity, so carefully

affections have their roots in the animal propensities, though they exist of course in measure where these are not strong. The Americans love their children, I should say, much more morally and intellectually than physically, which is the reverse of all coarse and powerfully animal natures. The American women do not care to have children, and have, I think, generally (compared with women of other nations) little baby and little nursery love; for all which their general infirm health and terrible climate and miserable lack of domestic assistance for the proper care of their children (rendering the periods of their infancy one of absolute slavery to the mothers) would be reasons enough.

I believe the climate has been assigned as the reason of the comparatively unsensual character of the Red Indian savages; and I have always thought that part of the dislike of the Americans for the negroes as a race, was due to the fact that the negro is among the most animal of human beings. But I think many causes tend to make American women hard, or, at any rate, less tender, caressing, soft, and affectionate in their outward demonstrations than other women.

Of course the immense influx of foreign people, Irish and German, keeps modifying the American character in all respects the whole time; but then,

deprived of all intellectual influence or nervous excitement. There is no American childhood, and the athletic sports of Englishmen are comparatively little cultivated by Americans. Business life begins much earlier in the United States, and the carelessness of youth is shorter lived there than in any other country.

again, the American climate and institutions modify
the constitution of the emigrants and their children,
in the course of a couple of generations, very per-
ceptibly.

I had a long letter from Fanny Cobbe about ten
days ago, written, I thought, in a depressed tone of
spirits, which was well accounted for by all the annoyance and worry she has being going through. I wrote
back to her, asking her to come and spend the winter
here with me; but I do not know if she would be able
to manage, even if she felt inclined to do this. How
would she bear the sea-voyage and the horrible winter,
and, worse than everything to her, the barren intellectual destitution of the life I lead here? She is very
fond of S——, who loves and admires her, and I am
very fond of her, and would gladly do anything to
show my regard and esteem for her, and this was the
only thing that occurred to me as possible for me to
do. Of course her coming here would be a godsend
to me and to S——.

I do not wear a cap at all, my dearest H——, for
if I did, I should find but little benefit from having
cut off all my hair, especially as I could never endure
anything tied under my chin. My hair is cut about
a finger long, and all brushed back from my forehead,
and powdered, so I look like a coarse, ugly copy of
some of my uncle John's pictures. The mass of hair,
wet through with the heat, was odious to me, the
hair-pins all becoming rusty and spoilt with it, and
the skin irritated to a degree that seemed to me to
threaten erysipelas. I am certainly a most ill-favoured
object now, but have at any rate escaped from all

these worries. As the weather becomes cooler, I shall wear on my head the sort of three-cornered lace handkerchief my sister wears, which is tied so loosely under the chin as hardly to be felt, or else caps that I can fasten round my skull with an elastic band.

York Farm, July 29th, 1875.

MY DEAREST H——,

You ask me if I ever see the new quarterly magazine in which Fanny Cobbe writes. I have told you that I see no European publications whatever, and that having, after infinite trouble, signally failed to obtain one or two of the periodicals in which there were articles that you wished me to read, I had given up all attempts to procure any such thing in despair. It is one of the minor privations that belong to my life here, and is so trifling, compared with many others, that I only occasionally grumble at it.

My little Alice has got very cleverly upon her feet, supporting herself very well by one's knees, or holding one's finger. Her mother had a capital contrivance made for her, a sort of wooden pen, about seven feet square, formed of light rails and bars, and fastened with hinges at the corners. This she used to put on the grass in the shade, and, with a counterpane spread in it, to protect the child from damp and insects, it was a most admirable enclosure for the little lamb, who used to pull herself up and stand, holding by the rails of it, quite comfortably. I have just sent it off to her, with a large sort of tent umbrella, to put over it, because, though they have grass at Newport, they have few trees and little shade, and, properly protected from the sun, of course it is an immense advantage to the child to be as much as possible in the sea air. The accounts of her from Newport are that she is altogether flourishing, and I am thankful to think of her and her mother in cool comfort by the seaside.

I do not think my dear Mr. L——, or any other *such* Englishmen, can ever like the United States as a residence—I mean, wish to make a home there; and I sincerely hope that they have made arrangements for their final return to England next year. There is a great deal that he thoroughly admires and approves of in this country; but it is not a home for English-men or women born and bred as he is, and has grown less so within the last ten years and since the war.

I am very much affected by the news I have just received from Lizzy Mair of her sister, Mrs. Grant's, death. She was old, and had become infirm; but Lizzy's announcement of her death recalled the time when we were all young together, and my happy year of girlhood spent in her mother's house in Edinburgh.

God bless you, dearest H——, my friend of fifty years. It is just about half a century since "we were first acquaint."

Ever, as ever, yours,
FANNY.

York Farm, July 31st, 1875.

MY DEAREST H——,

Winter.   My grandson, about whom you ask so par-ticularly in the letter I have received from you this

morning, is not at all a "precocious American young
man," but an uncommonly clever and gifted boy.
Like most of his country people, he is deficient, I am
sorry to say, in animal spirits, and this and rather
unusual *reasonableness* prevents him from appearing,
or, indeed being, young of his age; but he is thoroughly
well bred, and has no pert unpleasant precocity at all.
Certainly people can never shake off or absolutely
change their original physical organization, which is, I
suppose, what you mean by their "natural disposition,"
however much by strenuous and long-continued effort
they may succeed in modifying it. . . .

As for the difficulty of the "servant question"
here, you can form no conception of it. The W——s
are keeping at this moment in their house a man-
servant whom they know to be a thief and a liar,
because he is good-tempered and clever, and under-
stands his work, and the trouble and difficulty of
replacing him would be something that they cannot
face. One must have lived here to imagine the state
of things in this respect.

A new source of income, when at my age one is
suddenly deprived of a considerable portion of the old,
when one lives up to one's revenue, and indulges no
superfluity that will admit of retrenchment, is a
seriously fortunate circumstance. It so happened that
just at the time when my yearly income was suddenly
and unexpectedly reduced, I received an offer, as I
have told you, from one of the principal American
magazines, for any prose matter I would give them,
and for as long as I chose to send them articles. Of
course I could not now undertake to *write* to eke out

my income, any more than I could now undergo the fatigue of reading to do so; but the large mass of ready-written matter which I had in my hands was an obvious means of helping myself. The task of recopying it all is very tedious, but the manuscript, as it is, could not go out of my own possession, and I am only too thankful that I had such a resource to turn to in my dilemma.

I am as well as I can be here at this season; but the idea of your *fire* makes me *shudder*.

York Farm, August 17th, 1875.

MY DEAREST H——,

I wrote to you yesterday, not having heard from you for some time, and fearing, from what appeared to me a much longer silence than usual, that something was amiss with you. The letter I now have from you is, on the contrary, one of the brightest I have had for a long time, and I am sure, though it may be unconsciously to yourself, that it must have been dictated under the influence of the happy expectation of Mrs. St. Quintin's visit. I am so very, very glad she is coming to cheer and comfort you.

I have heard nothing of my dear Mr. L——'s experiences in England but one or two incidents of his London society life, and since his return to America I have not seen him, as, of course, he went immediately to Newport, to his wife and child, on landing, and I shall see none of them till they come here again, on their way to the South, in November or later.

I answer your questions as they come, dear H——,

and therefore beg to tell you that my hair is already growing, and that I shall not cut it again, as the summer cannot last much longer in its intensity, and I am a painfully hideous object to all my friends here, who do not at all approve of my short shock of grey hair, with its perfectly white lining turned back from my forehead, which is yellow-brown, and seamed with many a deep line of age and care.

The portion of my Memoirs that I have recopied for publication has only reached my first summer at Weybridge, on my return from school in Paris, when I was about sixteen. I could not put it as it was in the printer's hands, and therefore have undertaken the task of copying it, in which I have just now obtained the assistance of our village grocer, an unfortunate man, who, after the example of many of his richer commercial brethren, has been trading upon credit without capital, and far beyond what honesty or prudence would warrant. He has failed, and has just been sold out of his shop. Of course the man was in great distress, and until he finds some steady occupation, which he is looking for, I make him come here for two hours and a half every morning, and he writes for me under dictation, which relieves me for the present from my heavy task of penmanship, and gives him five shillings a day wherewith to buy food for his wife and child.

" What is our identity ? " say you. Why, I suppose that one of our qualities, or those of our qualities, which preponderate most strongly over all the rest, and distinguish us from other human beings. Of course, we are made up of inherited mental, moral, and physical conditions, which can be traced, in most cases, to our progenitors, to which each one of us adds either some specific different quality or different combination of the inherited ones, which portion of his or her being constitutes, I take it, the element of his or her *individuality*. There are no two faces exactly alike, although all faces have precisely the same number of features. In the tree of fullest foliage no two of its thousands of leaves are precisely alike. The *difference* constitutes the *individual* and is its identity.

The church at Stoneleigh is not between two rivers, but close to a narrow sluggish stream, called by the unpicturesque, but very appropriate, name of the "Sow" (especially since it has been made a mere sewer for the impurities of Coventry). This stream runs just by the Stoneleigh graveyard, and about a quarter of a mile from the village. After entering the park, it meets the Avon, and these are the two rivers which you remember in that neighbourhood.

Ever since the beginning of August now we have had intense heat, with almost incessant rain. We are obliged to keep all the windows open, otherwise we should be stifled, and the consequence is everything in the house is saturated with damp—the armchair back against which you lean, the sheets on your bed, and the linen in your drawers.

I have only been able to walk out twice since the beginning of June, except to church, whither I crawl on a Sunday, the distance being a quarter of a mile, to accomplish which I never allow myself less than half an hour. Last Sunday I had the opportunity of observing a most disgusting phenomenon on my way thither and back. The road was literally *alive* with those horrible Colorado beetles, or "potato bugs," as they more commonly and agreeably call them here. They were marching along the highway by scores and hundreds, in companies, like a disbanded army. I never saw anything more horrid. They have so completely stripped a potato field of several acres on this farm of every vestige of green, that I walked through the naked *twigs* the other day wondering what strange kind of crop the farmer had put into the ground.

York Farm, August 24th, 1875.

My beloved H——,

I believe my theory, with regard to the national physical characteristics of the Americans, true in spite of your medical book upon the subject. In speaking once with Monsieur de Mussy, who was then my doctor, and saying that every fifth man in the United States was supposed to be diseased with dissolute living, he replied that every third man was the average of such cases in France, and he presumed in England, and that, you see, is a difference of nearly half the number in favour of American morality. I imagine one reason of the general want of health in this country is not so much the amount of profligacy as the early age at which dissolute habits are indulged in here by mere boys. The absence of all effectual authority leaves them almost as mere children, to follow the impulse of their inclinations without restraint, and the injury done to the constitution at such an early age is, I imagine, greater and of worse consequence than when the system at a more advanced age would be in some measure consolidated. The early, almost boyish, constant use of tobacco, too, destroys the nervous system, and that obtains here earlier than anywhere else, I think, not only in the habit of smoking, but of chewing tobacco, one or the other, or both, of which practices are indulged in by the majority of Americans, almost from their boyhood.

I think it strange that I have never heard from Fanny Cobbe, in reply to the letter I wrote to her, begging her to come and spend the winter with me. It was a letter that she was sure not to leave unanswered, and I begin to fear she has never received it, which I should regret very much, as it contained the full expression of my sympathy with all her annoyances, and an affectionate expression of my great regard for her, as well as certain explanations upon the subject of my present publication of my Memoirs, which seemed to me due to her, as she had promised to take charge of my papers in the event of my death. She has taken no notice whatever of this letter, and I am afraid it is among the "missing."

We are all rather depressed by the approaching departure of our boy for school. He makes a wonderful light and warmth in our rather sad-coloured existence, and I think with dismay how terribly his poor mother will miss him.

You say that it must be pleasant to me to fancy myself like my uncle John. My uncle John was your idol and beau-ideal, and it would have been pleasant to *you* to have fancied yourself like him, but I cannot say that it gives me any particular satisfaction to be, as I have all my life been a very plain likeness of my very handsome family. On the contrary, it is rather aggravating to suggest an association that instantly turns to one's disadvantage. I should have been quite good-looking enough to pass in a crowd but for my good-looking relations. The likeness between myself and Mrs. Siddons, and myself and my sister was very great, and yet the whole configuration of our face and features was different, for theirs were long and regular, and mine snub and irregular. The degree to which this resemblance, without similarity, may exist, was curiously exemplified with my grandson the other day, who is not like John Kemble, but who, suddenly looking in at the window, produced an effect so like a full-face picture of my uncle John in Macbeth, that everybody was struck with the resemblance, and cried out at it. Likeness seems to depend on so many indescribable things. S—— and F—— are occasionally spoken to for each other, by persons who do not know them intimately, though I cannot see the least likeness between them. I suppose my strong resemblance to my grandmother, Mrs. Roger Kemble, must give me a latent likeness to her children, my uncle and aunt, which accidents of dress or expression occasionally bring out. Inheritance in that, as in all our qualities is a wonderful thing, but I shall comb down my hair in a day or two now, and then, all fancied or real likeness to my uncle John will disappear again, I imagine.

I am thankful to say that the weather is so changed, as to be quite tolerable within the last two days, and to suggest a hope that the heat is over for this year.

The mornings and the evenings and nights are cool, and there is an autumnal look and feeling in the air, that makes one hope that we are released from broiling, boiling, frying, roasting, and stewing for this year. ·It is very sad thus to have to rejoice at the departure of the summer, especially when one has before one such a winter as ours is, but the beautiful autumn lies between this and that, and the autumn of this climate is incomparably beautiful. No season that I have ever seen anywhere is as lovely but the spring in Italy.

York Farm, September 2nd, 1875.

My dearest H——,

It is a most useless practice to speculate about other people's affairs, and I am gradually giving up that bad habit. Moreover, I think as little as possible of the irregularity of the miserable postal arrangements, by which we are constantly suffering here, although vexation of every sort is perpetually arising from it. It is now long ago since you wrote me word of Fanny Cobbe's late annoyances. I wrote to her directly such a letter as I am sure she would have answered, proposing to her to come and spend the winter with me. I have never had a line from her in reply, and certainly the letter has never reached her. A young lad, a schoolfellow of my grandson's, came on the other day at considerable inconvenience and expense, a distance of ninety miles, to pay a visit to friends, who were away from home, and had written to tell him so, and to warn him not to come. Within the last fortnight I have lost a letter from Newport, from F——, and S—— says she is positive that within the twelvemonth she has been at Branchtown, no fewer than seven of her letters have gone astray. There is no remedy whatever for this, and I bear it just as I am obliged to bear the sores with which I am covered from head to foot from mosquito bites, and which, as Ellen very justly observes, if I were to die, might make people suppose I had fallen a victim to the plague. I am thankful for every letter I get from you, and for every one of mine that I hear reaches Fitzwilliam Place.

Tell me if you ever knew that the Grove, opposite Cassiobury, which belonged to Lord Clarendon in our time, had once belonged to your family? A notorious, ill-conducted actress, of the name of Bellamy, a contemporary of Garrick's, speaks in her life of the place being owned by the Lord Doneraile of her day, and of the happy hours she spent in the adjoining park of Cassiobury, with her " dear Miss St. Leger." Did you know that neighbourhood had been haunted by an ancestress of yours, and another player woman ?—I suppose perhaps your grandfather's sister, or possibly daughter—she married a Colonel Burton, I believe. Do you know this? I think if you had you would some time or another have mentioned it to me, and I am sure you never did. I wish I knew what that Miss St. Leger's name was. . . .

You speak of the blight having appeared among the potatoes in Ireland, and I have been in daily dread of hearing that this horrible pest, the Colorado beetle, or potato bug, as they call it here, had got a footing in your Ireland, where, I am afraid, little less than

another potato famine would be the consequence o
its appearance. They have infested this part o
Pennsylvania in such numbers as to recall the terrible
denunciation of the Old Testament, "I will send my
great army of the palmer worm and the caterpillar on
you." The tenant who rents this farm of about forty
acres from F——, planted six acres with potatoes, and
walking through the field the other day, I could not
help wondering what curious crop it was sown with.
I had no more idea that I was walking among potatoes
than that the field was sown with wheat. After
devouring the potatoes, they betake themselves to the
neighbouring vegetables, egg-plants, tomatoes, etc.
For the last few days they have appeared to be
emigrating in a body, the garden walks and high-
road have swarmed with them, and thousands have
crawled up the walls of the house, so that I have had
dustpans full of them scraped off two or three times a
day. They come into the bedrooms, as well as all the
rooms on the ground-floor, and I am terribly afraid
they are prompted by some instinct to climb up to
the roof of the houses, to seek some place of safety to
lay their eggs and hibernate, and descend again in
force next year upon us. There is something disgusting in these crawling creatures coming into one's very
house and on one's clothes. I expect to find them in
my soup presently, "potage à la pomme de terre bug."

My opposite neighbours and myself are all rather
sad just now with the approaching return of our boy
to school. He leaves us next week, and will carry
away every ray of brightness from his mother's
atmosphere. His father dotes upon him, and will

miss him terribly, and so shall I. It cheers my heart only to hear him knock about the croquet-balls on the lawn over the way. I have been trying to stretch my old, swollen, rheumatic hands, endeavouring to practice Mendelssohn's Scotch and Italian four-hand symphonies to play with him. His extemporaneous voluntary playing on the piano is really indicative of a high order of talent. . . .

We have had a terrible month of August—incessant rain and stifling heat; and now the rain has ceased, and we are again having fearful broiling hot weather, the thermometer nearer ninety than eighty all day long, flies and mosquitoes, like the chorus in Goethe's "Faust," hunting one in the house from room to room and out of doors, these multitudes of crawling creatures making one's physical life almost a burden. The nights are longer now, which is some relief, and every day I gasp out, "It must soon be over; it cannot last much longer." Not having been able to go away, or even to hire a carriage for the refreshment of occasional driving, I have felt the oppression of this dreadful season in this small house, with its little rooms and low ceilings, terribly, and have made up my mind not to attempt passing another summer at this place.

York Farm, September 14th, 1875.

My dearest H——,

There is a great cricket match between English and Canadian and American players going on in this neighbourhood, and Mr. L——, who is always much interested in such matters, arrived here yesterday to spend the cricket week. I had scarcely had time to shake hands with him, when I got a message from S——, begging me to go over the way to her, which, of course, I did directly. She had been in New York all last week, servant-hunting, having neither man-servant nor cook at present. The cook she had brought with her from New York on Saturday had gone away yesterday, Monday morning. Mr. L—— was to dine with her that evening, and she had invited people to her house to see the cricket match at the end of the week. . . .

[One of my earliest experiences in housekeeping in my married home in America was the warning given me by my cook the very day of my first "dinner-party." I shook in my shoes at the ominous words, "I wish to go." "When ?" said I, with my heart in my mouth. "Well, just as quick as I can." "Certainly," said I, in quavering accents. "You shall go immediately." I paid her her week's wages, sent her off instantly by the railroad, had a good fit of crying, called my remaining household together, and besought them to send up a dinner of some sort for me; and, when my guests arrived, threw myself upon their merciful sympathy, reminding them that the same fate might overtake any, or all of them, any or every day of the week. I did my best to entertain them with a "feast of reason and a flow of soul," but I doubt if I succeeded quite as well as Madame Scarron, to whom her servant addressed the whispered compliment, "Ah, madame ! encore une histoire, car le roti manque !"]

Conceive living in such a condition of helpless

discomfort and perpetual domestic *warfare,* so to speak, the whole time. I see no end to it but their giving up living at Butler Place, and returning to lodgings in town, where, at any rate, they have restaurants to send or go to for their food. But they have spent a great deal of money in altering, improving, and fitting up the place. The house is charming and comfortable, and is, or ought to be, a delightful home. He is now again practising his profession very zealously in this his own neighbourhood, where he was born and has lived the greater part of his life, and is very generally liked and looked up to. In town he would have to begin making a practice, well known as his name is, and it might seem like an invidious rivalry with his brother, who is a very popular physician in Philadelphia. Visiting his country patients thence, would, I should think, be out of the question. It is impossible for them to part with this estate, which is strictly entailed upon their children and F——'s, so strictly, that there seems an insuperable difficulty in their selling any part of it. As for letting the place, that is almost hopeless; besides which, tenants here, with the help of their children and Irish servants, pretty nearly destroy the houses they hire and all their contents.* . . .

The want of common honesty in this country *has*

* One of the first hotel-keepers in Rome complained piteously to me of a wealthy American family, occupying the Piano Nobile of his house, whose children habitually dragged his magnificent gilt and silk brocade Louis Quinze armchairs on their backs over the floor for carriages, of which nuisance he complained in vain to their parents.

become such, that it is seriously affecting all business transactions everywhere. Nobody knows who is to be trusted, and a general paralysis of credit and deadlock of commercial and financial activity is the result of the all but general bad faith of men in business. Hard-handed robbery and red-handed murder were the crimes of nations in their early feudal childhood. Greed of gain and utter unscrupulousness in all, and any pacific modes of obtaining it, and boundless extravagance and vulgar folly in its expenditure, are the besetting sins of this, one of the foremost of civilized people in this, the hundredth year of their national existence. The evil has now attained such proportions, that I suppose it will before long produce a reaction in favour of common honesty and decent integrity. In the meantime, one has a rather uncomfortable feeling of being in a *"durty"* place and among *"durty"* people.

My dearest H——, I am so glad you have your dear Mrs. St. Quintin with you. I am sure she and E—— must get on admirably together: they are both such fine flowers of fine Toryism. I am glad she saw Ardgillan, which I used to think so charming. . . .

It is grievous to think of poor Fanny Cobbe's worries and trouble. I read her Town and Country Mouse Paper, and thought her description of Newbridge touching and charming. How well I remember your taking me there, the first time I ever saw her, and the impression made on me by her sweet sunny countenance and curious fine turquoise set in diamonds (it deserved to be Jessica's, and *not* to have been given for a monkey) on her beautiful hand. She has written to decline coming to winter with me. In my great desire to testify my regard for her, I could think of nothing else, and judged it probable that she might here find employment for her pen, and make arrangements for supplying some of the periodicals with matter, for which she would get good remuneration. She says she cannot put the Atlantic between herself and M—— L——; and as I have seen an article of hers in the *Spectator*, I hope she has found employment that will suit her, and us, and the public. . . .

My health, after which you ask, is quite as good as a person of my age has any right to expect in such a climate as this. A few days ago the thermometer fell *forty degrees in twenty-four hours*, from near ninety to very little above fifty. The great heat is probably passed, and this tremendous change, welcome in itself, brought me not unnaturally a visitation of sciatica; but I am very fairly well, only bitten into deep pits and holes by the mosquitoes all over my arms, hands, feet, face, neck, and shoulders; in short, my whole *public* body.

God bless you, my dearest H——. I rejoice to think of your having your dear sweet friend, Mrs. St. Quintin, with you. I think she is like warm moonlight.

Ever, as ever, yours,
FANNY.

York Farm, September 19th, 1875.

MY BELOVED H——,

How glad I am to think of Mrs. St. Quintin cheering your darkness; how glad that I know her sweet face and voice, and can imagine her sitting beside you, as I had hoped to have done this year ere this, but the possibility of my leaving America at present seems to me to decrease. . . .

The W——s have neither cook nor man-servant in their house. Yesterday a woman, engaged as their cook, actually did come out (they quite as frequently as not engage to take a situation and never either come near the place or send reason or apology for not doing so); so I live in trembling hope that perhaps for a week or two they may have a respite from this incessant domestic torment.

M——has just mentioned in her note to me the death of one of the first acquaintances my father and myself made when we came over originally to this country—a gentleman of the name of Kemble, who said he was of the same family as ourselves, but whose own people had been settled in New York and on the banks of the Hudson, at a beautiful place called Cold Spring, from early colonial times. He died at the age of ninety, a man of remarkably fine character, upright, honourable, benevolent, simple—a *fine gentleman,* such as is rarely to be found now in the length and breadth of this land. I visited him more than once at his beautiful country place on the Hudson, and had a very affectionate respect for him. His life and character were very noble, and I am glad we had the same name and came of the same stock, even so far away as it was. On one occasion, while visiting Mr. Kemble at Cold Spring, I observed in one of the rooms the same coat of arms as ours, with this curious difference, that the shield and crest were turned in the opposite direction.

[Mr. Gouverneur Kemble was at the head of one of the government cannon foundries of the United States, the great ironworks of which were on his estate at Cold Spring.

The individual bearing the name Kemble, with whom I should have been proud to claim even remote kindred, was a young gentleman (a midshipman) in our navy, who being in charge of one of his ship's boats, was in such peril that the sailors with him jumped into the sea and swam to shore, the boatswain advising him to do the same, saying, " You are a fine swimmer, sir, and can easily save yourself." He refused, however, saying his duty forbade his leaving the boat entrusted to his command, and he was drowned. I honour *our* common name for that young hero's sake.]

York Farm, October 1st, 1875.

My beloved H——,

I have now been two years here without stirring (except for a wretched *try at a trip* to the seaside two months ago), and feel quite a sort of nervous helplessness at the idea of travelling again—I, who have literally spent my whole life in wandering from place to place and have crossed the Atlantic seventeen times. This small journey seems quite a formidable expedition to me, and that sort of cowardly feeling of incapacity and disinclination for the smallest effort or unusual exertion is the growth of a two years' habit over that of thirty preceding ones, and is a greater sign of age than white hairs, wrinkles, or loss of teeth. I really think M—— is unfit for such an exertion, which physically I am not, but she is bent upon it, and there never was so small a body with so great a will. . . .

I am still occupying my time with preparing my Memoirs for the press. This has nothing whatever to do, however, with what I am publishing, as I do not intend extending that record beyond the period of my leaving the stage, if even I continue it so far. That would only take me to the year 1832, and you may judge what a task the whole selection and copying of matter is, when I tell you that at present I am still extracting from letters of only 1843.

I wonder if I told you that, at Mr. L——'s instigation, I had bought myself a printing machine, by means of which I print, instead of write my daily task of copying, and as it is a very ingeniously contrived machine, which is worked merely by striking keys as one plays on a piano, it is a great relief from the fatigue of constant writing. It is an admirable invention, and affords me a great deal of satisfaction in the process of working it. I got it principally in hopes that S——, who writes a great deal too much, would use it, but she says it would fidget her to such a degree that the nervous irritation it would cause her would quite militate against any relief from fatigue in employing it. This has been a great disappointment to me, as I should never have gone to the expense of such an apparatus for myself.

Of course, in so far as a lawyer may be a *pleader*, the practice of his profession is liable to the same admixture of personal effect as the clergyman's or actor's. His face, figure, voice, gesture, and deportment must naturally act upon his hearers to some extent, but the hearers whom a lawyer desires to influence are *men*, and his matter, matter of *fact*, and not of fiction or imagination and emotion. This dramatic element may be injurious to a pleader, according as he uses his power consciously for or against the truth; it *must* be injurious to a preacher, if he uses it consciously at all. It is the chief part of an actor's business, which is one reason why I think his business a poor one.

Lenox, October 6th, 1875.

My dearest H——,

You will learn where I am by the date of my letter in this formerly familiar dwelling of mine, whither I came to-day from Boston, where I parted with M——, who is going to spend a few days at Newport, which I shall pass here, after which we meet again at Boston, and return together to Philadelphia. I shall be away from York Farm about ten days, and your letters will not be forwarded to me, as I had much rather wait a few days to receive them, than run the risk of losing them involved in their following me through two or three American post-offices.

F—— and Mr. L—— are staying here, and I knew my coming would be a pleasant surprise to her. There are still some old friends of mine here, and several younger members of the Sedgwick family, to whom I am much attached, and whom I am very glad to see again, and I am charmed to be once more in the picturesque country, of which I am so fond, and where I have spent so many happy days.

The autumn is now in its full beauty, and nothing can exceed the splendour of the many-tinted foliage— this Joseph's coat given to the youngest of worlds, or, rather, of nations (for this world, science says, is the *older* of the two). The weather, too, is exquisite, wonderfully brilliant and soft in its radiance, and though delightfully warm and sunny, not in the least oppressive. This is the only pleasant season of the American year, unequalled, as the Italian spring in its way. It is really delightful, and often protracted with us in Pennsylvania till the end of November; not up here, though, where it is every now and then already slightly *chilly*, and ere long will be unpleasantly so.

I am tired, dearest H——, with my six hours' railroad journey, and will bid you good night, as it is just twelve o'clock. I do not like to think that it will be a whole week before I hear from you. God bless you, dear.

Ever, as ever, yours,
FANNY.

[During this visit of mine to Lenox, I made the acquaintance of Mr. Bret Harte, with whose original stories I had been deeply interested and delighted. He was staying in the same hotel with us, and did us the favour of spending an evening with us. He reminded me a good deal of our old pirate and bandit friend Trelawny in his appearance, though the latter was an almost orientally dark-complexioned man, and Mr. Bret Harte was comparatively fair. They were both tall, well-made men of fine figure; both, too, were handsome, with a peculiar expression of face, which suggested small success to any one who might engage in personal conflict with them. I had been told that Mr. Bret Harte was an agent for some Eastern Express Company, travelling for whom in the savage western wilderness, among the worst kind of savages, the outcasts of civilization, he must often have carried considerable sums of money about his person, and always have ridden his long lonely journeys with his life in his hand.

He told us of one of his striking experiences, and his telling it made it singularly impressive. He had arrived at night at a solitary house of call on his way, absolutely isolated and far distant from any other dwelling—a sort of rough roadside tavern, known and resorted to by the wanderers in that region. Here he was to pass the night. The master of the house, to whom he was known, answered his question as to whether any one else was there by giving the name of a notorious desperado, who had committed some recent outrage, and in search of whom the wild justices—the lynchers of the wilderness—were scouring the district. This *guest*, the landlord said, was in hiding in the house, and was to leave it (if he was still alive) the next day. Bret Harte, accustomed to rough company, went quietly to bed and to sleep, but was aroused in the middle of the night by the arrival of a party of horsemen, who called up the master of the house and inquired if the man they were in pursuit of was with him. Upon receiving his repeated positive assurance that he was not, they remounted their horses and resumed their search.

At break cf day Bret Harte took his departure, finding that for the first part of his journey he was to have the hiding hero of the night (thief or murderer probably) for his companion, to whom, on his departure, the master of the house gave the most reiterated, detailed, precise, and minute directions as to the *only* road by which it would be possible that he could escape his pursuers, Bret Harte meanwhile listening to these directions as if they were addressed to himself. They rode silently for a short time, and then the fugitive began to talk—not about his escape, not about the danger of the past night, not about the crime he had committed, but about *Dickens's last story*, in which he expressed such an eager and enthusiastic interest, that he would have passed the turning in the road by which he was to have made his escape, if Bret Harte had not pointed it out to him, saying, "That is your way." I wish I could remember what story of Dickens's it was, and that he could have been made acquainted with this incident, worthy of a record in one of his books.

It is perhaps a cause of some slight monotony in Bret Harte's admirably touching and powerful pictures of the life and dwellers in the western deserts, that his men and women are almost universally and inevitably male or female " good-for-noughts." It is part of his great merit to make one feel how much good may remain in " good-for-noughts."]

York Farm, October 16th, 1875.

MY DEAREST H——,

I arrived here yesterday on my return from my expedition to Boston and Lenox, and found among many letters awaiting me, yours of the 26th of September. I have written to you twice since I have been away from home, once from Lenox, and while on my way here a letter only posted on my arrival.

I remember well reading at Plymouth while you and dear Dorothy were there. The climate of Devonshire never agreed with me, being bilious and relaxing to my system, and almost always giving me headache, just as Rome does for the same cause, but I thought Plymouth very beautiful, and recollect with pleasure going to Mount Edgcumbe. I am not sure whether you were with me, and to Saltram to see my old friend, that charming and most entertaining woman, Lady Morley.

Yesterday M—— and I regained our respective homes, and I have been very busy this morning in answering an accumulation of letters of one sort and another, which were not sent after me, and in restoring to their usual places on the various tables in my little rooms, all the knick-knacks, miniatures, photographs, bits of china and small friendly remembrances with which they are generally covered, where they serve pleasant purposes of ornament and suggestive reminders of those I love. I put these all carefully away on my departure, because during my absence the house was cleaned, and the summer matting taken up from the rooms, and all the carpets laid down. Tiresome as this double process is every year, it has an obvious advantage over the custom, rendered possible by our milder English climate, of retaining carpets and curtains unmoved, not only during one year, but certainly, in the case of all lodging houses, hotels, and smaller middle-class residences, for a succession of years, a practice which, combined with the damp and fog of our atmosphere, and the coal smoke for ever loading it with blacks and other impurities, might well draw down the anathema of Florence Nightingale, or any other enlightened hygienic teacher. My little house is quite pretty, and though decidedly *queer* in some of its peculiar arrangements, quite comfortable. S—— has filled all the vases in the drawing-room with the last flowers of autumn from her garden, and my gardener has taken up all the flowering plants from the beds for the winter, so that the little green-house, into which the drawing-room and dining-room open, is filled with refugees, who are now housed for the cold season.

My welcome home was from my servants, who are kind-hearted people, and good *friends* of mine, whom I was glad to see again, and from a beautiful dog of Mr. L——'s, a splendid large, curly, chocolate-coloured Irish retriever, which has been left with me all the summer, and of which I am very fond; the poor creature, though a general favourite in the house, and petted and spoiled by all the servants, was overjoyed to see me, and will hardly move from my side. . . .

Among the letters I found waiting here was a formal official request, on the part of one of the managing committees of the projected centennial exhibition, to be held next year in Philadelphia, that I would give a reading for money for some additional building they propose putting up, which reading I was to deliver in the Philadelphia Opera House, an enormous building where my strength was taxed to the utmost, ten years ago, to make my voice heard. I have declined the compliment of this invitation upon three grounds : want of strength, want of voice, and want of articulation, in consequence of loss of teeth. I must say I think the request a little unreasonable, as the raising of funds for this purely patriotic purpose ought, it seems to me, to be accomplished by Americans themselves ; perhaps, however, if I had more sympathy with the whole enterprise, I might think more amiably of their application to me to raise money for them by such an impossible exertion as it certainly would now be to me to read to seven thousand people. . . .

Good-bye, my dearest H——. My Caliban gardener is calling me for some consultation, and there are sundry household details to be attended to after my fortnight's absence. God bless you.

Ever, as ever, yours,

FANNY.

York Farm, October 22nd, 1875.

MY DEAREST H——,

I have been wanting to write to you for the last two days and have been prevented from doing so, and will do it now before I go to bed, although it is past eleven o'clock, because to-morrow F—— and her husband and baby arrive from New York, and I shall be cumbered and busy about many things, and even if I begin a letter to you, doubt much if I shall find leisure to finish it.

I am troubled, but not surprised at what you say about Fanny Cobbe. Several years ago, when I saw her in London, she appeared to me to be overtaxing her strength, and I think I either wrote to you or told you so at the time. . . . But nothing is easier than to comment on one's neighbour's affairs, and I used sometimes to regret what struck me as her over-active mode of life, simply, I suppose, because it would not have been mine. . . .

I should think this question of vivisection must be in every way very trying to Fanny Cobbe, both on account of the labour and exertion she bestows upon it, and also the passionate sympathy she feels in the subject, she certainly, with regard to that, is spending herself in a good cause, and I would sooner give her leave to overwork herself for that than for many another. . . .

There is an excellent paper in the *Spectator* that I have just been reading, upon the excess of shallow mental culture and superficial intellectual education, calling itself " progress," which I have read with very cordial agreement. Too much eager interest in too great a variety of subjects seems to be quite a characteristic of people's minds now, and I think it is quite as fatal to any sound result of real progress as the opposite extreme of narrow stagnation ; but I always rather cherished stupidity and monotony as pleasant preservatives from undue nervous excitement, and though now I have almost a surfeit of dulness in my daily life, I hold it the wholesomer excess of the two.

I remember your giving me one of those "Essays for Priests and People" to read, and telling me that some of them were by that Mr. Hutton with whom I had at one time a slight acquaintance. I wonder if he wrote the article on superficial over-education that I have just read with so much pleasure. I recollect stopping at the office of the *Spectator* as I came up from Warnford one day, to give them the lines I had just written in the railroad carriage on the taking of Richmond by the Northern troops, and being told by the person who received me of the murder of President Lincoln, which drew from me such a cry of surprise and horror, that it brought Mr. Hutton out of his room, and he put me into my cab, unable to speak and almost to stand with the shock of those terrible tidings. He is related to my Dublin friends (a cousin, I believe). The whole family were Unitarians; but I have heard that Mr. Hutton is verging towards Roman Catholicism, and I thought I had perceived a similar tendency in the paper.

God bless you, dear. Good night. I must go to bed. You cannot imagine how full of thankfulness to God I am at being thus surrounded with my children. Poor S—— just now has her full complement of servants, and is in a state of comparative rest and comfort. She looks well, and is in good spirits. Good night, once more, dear.

I am ever, as ever, yours,
FANNY.

York Farm, October 26th, 1875.

My dearest H——,

I have to-day sent you the last published sheets of my " Old Woman's Gossip,"* from the *Atlantic Monthly.* If I had imagined that it could have afforded you any entertainment, after hearing it once, and in such a much more detailed form, I should not have left it to Fanny Cobbe to send it to you, and you shall in future receive it, whenever it comes out, since it gives you pleasure.

Of the hairs of my head, about which you express such an affectionate interest, I can now report that they are long enough at the back to be twisted up with a small comb, and decorously covered and adorned with two or three plaits of my own grey growth, so that the posterior of my head is no longer in any respect offensively singular, nor is the *front* much *behind the back* (isn't that good Irish?) in propriety, as it sits in two tolerable curves across my forehead, the ends of which are kept behind my ears (I don't mean the ends of my forehead, but of my hair) by a black velvet band round my skull, to which (the band, not my skull) caps and usual she headgear can be pinned, and so I appear a good deal like other women.

I am rejoicing just now in a most delightful sense

---

* " Old Woman's Gossip " was the title that appeared to me appropriate for my articles published in the *Atlantic Monthly Magazine.* When Mr. Bentley kindly undertook the publication of my early Memoirs, I proposed it to him as the title, but he did not accept it. I then suggested, " Elderly Female Twaddle," which seemed to me suitably descriptive ; this, however, being also rejected by him, the " Record of a Girlhood " was chosen, I do not remember whether by myself or by my courteous publisher.

of heart riches, in the nearness of all my dearest, except my boy grandson. Dear J. L——, and F——, and the baby are here, and as my poor dear S—— is just now enjoying a lull in the "still vexed Bermoothes," of her kitchen and pantry, we are all happy enough. . . .

I console myself for my little baby's delicate appearance by her great spirit and vivacity, her quick bright intelligence and sweet temper; she never cries or frets, and in spite of her sentimental dark grey eyes and white cheeks, is *au moral* decidedly a "jolly baby." She is cutting teeth very fast just now, poor little soul (that is to say, in the sense of *suffering*, her soul is cutting its first teeth), and that has to do, no doubt, with her not looking more "robustious." She does not talk, but *jargons* delightful incomprehensibilities, with a great variety of inflexion and most emphatic accent. She will be very tall, I think, for she has very long legs, with which she crawls at an amazing pace. She stands, and is very eager to walk, which she does with support, and will soon do alone. She is an unspeakable treasure and delight to us all. They only stay with me till next Monday, and then go over the way till the beginning of December, when they start for the plantation. In spite of their being my guests, I have had a very quiet day to-day, for the father and mother went off on various errands to Philadelphia after breakfast this morning, and have not yet returned, and the baby has been over the way visiting her aunt almost all day. She has just been brought in and reported herself to me, and the father and mother will be back to dinner. . . .

Dr. W—— fortunately is less exacting, with regard to his own personal comfort, than any one I ever saw; and these domestic difficulties are endured by him with patience beyond all praise. He told me the other day that in the course of his practice he saw and heard of no end of worries and vexations, with regard to household affairs, by which the health of many of his female patients was seriously affected, and you know our friend, Dr. M——, told me that a lady had said to him that she was ill of "cook fever." Kate M——, one of the sweetest-tempered and most reasonable women I know, and one of the best household managers, told me, when I was in Boston lately, that friends of hers had had four cooks in three weeks, and she herself seven in the course of one winter.

York Farm, November 1st, 1875.

My dearest H——,

My journey with M—— was very successful, and we were both of us, I think, the better for it, though I have now been unused to the exertion of travelling so long, that after my first day's short journey to New York, I was so tired that I thought I must give up the whole expedition and turn back; I did not do so, however, and bore the subsequent much longer journeys very well. I wrote to you both from Lenox and Boston, and gave you the accounts of my doings and seeings there. I have not been feeling at all well since my return to this place, but do not attribute that to my journey, which in most respects was beneficial to me, but to the oppressive heat that we have been again suffering from. Not a week ago, days with the thermometer at eighty, and yesterday down to fifty and a *snowstorm*.

The travelling by railroad and the extraordinary overheating of the carriages affects me very uncomfortably, and I cannot say that I think travelling in this country a pleasure at all.* Perhaps now I have grown too old to enjoy it anywhere, as I used to do. One thing is very certain, and that is, that, like everything else, it is dearer in this country than anywhere else in the world. My journey of twelve days, with my maid, cost me between thirty-five and forty pounds, more than a whole month's travelling in Switzerland would have done.

My Memoirs are just now going on rather slowly, for having F—— and Mr. L—— in the house, I cannot reckon upon any precise regularity in any of my proceedings, and so am unable to have my amanuensis. Which amanuensis is a drunken, bankrupt, village grocer, of whom my son-in-law is one of the defrauded creditors—Mr. L—— having intrusted him with about forty pounds' worth of the plantation rice, to sell on commission for him, which rice, indeed, was

* The railroad carriages in America are constructed as those in Switzerland, and are heated by cast-iron stoves, which I have more than once seen *red hot*, while the windows, screwed down so as to prevent their being opened, were opaque with the hard frost, ice, and snow, with which they were covered on the outside. I have more than once been obliged to leave the suffocating atmosphere of the "cars," and go and stand on the platform outside, holding on to the iron bar, which froze my hands through my gloves, and steaming over the white prairies covered with snow like the Russian steppes.

sold, but was never accounted for, and as the man is a bankrupt, never will be. So, while the creditor is living with me, I do not invite the defaulting debtor to come and write for me, and so I crawl along at present with the copying by myself. I carry on two processes at the same time, of preparing what is already written for publication, and continuing the original composition, which, however, is little more than an occasional comment on, or explanation of my letters to you. From these I am very anxious to copy such portions as I wish to preserve, destroying the originals, as, although I did burn such of them as I thought likely to give pain to any one, there are still in those that remain a great many passages which I wish to obliterate; so that I go on copying and curtailing these, while preparing the earlier portion for the *Atlantic Monthly.* I have only got as far in this task as our residence in London in Harley Street, so you see I have nearly twenty years' letters to go over, and to winnow. . . .

I continue to take the *Spectator*, and think that I have recognized Fanny Cobbe's hand in several articles in the later numbers. The paper itself, however, seems to have grown stronger in the Roman Catholic tendency of a good many of its articles, or rather, perhaps I should say, there is an indirect under-current of Roman Catholic modes of thought and feeling in the treatment of various questions, which I thought I perceived some years ago, and which appears to me to have become gradually more prominent and perceptible.

I was not in Italy the year of Fanny Cobbe's

campaign against vivisection in Florence; but have often heard her refer to the violent opposition and personal enmity which her exertions in the cause of humanity drew upon her.

You ask me if I often write to L——? No, I do not; for you know that I hardly ever write to any-body who does not write to me, and L—— detests writing so cordially, that I do not care to compel her by a challenge to answer me.

My dearest H——, I must close my letter, as I have a visitor in my house, to whom I must go and give my attention. Lord Houghton (Monckton Milnes) is here for a couple of days, my children having insisted on my asking him, because he was among my former early friendly acquaintances, and because he has expressed a great desire to come out and see me. My house is so little calculated for the reception of guests, and my whole general solitary way of living is so very small and restricted to my own mere daily necessities, that I quite shrink from the idea of asking any one to visit me, knowing how impossible it is for me to make any one, what I should consider, decently comfortable. However, as I said before, my children insisted that I was bound to invite Lord Houghton here, and so here he is till the day after to-morrow, and I must go and do my hostess's duty of talking to him, in the forlorn hope of amusing him.

York Farm, November 12th, 1875.

My dearest H——,

I was beginning to think it a very long time since I had heard from, or written to you; the former circumstance made me anxious, lest you should again be suffering from one of your bad colds and coughs, and unable or unwilling to make the effort of dictating. As for my not having written during the past week, it has been really for want of sufficient time. My children did not leave my house until the very day that Lord Houghton came into it, to pay me a visit of some days, and since his and their departure, I have been very busy bringing up the arrears of my manuscript for the magazine in which it is published, and copying letters of the time which we spent in London, in 1841, when my sister came out on the stage. . . .

I do not know what the average duration of life is in America. I have an idea that the climate is more unfavourable to robust health than to longevity; and I know several instances in this neighbourhood of prolonged existence of persons who are extremely delicate, indeed, confirmed invalids. . . . I cannot tell you how I am bearing the beginning of winter, for at present we are, and have been for a week past, suffering from the heat. All day long we are sitting with the doors and windows wide open, and this evening the fire in the drawing-room was allowed to go out, and the room was still oppressively hot. I walked nearly four miles this morning, with nothing but a black silk mantle over my black silk gown, and suffered very much from the heat. The splendid and soft brillancy of the weather is quite amazing, and, but for the heat, would be delightful. As it is, it is lovely to look at; but this is the most treacherous climate imaginable, and with the ther-

mometer at eighty to-day, we may have a snowstorm
to-morrow; we had two about a fortnight ago. Everybody is suffering from coughs and colds, and the
danger of catching them is much greater now than in
midwinter, when the house is not all full of draughts,
and one is not constantly throwing off one's superfluous
apparel.

My children have come and gone, and are now
staying over the way till the 27th of the month, when
they go down to Georgia for the winter.

God bless you, my dearest H——, I am beginning
once more to think it possible that I may see you
again next summer, but dare not trust myself to dwell
upon it.

York Farm, November 25th, 1875.

My beloved H——,

I am perfectly amazed at what you tell
me of three of my letters reaching you at once, and
cannot imagine by what irregularity of our delinquent
post-office such a thing occurs; moreover, it proves,
of course, that you have been kept a most undue time
without some of those letters. It is very vexatious,
and chiefly because it is obvious that letters thus
arbitrarily despatched may be quite as arbitrarily, or
carelessly, withheld altogether. However, there is no
help for it, as everybody has to submit, without
redress, to the same grievance.

To-day is a national festival, partly religious,
partly social, called "Thanksgiving Day." It is
appointed annually by the President, at the end of
the autumn, and is observed throughout the whole

country with church-going and family gatherings,
much after the fashion of Christmas. The practice
originated in New England, where the Puritans
refused to celebrate Christmas, as an Episcopalian (*i.e.*
idolatrous) festivity, and so choose the anniversary of
the arrival of a vessel, laden with corn and provisions,
which arrived when the early colonists were almost
perishing with hunger. Subsequently, through all
New England, a day of thanksgiving was annually
celebrated, which combined the memory of this
particular blessing of the rescue from starvation of
the first settlers, and the acknowledgment of God's
goodness in the yearly harvest and fruits of the earth.
From New England the custom spread, or was carried
by emigrants to the other states, and has now become
national and universal throughout the country.

My children and grandson, who is here from
school, dined with me, and had an *execrably* bad
dinner, such as my poor little English cook often
treats me to. In spite of which, as she *can* cook
decently, and does so sometimes accidentally, and is
never insolent, and is content to remain in her situation, and to accept reasonable wages—being twice as
much as she could get in England, the possession of so
superlatively excellent a domestic is a rare good
fortune, for which I am envied far and near by all my
friends, acquaintances, and neighbours; and I am very
certain, that, if she choose to leave me to-morrow, she
could get four guineas a month from any one with
whom she would condescend to accept service. But
to-day being, unluckily, what Ellen calls, "one of
Miss Waterfalls bad days," the soup was vile, the

turkey overdone, the beef underdone, the custards thin enough to be drunk, and the trifle thick enough to be dug. S—— returned home almost immediately after dinner, in torture with neuralgia in her head, having been all day long servant-hunting in Philadelphia. F—— had been in town on business and shopping, and was tired, too, so that we were not a very brilliant party.

The L——s sail for Georgia the day after tomorrow, having determined to go by sea, as less fatiguing for F—— and the baby than the long land journey. . . .

I began this letter two days ago, and it is now Saturday morning, and I am just going over the way to see my children set off for the South. We shall miss them very much—the darling baby and the dear dog, who is an especial pet of mine, and almost as fond of me as he is of his master.

Dear H——, I wrote this much, and now it is "past ten at night," as the ballad says, and I had a very sad day, with the heartache of parting in the morning, and a lonely, desolate-feeling evening. It is my birthday, which my kind and affectionate friend Ellen remembered, though I did not. I am sixty-six, and I do not care much to be wished many happy returns of the day. One's birthday is not an especially cheerful anniversary, when once doll and plum-cake time is passed, and certainly to-day has been a doleful one to me.

I feel very anxious about F——, for though I think her decision to go by sea was wise, for the dreadful fatigue of the land journey was certainty, and they may have a fine voyage, but so near her confinement, I dread the terrible strain of any sea sickness for her., However, the new moon has come in to-day with bright weather, and the voyage is only one of forty-eight hours, so I trust they will have a smooth passage to Savanah where they will stay a few days before going on to the rice plantation.

My grandson is at home, earlier than he was expected, having been dismissed, with the rest of the school, on account of an outbreak of scarlet fever among them; so their holidays began a month earlier than usual, which our boy and some of his companions whom we have seen regret, as it alters the time of their vacation, without lengthening it, and will lengthen their next term at school by a month in the summer, so they are not pleased with the case of scarlet fever, which has scattered them prematurely to their homes.

In speaking as you do of S——'s household difficulties as a "few clouds" occasionally passing over her, you can form no conception of what her life is. Her health is positively sacrificed to the incessant torment, irritation, vexation, disorder, disgust, and physical fatigue of her household worries.

Good-bye, my dearest H——. How little one's letters can do, to convey really accurate ideas of one's existence! You speak of M——'s "vigour;" she is the most fragile, tiny, delicate, diaphanous, evanescent-looking creature imaginable; but she has heroic courage, and the most absolute will I ever met with, and she lives upon those. God bless you, dear,

I am ever, as ever, yours,

FANNY.

York Farm, November 30th, 1875.

MY DEAREST H——,

I think you must have imagined me more intimate with Lord Houghton than I am, though I have known him ever since I was a girl, but only as a friendly acquaintance that I met frequently upon cordial terms. He was everywhere in London society at the time when I was living very much in it, and I therefore saw him almost wherever I went. He has always been kind and good-natured to me, but, beyond thinking him so, I never felt any great interest in his society, or special desire for his intercourse. He is clever, liberal-minded, extremely good-natured, and good-tempered, and with his very considerable abilities and genuine amiable qualities a valuable and agreeable acquaintance. I was unwilling to ask him to my house for any more important occasion than driving out and taking luncheon with me. My house is not in itself comfortable enough, nor is it sufficiently well appointed, in any one particular, to admit of my asking any one to it accustomed to the luxurious comfort of English people of Lord Houghton's class. I cannot be sure of having even the plainest dinner sent to my table decently, and all the paraphernalia requisite for entertaining, glass, china, etc., is in such a state of dilapidation—cracked, old, odd, insufficient, or unpresentable, that, though it answers very well for me by myself, it is altogether unfit for purposes of receiving company, even in the humblest way.

I did not consider that I had the means of lodging Lord Houghton comfortably, even though in order to lodge him at all I gave up my own bedroom, and dressed in a room without a fireplace in it. All these things made me reluctant to ask a man, who is now old and infirm, a martyr to neuralgia, gout, and rheumatism, to stay in my house. However, I did so, because my children wished that I should. He stayed but two days; that is, arrived on a Wednesday, when my four children dined here with him, the next day Mr. L—— gave him a man's dinner in Philadelphia, the day after that S—— asked some people to meet him at dinner at her house, and on Saturday morning he left me, having been, I am afraid, miserably uncomfortable, for the room I gave up to him, suddenly and most perversely, took to smoking, which it had never done before in its life, and he was obliged to occupy what was to have been his bedroom. I had no conversation of any particular interest with him, for he is very deaf, and, having lost his teeth, speaks so indistinctly that I, who am also very deaf, could hardly understand half he said; so you see his visit was no particular satisfaction or gratification to me, nor could it possibly have been either to him. He has run all over the United States in a wonderfully short time, and people say that he means to write a book about them; this being pretty generally expected of him, I believe. He has been courted and flattered in the most fulsome manner, crowned with flowers, crowned with laurels (literally, not figuratively), given dinners to in public and private, and harangued, lauded, and complimented to a degree that was really absurd. I suppose it has not been pains thrown away, for I hear he praises everything in the country, from the debased currency to the degraded government.

I think S—— is extremely fond of her little niece. I do not know that she would habitually like to have her literary occupations interfered with by demands on her attention by any young child; but as little Alice was only her inmate for a short time, I think she found her a very fascinating plaything. The little creature still continues pale and delicate looking, and has a fitful and capricious appetite, in spite of which she hardly ever cries or frets, and is full of fun and spirits. She is beginning to talk and walk about, and is extremely delightful to me, whom she has learned to designate as "Gannie" with much glee whenever she sees me. They all went away last Saturday, and left me forlorn. I miss them terribly, and am quite bereaved in the loss of my dear Irish retriever, which has been living here all the summer, and had become my constant companion, lying by the fire in my dressing-room, to which I always betake myself at ten o'clock, until past midnight, when just before getting into bed I used to put him outside my door, where he slept till morning.

It is past twelve o'clock, and I am very sleepy; with you it is only about six, and perhaps you are not yet very sleepy. Good night, God bless you,

I am ever, as ever, yours,

FANNY.

York Farm, December 12th, 1875.

MY DEAREST H——,

The interest that you take in Lord Houghton's visit to me surprises me, and so very much surpasses what I felt in it, that your questions about it seem to me curious. His visit was rather a distress to me than a pleasure, for I am in no respect so situated as to be able to accommodate visitors of Lord Houghton's class and kind—accustomed to luxurious comfort. I never invite any company or see any one whatever, and, therefore, to make my table furniture sufficiently decent, for the one day he dined with me, I was obliged to spend eight guineas in plates, finger-glasses, and salt-cellars, of all which necessaries of civilized life I had an insufficient supply for a dinner of six persons—my four children, Lord Houghton, and myself.

I suppose, though I said nothing to him upon the subject, that he might easily conclude that I like living in my own country better than in this. He kissed me when he went way, and asked me when I was *coming home*. But I do not know whether my life here struck him as happy, or pleasant, or the reverse; and can tell you nothing of his impressions in that respect.

[Lord Houghton, in the latter days of our always friendly intercourse, often laughingly referred to the beginning of our acquaintance, which took place at an evening party at my father's house, when my brother John introduced Mr. Monckton Milnes to me as an early and intimate college friend of his, winding up a catalogue of his mental gifts and moral qualities by his recent highly successful personation of Beatrice, in an amateur performance of "Much Ado About Nothing." "How durst you?" was my instantaneous exclamation, and, Lord Houghton declared, the only words I addressed to him; but though they certainly

were the first, I do not think they were my only
greeting to my brother's friend, although it is not
impossible that my sense of the inappropriateness of
such a representation of Beatrice may have gained
some acuteness by the fact that Alfred Tennyson, who
was also one of our guests that evening, had accidentally said to me, by some curious chance, " You remind
me of Beatrice "—assuredly not by the wit and wisdom
of my dialogue and discourse, but, I think, by the
fashion of my head-dress, which struck his fancy as
like something that might have been worn by the
" merry hearted," fine Lady of Messina.

After Lord Houghton and myself had both left
America and settled in London, I saw him frequently,
and he very often kindly sent me courteous invitations to dine with him, which I invariably declined,
as I never went into any society. This Lord Houghton
resented, with a tone of friendly vexation, reproaching
me for dining at the deanery on Dean Stanley's invitation, " Who," said Lord Houghton, " is a much more
modern acquaintance of yours than I am ; " which
indeed was true. But Dean Stanley's invitation was
a command to me, hardly less imperative than that
of royalty. The last of Lord Houghton's kind invitations to me was enforced by " to meet the Princess
Louise." I was obliged, however, to decline even that
great honour, and did so, wondering if the royal lady
chose her own company, and, if so, why she had chosen
mine ? Upon expressing my surprise at receiving such
a mark of distinction, I was more than once assured
that royal personages were nowadays only persons
"just like any others," which the respectful super-

stitions of my early days quite prevented my understanding; but in my early days, and in earlier days, "reverence" was still "the angel of this world."

The last time I ever saw my friend, Lord Houghton, was during a few days that I spent with him on a visit to our common friend, Mrs. Richard Greville, in the course of which she asked us to go with her and call upon Alfred Tennyson, who was then at his place at Blackdown, some miles from Guildford, near which town Mrs. Greville's cottage was. I consented with great pleasure to make this expedition, but was much dismayed at finding that the vehicle, in which we were to drive a considerable distance, was a light Irish jaunting car, out of which I expected to be shot at a tangent round the first corner we turned; though Mrs. Greville, Lord Houghton, and myself were all portly bodies of sufficient weight to steady the craziest-minded Irish carriage. Upon my expression of nervous distrust in its carrying capabilities, our hostess very amiably sent for a fly, in which we made our ascent to the Parnassus at Blackdown; but if the fly could not fall, neither could it go, and, towards the top of our hill journey, Lord Houghton got out to open innumerable gates, and Mrs. Greville preferred walking to crawling on wheels. Our return was even more ignominious, for, before we got to Guildford, our fly refused to stir, and we eagerly hailed an empty cab on the road, which the providence of some local races furnished us, and reached home, Mrs. Greville and I inside, and the poet and peer by the side of the driver.

Our visit to Alfred Tennyson was my last interview with him, and one of peculiar interest. The room

where he received us commanded a fine view of the
downs and the distant shining of the sea; while the
situation of the house itself, half-way up a hillside
covered with fine trees, gave a striking effect to a
sudden storm that darkened the sky and swept the
downs and lashed with violent rain the window panes,
against which the oaks bent and bowed themselves,
writhing and struggling with the wind; while Alfred
Tennyson, to whom Mrs. Greville had made an urgent
request to read something to us, declaimed in his
sonorous monotone the imprecations of his "British
Boadicea, on her Roman Enemies." When he had
finished reading, he brought me a Shakespeare, which
was on his writing-table, and, putting it in my hands,
desired me to read something to them. "What was
this for?" said I, taking a pen from between the
leaves. "Oh, to write his criticisms on Shakespeare,"
said Lord Houghton. I took possession of it, and
determined to have it electro-plated, lest in my possession it should become again a common goose's quill,
and then read, where it had divided the leaves,
those wonderful computations of the worthlessness of
life and the terrors of death, spoken in the prison
scene of "Measure for Measure," by the Duke and
Claudio.

On one occasion when I visited Lord Houghton
and his wife (then still Mr. and Mrs. Monckton Milnes)
at Frystone, their place in Yorkshire, an incident
occurred that I have often thought might have figured
with comical effect in a novel.

One evening, when I was dressed for dinner, before
any one else, and was sitting alone in the drawing-

room, I overheard old Mr. Milnes, the father of my host, who was very little acquainted with me, questioning my many-years kind and attached friend, James Spedding, about my career and fortunes. They were walking up and down an adjacent room, of which the door was open, and I heard a story that I should have pitied, if told of another woman, related in the compassionate voice of the gentleman who had known me from my girlhood, and been my brother's school and college friend and companion. Plunged in very sad reminiscences, it was some minutes before I perceived that I was sitting, quite unconsciously, opposite a very good portrait of Lord Houghton, with the tears streaming down my face, apparently at its contemplation. What any of my fellow-guests, or my charming hostess herself, might have thought of such an apparent indication of feeling has often since made me smile. Luckily I recovered myself before any one came to misinterpret it.

Sydney Smith and Monckton Milnes were very good friends, in spite of the rather sarcastic title bestowed by the former on the latter of the "Cool of the Evening," by which nickname he was often designated in familiar society, as describing the serene self-satisfaction and smiling self-sufficiency, which characterized him in his earlier years. Conceit is the proud privilege of youth; and Monckton Milnes had a justifiable share of that great gift of the imperturbable gods.

It was to him, too, that Sydney Smith gave the ludicrous answer to a kind inquiry as to what sort of night he had had when he was ill. "Horrible, horrible, my dear Milnes! Dreamed I was chained to a rock, and being talked to death by Harriet Martineau and Macaulay." There is another version of this— "Dreamed I was being preached to death by mad curates;" but the personal epigram is the better. Perhaps the great wit said both the good things at different times; perhaps he repeated himself, as the greatest geniuses occasionally do; perhaps he thought that the cherry could afford two bites; but the most spontaneously brilliant wit cannot always sparkle impromptu or flash extemporaneously.]

Our weather here still continues very mild; quite unusually so for the time of year. There has been a day or two of frost, and a few scurries of hail and snow, but no real cold. To-day was lovely soft and mild, like a Roman winter day, and the sky at sunset was, as it often is, as beautiful as the sky in Italy. The heavens are a perpetual heavenly delight to me here.

I am very much interested in the Eastern question and the present aspect of European politics; it is like coming to the last chapter of an eventful story, the virtual end of the Turkish power in Europe, and the probable formation of an entirely new one, by the consolidation under one government of those provinces between Turkey and Austria, seems like the beginning of a new era in that part of the world, and it interests me deeply. I am glad England has bought the Suez Canal, and keeps a hold upon Egypt. I think the changes likely to occur in the Ottoman Empire full of promise for the progress of civilization and improvement in the condition of the provinces in the south-east of Europe, that have been such miserable dependencies of the Turks.

My children are safe at the plantation. Mr. L—— wrote to me immediately on their arrival at Savanah, to which place they went direct from Philadelphia by sea, and had a most prosperous voyage. I had a letter from F—— yesterday, from the island, giving an excellent account of herself and the dear little baby, whose progress in the experiences of life now includes being put in the corner by her nurse for *naughtiness*, which chastisement for her sins, her mother says, she seems to regard as a capital joke. She is quite well, and as merry as a little creature can be. They give a most wonderful account of their orange crop, the abundance of which is something amazing, the branches of the trees have to be propped to sustain them under their burthen of splendid fruit, "golden" in the literal sense of the word, for they have already sold several hundred pounds' worth of it this season.

Cold does not agree with S—— at all, and the winter here tries her severely. Often as I have been tempted to wish that she had settled in Boston, where her life might have been in some respects more congenial and better suited to her, she would, I am sure, never have been able to endure the climate. Our boy is at home for his holidays.

God bless, you my dearest H——; how much, how constantly I think of you.

Ever, as ever, yours,

FANNY.

York Farm, December 31st, 1875.

My beloved H——,

It is a quarter to twelve at night, and we are at the edge of the New Year. God bless you dear, dear H——. These divisions of our time (really without significance as they are, except what we ourselves invest them with) appeal to our imaginations and feelings, and affect our heart in spite of our reason. A new year begins with every day, but we call the 1st of January New Year's Day, and old associations hallow it, especially to us. God bless you in the coming year, my dearest friend, and comfort and support and cheer your darkness and infirmity, and strengthen and sustain her who sustains and ministers so faithfully to you, for I know how devoted she is in her service of love, and how little she shares it with any one. May I be permitted in the course of this year to embrace you once more, my dear friend; but, in and above all things, may we be enabled to accept God's will.

My children, that is, S—— and her husband and boy, came from over the way to spend the evening with me, but were so tired with sitting up late for children's festivities for the last two nights, that they were all tumbling off the perch, and left me at a little after ten, so I shall see in the New Year alone. At this season of the year I never go to bed before one o'clock, though I leave my ground-floor rooms and come up to my dressing-room at ten, that the servants may shut up the house and go to bed; and then I write or read till an hour past midnight, when I go to my bed till eight, when I am called—seven hours' sleep being still my normal allowance, though I now find it difficult, not to say impossible, to sleep *steadily* for seven hours. . . .

What a real misfortune it is to be utterly without animal spirits ! The Americans, as a nation or race, are more deficient in them than any other people I have ever lived among, and their early gravity is something portentous. . . . As for S——, she is worried, ill, and I sometimes think she will be worried to death by the incessant struggle *to live*. Dr. W—— occasionally says that if it was not for his boy, whom he does not wish to bring up out of his own country, and whom he will not leave at school here, he would give up America altogether, shut up their house, or let it, and go and live abroad ; and I often think they really may be compelled to adopt that course, for their health, comfort, and happiness seem to me literally destroyed by the impossibility of keeping a decent household together.

The question of vivisection is not agitated here, because it is practised so commonly and with such reckless cruelty by mere medical apprentices, that it is accepted as a thing of course. There is no law and no restraint of custom, and no influence of public opinion to limit the abuse of the practice. Social cowardice, everywhere prevalent enough (but here peculiarly predominant), prevents men from opening their lips about it, for fear of incurring personal unpopularity.

You say that the evil tendencies of men are oftener exerted against their fellows than against the brute creation. But medical students are *boys* rather than

men, and there is no more common form of the love of
power in boys than cruelty to animals; and in this
case there is the fine pretext of the pursuit of science
to justify it. It is a subject I never speak and cannot
bear to think of. Fanny Cobbe made some attempts
to get some information upon the practice of vivisection in this country, but though I know nothing of
the result of her inquiries upon the subject, I should
feel greatly surprised if she got any satisfactory answer
about it.

I am very glad to hear that Lady Jane and her
children are recovering, and rejoice at your nephew's
improved condition. He always seemed to me the
very beau-ideal of sound health and the cheerful
bright good nature and sweet temper that generally
accompanies a fine physical organization; and I was
very sorry to hear of his late indisposition. I did not
know how to imagine him anything but blooming and
beaming in perennial health and strength.

Dear E——, may God give you and H——, to
whom I send my dearest remembrance, a good New
Year. I cannot write to *her* of my constant thoughts
of and prayers for her, nor of my earnest hope that I
may see her this year. How much I long to do so
you will easily believe; but I fear to speak or to think
much about it myself, for who can tell what may be
ordained for us ?

York Farm, January 10th, 1876.

My beloved H——,

Yesterday morning the thermometer at *sun-
rise* was at sixty-eight *above* freezing; yesterday

evening it was at seventeen *below* freezing. What do
you think of a climate which inflicts such sudden and
extreme changes upon unfortunate mortal bodies?
To-night it is severely cold, and I suppose the winter
is come at last. Nor, though I think a variation in
the thermometer of forty degrees in twelve hours
rather unreasonable, am I sorry that the unnatural
heat from which we have been suffering has given
place to seasonable, normal cold; but, to be sure, the
suddenness of the change was tremendous.

You ask me in your last letter to how late a period
I think of extending the publication of my " Gossip."
Certainly not beyond my marriage, and probably not
beyond my coming out on the stage; but this would
depend in some measure upon my stay in America or
return to England.

The reason that induced me to publish those
Memoirs was the sudden serious diminution of my
income, by the loss of three hundred a year, caused
by change of investments from securities which returned ten per cent. to others which gave me only six
or four. The great expense of living here made this
diminution of my means a subject of distress and
anxiety to me, for I do not live in a manner that
admits of much retrenchment, and I am altogether
incapable of the exertion of my former mode of earning money by reading. I was glad, under these circumstances, to accept a very liberal offer for my
" Gossip," and shall be guided in my continuation of
the publication by my circumstances (financially
speaking); but do not think I shall extend it beyond
the time of my leaving the stage.

You say you do not feel sure that you have lost any of my letters; but I feel certain that I have lost some of yours. About a month ago, I think, there occurred an unusual interval between your letters, and then you referred to Lady Jane Taylor and one of her children having the scarlet fever, and of some terrible accident which had befallen Miss Olivia Lambert, as to things of which I must be already aware through your letters; whereas I had received no previous mention of them, and now have not the least idea what did happen to Miss Lambert to deprive her of the use of her hands. I do not think you can have imagined you had written to me upon these subjects without having done so; but the first letter that reached me, in which they were referred to, clearly indicated that one previous to that, mentioning them, had not come to my hands. I hate to think of the possibility of our losing each other's letters; but know, from the utter carelessness of our village postmaster, that there is no security for their safety.

We have a great deal of very malignant small-pox in our neighbourhood just now, and Dr. W—— has been very busy vaccinating all his neighbours, the household at Champlost, with M—— at their head; so this morning I walked over to see how she was. . . .

Dr. W——, who, poor man, is cookless at present, has dined with me every day since she went away, an arrangement with which I am only too delighted and thankful for, for he is charming company, and his coming relieves most agreeably the tedium of my entirely solitary evenings.

York Farm, January 17th, 1876.

MY DEAREST H——,

Thank you for your wish of a Happy New
Year to me. There is enough to be thankful for in
every day; but the wish of a happy year conveys
what one no longer believes in. The days, as they
come and go, one by one, are full of mingled trials
and blessings, and I pray God to make me thankful
for both; but my chief endeavour is not to look
beyond the day, of which the evil and the good are
both sufficient. I hope most earnestly that F——
and Mr. L—— will return to England this summer.
For myself, I know not what to hope or determine.

I long extremely to see you once more, and am
deeply troubled at Ellen's prolonged postponement of
her marriage, occasioned by her protracted stay here
with me. I am very uncertain as to what I ought to
do about her, but hope I may be able to determine for
the best.

My sister wrote to me on my birthday, and gave
a fairly good account of herself and all her belongings.
She was going to take a house in London for a few
months; she said she should try and make it gay and
pleasant for her children and theirs, but that she was
at her best only when she was alone with her husband
at Warsash.

I have no news of F—— yet, but am anxiously
expecting to hear every day. I am only waiting for
that to go to Boston, where I have promised to visit
several of my friends, and to stay with one of whom
I am very fond, whom I have known ever since she
was a school-girl, and who has urgently begged me to

pay her a visit. I should also pass a day or two with
Mrs. Minot, who was a young girl travelling with her
aunt, Miss Sedgwick, when you and Dorothy met
them in Germany.

I wrote you word, in my last letter, what an extraordinary winter we were having in point of weather
—two days ago the road was covered with a perfect
procession of waggons carrying loads of blocks of ice,
from ten to twenty inches thick, to fill all the farm
ice-houses; to-day it is quite warm, and the ponds
and brooks are free, and there is not a trace of frost
to be seen anywhere. The ice-houses that are filled
are lucky: mine is not; but I feel no anxiety about
it—we shall have bitter cold again, no doubt, in
a day or two. Last year we had the severest frost
and deepest snow of the whole winter far into the
month of April.

I have just come home from dining with M——,
which I do every Monday; her other neighbour and
intimate friend, Mrs. T——, a very charming person,
frequently joins our party and calls them "les causeries
du Lundi."

They had seen in the newspapers the account of
Lord Leigh's accident, of which I got the first news
from your letter. He is a terribly heavy man to be
thrown from his horse, and especially upon his head.
I am sure his brother will be greatly troubled about it.

Nutwood, January 30th, 1876.

MY DEAREST H——,

I have left my small house and come on to
the neighbourhood of Boston, to see a dear friend,

who, though my junior by many years, cannot stand
or walk without crutches, which is in itself a great
improvement on her chair-bound helplessness when I
was last here.

I passed through Boston last autumn, but stayed
too short a time to admit of my seeing my many
friends, and I am now receiving visits from them all,
and have become so entirely unaccustomed in my
York Farm existence to any intercourse with my
"friends and fellow-creatures" (into which two classes
I divide the whole human race), that I am really quite
exhausted, when the evening comes, with the unusual
amount of social intercourse I have enjoyed in the
course of the day. In a day or two more I leave my
present abode, to go and pay another visit in this
neighbourhood, and expect to be back in my own
home about the seventh of next month.

I drove this afternoon through the neighbourhood
of this place, which was once very familiar to me, and
about which I used at one time to ride a great deal.
I went to a hill which commands a very beautiful
panorama of the mountains, the sea, and the city, and
I was greatly struck by the unusual aspect of the
whole landscape, which, at this season of the year, in
this region, is generally buried in snow, but which
to-day was basking in bright sunshine, without a
trace of white to be descried in any direction. The
winter this year is really most extraordinary in its
mildness. I believe such a season is remembered by
nobody.

Boston, February 2nd, 1876.

MY DEAREST H——,

You bid me tell you of my health, and I can report very fairly well of it, though I am suffering inevitably a little from change of hours, of diet, of water, etc., all which are apt to be more or less drawbacks to the advantages of change of air and scene, when people are as old as I am and accustomed, as I am, to live with unvarying regularity in every respect.

I think you will surely remember having heard or read of Dr. Howe, of Boston, the philanthropic and devoted governor of its blind asylum, the admirable man who brought the poor deaf, dumb, and blind girl, Laura Bridgeman, out of her strange and terrible fleshly prison-house, into intelligent communion with the outer world and her fellow-beings. His redeeming of that creature from the hard tyranny of her triple impotence, was a miracle of Christian patience and love. That man is just dead, and I never heard anything more touching than the description of the demeanour of Laura Bridgeman during his funeral, not so much from any demonstration of sorrow, for indeed she made none, for her face did not vary in expression or exhibit any emotion, but there was something inexpressibly touching in the mere description of her pausing by his bed, to which she was led, and feeling his face and hands, and then at the funeral service standing by his bier, over the surface of which she passed her hands repeatedly, as if seeking to find him. It seemed to me one of the most pathetic incidents I almost ever heard described.

I leave this place to-morrow, to spend a couple of

days with Kate M——, and then return for a day to
Boston, after which I go back to Branchtown, where I
must look after my poor widowed son-in-law, who, I
suppose and hope, will come and spend his evenings
with me, while S—— is away from home.

The winter here has been extraordinarily mild until
to-day, when one of those frightfully sudden and
excessive changes of temperature, for which this
climate is nefarious, took place.   A friend of ours left
his house on horseback this morning to visit us, and
rode for some time on roads so soft as to be muddy.
Suddenly the wind changed, and rose almost to a
hurricane, the temperature fell, and the road froze so
rapidly as to become one sheet of ice, and he was
compelled, in order to avoid breaking his neck, to dis-
mount and lead his horse to the first blacksmith,
where he could get him roughed to prevent his slipping
and falling on the sort of looking-glass to which the
whole road had turned.

York Farm, February 9th, 1876.

MY DEAREST H——,

I reached my home yesterday afternoon, on
my return from Boston, where I had a most delightful
visit, meeting again all my kind old friends and
acquaintances.   It is undoubtedly a considerable proof
of my love for my children that I live here, instead of
in or near Boston, where there are so many people for
whom I have such a strong regard, and whose intercourse is so delightful to me.   However, I hardly
suppose that I could afford to live in Boston, which is
the dearest place in America, and therefore in the

known world. The friend with whom I have been staying pays her cook thirty shillings a week, and tells me that two guineas a week is a frequent rate of wages paid to cooks in Boston; her parlour-maid receives a pound a week, and so on. My bill for my maid and myself, for two days at a hotel in Boston, was nine pounds; so how anybody can afford to live there who is not, as the French say, "*cousu d'or*," passes my comprehension. . . .

Sir Michael Hicks Beach was one of F——'s visitors at the rice plantation, when Mr. L—— first went there. On one occasion he was very kind and compassionate to a dog of hers who was suffering, which gave her a very agreeable impression of his amiability.

I returned home to find S—— gone down to Georgia to stay with her sister, so I and my son-in-law shall have to make the best we can of each other's company.

I am sorry to say the late American tenants of Widmore have lost a great deal of money since their return to America. The incessant fluctuation of people's fortunes, and uncertainty of their means, is one of the most unpleasant characteristics of social existence here; nobody ever seems to be sure of being in the same place, so to speak, two years together.

York Farm, February 17th, 1876.

MY DEAREST H——,

I got a letter from S—— yesterday from the rice plantation, where she had just arrived. Besides the pleasure of seeing her sister and Mr. L——, she seems to be enjoying the delightful mild southern climate, the wild solitude by which they are surrounded, the lovely profusion of flowers in full blossom in the woods, and bears admiring testimony to the homelike charm of the pretty, tidy, comfortable, pleasant abode the L——s have contrived to make on that most unlovely rice swamp. How different from the wooden overseer's shanty (it could not even be dignified by the title of a cottage), unpainted without and unfurnished within, except by spiders and centipedes, which I inhabited during my stay there!

I am delighted she has gone; it will do her a great deal of good, as well as being so great a pleasure to them. Poor Dr. W—— is very forlorn in her absence. He comes and dines and spends the evening with me, and half the time rejoices that his wife is gone to the South, and the other half growls and grumbles that she is not here.

My printing machine is in one respect a great disappointment to me, for S—— says that it irritates her nerves to such a degree that she cannot use it, which I am very sorry for, as I should not have got it for myself.

Good-bye, my dearest H——. I am thankful that you can still find so much interest in my letters.

Ever, as ever, yours,
FANNY.

York Farm, March 1st, 1876.

MY DEAREST H——,

I can do nothing but think with acute vexation of your disappointment in getting a letter

I intended for F—— directed in an envelope to you, while your proper epistle went wandering off to Georgia, whence F—— sent it back a couple of days ago, and I immediately despatched it to you with a few lines, explaining the mistake, and expressing my contrition and concern at my carelessness. I suppose my mind was perturbed and confused in consequence of a letter from F——, to which I wrote a reply immediately after writing to you, and putting both the letters into envelopes at the same time, misdirected them. For in F——'s last letter she tells me that they have determined not to return to England this year; not, indeed, until the spring of 1877. I regret this change of plan on my own account, as well as theirs; but what concerns me is of the least importance, though now I do not quite know what will become of me.

Ellen has promised her mother to return to England this year, whether I do or not, and I shall lose in her not only my attached friend, but my excellent, efficient maid and housekeeper. My little English cook, too, returns home with her, and my man-servant is going back to Ireland to his own family. Without their assistance and Ellen's help, any attempt on my part to keep house in this country is quite out of the question. Thus I am thrown into a perfect sea of uncertainty, and have not a notion what is to become of me; but I do not trouble my head much about it, for I cannot help myself, and it is no use worrying about uncontrollable circumstances. I am thankful that Ellen has determined to go home. Her loss to me will be quite irreparable; but I have been extremely distressed at involving her, through her attachment to me, in such a protracted stay in this country, and in the consequent anxiety and disappointment of her mother and the good fellow to whom she is engaged, and serious injury of her health, so that I am really thankful that she has determined to leave me.

There is a great deal that distresses me in again postponing my return this year, but it is no use thinking about it. " 'Tis vain to mourn inevitable evils."

S—— is still in Georgia, and we do not expect her home before the end of next week. She has been absent for six weeks—an excellent thing for her—but her husband finds her absence rather oppressive. He dines and spends his evenings with me, and we shall both be glad to have S—— at home again, for our sakes, not for hers. I dread to have her come back to the incessant domestic worry of her hateful housekeeping.

I am still going on with the publication of my Memoirs, and have lately sent you two numbers of them.

My grandson is at present going on very satisfactorily at school, working hard and behaving well, and his father occasionally expresses comical apprehensions lest the boy should be becoming *too good*, a process which may be considered unnatural, and therefore, perhaps, unhealthful at so early an age. . . .

Oh, my dear E——. It is sadder to me than I can express to think I shall not see her this year. I had so earnestly and confidently trusted to do so; but what is the use of afflicting her with the expression of my regret. I had hoped to have come and lightened your burden for a while. It may not be!

York Farm, March 5th, 1876.

MY DEAREST H——,

We are now having our winter snow, not indeed deep or heavy, or long lying, but more than we have had yet this season, and ice and frost that again revive my hope of getting the ice-house filled before the spring fairly comes, and we are left unprovided with what is here such an indispensable necessary of life, that we shall have to purchase it daily, if we have not our stored supply. It does not cost much more, bought in this way, but it is far less convenient than having one's own ice-house well filled, the expense of which is about fourteen pounds. The poorest people here afford themselves this luxury, and in the city it is quite curious to see the ice cars early in the morning going round and leaving a huge block of crystal clear *cold* on the doorstep of every house. There are in various localities great storehouses of ice, from which this general distribution is made, and a short time ago one of these great ice-houses, on the Hudson river, took fire and was burned, with thirty thousand tons of ice in it, which seems a strange catastrophe, as such a mass of ice, one would have thought, would have put out the fire as it melted.

Our last report from the South was a very cheerful letter from S—— to her husband, from the plantation. We are in hopes of having her back at the end of this week.

My visit to Boston was beneficial to me after I

returned home.   I was not very well while I was
there, the extreme regularity of diet and hours with
which I live, and my whole daily external existence is,
I presume, favourable to my general health while it
is uninterrupted, but I think it makes me more sus-
ceptible to the irregularities unavoidable in travelling
and living with other people in other people's houses.
While I was in Boston I suffered from the necessary
change in all my habits, but after my return here I
think I was decidedly the better for it, and my stay
among my friends was exceedingly cheering and ex-
hilarating to me, though it revived the regret that I
always feel that I live at such a great distance from
so many people whose intercourse is delightful to and
good for me. . . .

[During the time that I spent in Boston, the
persons I knew best, and saw most frequently there
were Dr. Channing, Prescott, Motley, the historians ;
Felton, the learned Greek professor ; Agassiz, the
great scientific naturalist ; Hillard, Emmerson, Oliver
Wendell Holmes, Lowell, and Longfellow.   Such an
extraordinary contemporaneous collection of eminent
and remarkable men, in a comparatively small city,
ought to have resulted in a society that might have
been the admiration and envy of the greatest civilized
capitals of Europe.   Paris, and London, might have
been proud of such a company of exceptional intellects,
and sent pilgrims from among their most distinguished
men to the Puritan capital of Massachusetts.

With such material for the most charming and
brilliant society, it has often been a subject of curious
surprise to me that Boston had nothing that could be

called so, nothing comparable to that finest product of mature civilization, the frequent easy and delightful intercourse of highly cultivated and intelligent men and women. They were all intimate or friendly acquaintances with each other; their wives, sisters, and daughters were in almost daily intercourse, and yet there was nothing that could be called society, in the true sense of that word, in the Boston of my day.

I had the honour, pleasure, and privilege of the acquaintance and friendship of all these distinguished men, and was received by them with the utmost courteous kindness in their homes and families; but a general society of them, attractive and interesting, such as their combined intercourse ought to have produced, did not exist among them. Three reasons may have tended to this result: the men worked too hard in their business abroad; the women were too hard-worked in their duties at home; and I think the New Englanders inherited from the old ones the want of both taste and talent for society, and from their Puritan ancestors a decided disinclination and incapacity for amusement in general, for amusing others, and being amused themselves.]

I am quite as well as any one can expect to be at my age; the dull monotony of my life here throws me, no doubt, too much upon my own resources, which naturally dwindle more and more, as mental and physical powers decay, but I have plenty to be daily thankful for, and my whole existence is such as should content and more than satisfy a reasonable person.

You say that you wish you had anything satisfactory or cheering to tell me, and Heaven knows how much, when I write to you, I wish the same; but I have nothing to write about but myself, and the expression of my deep, deep sympathy with you, would, I fear, be enfeebling and distressing, instead of strengthening to you, my dearest friend. I love you most dearly, I think of you daily, I pray God to comfort and sustain you, and lighten your darkness with a sense of His mercy; and I am ever, as ever, yours.

York Farm, March 8th, 1876.

My dearest H——,

I have your two letters of the 14th and 12th, the latter having arrived after instead of before the other, as it should have done.

You ask me what the Americans think about our Queen becoming an Empress, but as I see no Americans but my children and my dear M——, and never read the papers, I have little chance of knowing what is generally thought about it. I thought a letter to the *Spectator*, by one of the Trevelyans, contained a good suggestion with regard to the Queen's title, namely, that it should be "Queen of the British Isles and India," which I think is comprehensive, sufficient, and handsome sounding. For my own part, I like best of all the old-fashioned, ladylike, and most noble name of the "Queen of England."

S—— has just been spending a couple of hours with me, and I have had the first full talk with her since her return from the South. She advises me on no account to make my plans dependent upon those of the L——s, for theirs appear to her quite uncertain. She thinks F—— happier, better, more useful and more contented on the plantation than she can ever be anywhere else. She thinks the life agreeable to Mr. L——, who finds duties enough everywhere to devote himself to, for the satisfaction of his conscience and his heart, and who is actively interested and eminently successful in the management of the estate, and to whom the freedom and ease of the life, the wild picturesqueness of the place, the fishing, the boating, the hunting are all elements of enjoyment, and that there is much in his apparent satisfaction in his existence there, as well as his wife's passionate preference for the place to account for their protracted stay, especially as, she says, the improvement he has achieved in the whole place is something quite wonderful, and the lively, energetic interest he takes in what might be its future development most natural. She agrees with me, nevertheless, in thinking that Mr. L—— ought to return to England, and that his proper sphere and place is in his own country; but although this is quite my opinion, all she has been telling me makes me perceive, as I have not done hitherto, the impediments of many sorts in the way of their returning to Europe.

My printing machine is a most delightful creature, and I use it now entirely for copying the matter that I send to the *Atlantic Monthly;* it saves me the wearisome writing over again of all my manuscripts. I sit upright to it, as I should to my piano, and it tires neither my eyes nor back, as writing does, and I

think must be an unspeakable comfort to my poor
printers. They are now very generally used in lawyers'
offices and places of business where much copying is
done, and with persons expert in their use are quite
as rapid in writing as the pen.

M——'s other intimate friend and neighbour is a
lady who corresponds with an American friend in
London, and the latter, who writes to her every sort
of gossip, has informed her that there is going to be
(I suppose by this time has been) a grand fancy ball
at your Dublin Castle, and that a lady, who was a
famous American beauty, is going to it as the Suez
Canal, which seems to us *ultra mondaines* irresistibly
ludicrous. What is the dress, beyond a steamer on
her bosom? What is the costume of the Suez Canal?
Think of such a piece of nonsense coming all across
the Atlantic to us!

I have just been reading a couple of delightful
volumes of my delightful friend Ampère's letters, and
thought of you while reading of Madame Recamier's
blindness and his devotion to her.*   -

* From the abundant contemporaneous literature, letters,
journals, memoirs, etc., of which Madame Recamier may be
called the heroine, I think it appears that, besides a great
beauty, she was a considerable coquette. It is impossible not
to come to that conclusion in reading the scene between herself
and poor Ampère, when she (being then old enough to be his
mother) draws from him the secret of his desperate love for her
by her pretence of believing her niece to be the object of his
attachment. "Mais c'est vous, c'est vous!" exclaims the
young man, beside himself with this cruel experiment, and
breaking into tears of passionate emotion. One of Madame
Recamier's adorers said that no man ever read his prose or

York Farm, *March* 11th, 1876.

MY DEAR H——,

S—— returned from the South yesterday ; she was not expected till to-day, but by some accidental mistake found she could get home sooner, and did so. She says her sister looks extremely well, and is occupied and interested and busy the whole day long with the various details of her life there, which you know is that of a very large farm, with labourers and live stock, and gardening, and agricultural, and all sorts of rural processes constantly succeeding one another. Mr. L——, who for the last two years has been his own overseer, is also active and energetic, and busy from morning till night, and while superintending the management of the estate, is indefatigable and unceasing in his pastoral duties among the people. Altogether, the account of the life they are leading down there seemed both pleasant and good.

I have just received a letter from F——, by which I find that I did not, as I supposed I did, misdirect my letter to her as well as to you. I thought I had sent you a letter I had written to her, as I did send her a letter which I had written to you ; but the latter it seems is the only mistake I have made, and I

poetry to her without being convinced that she thought it the finest prose or poetry that ever was written or read. No wonder Saint Beuve said of her, "Elle écoutait avec séduction."

I was pressed by one of Madame Recamier's female worshippers to be presented to her, but on that occasion I was merely passing through Paris, and, not being enthusiastic about an introduction to the blind and elderly beauty of L'Abbaye aux Bois, neglected the opportunity, and now regret it.

wish I had made my blunder the other way, as she can far better spare a letter of mine than you can.

Dear H——, you say you feel it an exertion to dictate, and I cannot bear to think of your making a painful effort to communicate with me. I am sure E—— will have the goodness to let me hear how it is faring with you, and I will continue to write to you, and tell you all that concerns me, as long as you care to hear it. Your intercourse with me, my dearest friend, must not become a burden to you—it would be too sad to me, and I could not endure the thought of it.

Besides the articles published in the *Atlantic Monthly Magazine*, I am daily copying such portions of my letters and journals, kept and written at a later period, as I wish to preserve. I am anxious to destroy the letters themselves, retaining only such extracts from them as have no particular reference to myself or my own affairs, but merely describe things or persons of general superficial interest.

Last week my old friend Edward Fitzgerald (Omar Kyam, you know), sent me a beautiful miniature of my mother, which his mother—her intimate friend—had kept till her death, and which had been painted for Mrs. Fitzgerald. It is a full-length figure, very beautifully painted, and very like my mother. Almost immediately after receiving this from England, my friend Mr. Horace Furness came out to see me. He is a great collector of books and prints, and brought me an old engraving of my mother in the character of Urania, which a great many years ago I remember to have seen, and which was undoubtedly the original of Mrs. Fitzgerald's miniature. I thought the coincidence of their both reaching me at the same time curious.

I am extremely perplexed with reference to my plans. Ellen will certainly return home in October ; with her goes my good little English cook, and my good man-servant, who wishes to return to Ireland to see his parents. I must give up housekeeping, as without Ellen's assistance and such a household as I have had with my present people, I could not undertake the management of even such a small establishment as mine, and if I remain in this country shall have to leave this house, and the proximity of S—— and M——, and go and live in a boarding-house in Philadelphia. In short, I do not know what I shall or can do ; but as the time comes for doing something I suppose I shall find out what best it may be.

My health is fairly good. The thing I suffer most from is depression, languor, and debility, which I attribute partly to the climate, and still more to *anno domini*, the fertile source of ailing, failing, and general *gradual death*. I have little to complain of compared with many of my neighbours. The spring has begun, and I have left off sitting up till one o'clock in the morning, because I get up earlier than in the winter, my seven hours' sleep being still a sufficient allowance.

Good-bye, dear, I am ever, as ever, yours,

FANNY.

York Farm, March 15th, 1876.

MY DEAREST H——,

You ask me if there is no chance of the plantation being either let or sold. There was an offer of purchase made for it last year, which for some cause or other did not come to anything. Heaven knows how thankful I should be if it were only got once rid of, and Mr. L—— were free to return to England and resume his proper position and career there. He finds and he does abundant work of every sort, spiritual and temporal, where he is, and labours as assiduously in his ministry as a clergyman in Darien, and on the estate as he does in the management of the property and cultivation of the crops. He is good and conscientious, and indefatigably active and energetic, and wherever he is he will serve both God and man; but I am nevertheless most anxious that he should return home.

I have been relieved of one item of troublesome uncertainty by Ellen's having at length determined to go back to England. Her affectionate attachment to me induced her to separate herself from her own family, and to leave the man to whom she was engaged to wait for her for a space of two years, at the end of which time I expected to return to England with the L——s. The two years expired last October, six months ago, and we are no nearer returning than we were then. Ellen has been friend, helper, adviser, housekeeper, maid, servant, everything to me, and has sacrificed her own health, and all consideration of her own comfort, convenience, and happiness, to her devotion to me, and as the end of this self-sacrifice now seems to become utterly uncertain, I have felt the responsibility of keeping her here, even involuntarily as I have done, weighing upon me more and more, until it is a cause of distress and anxiety to me. It was, therefore, with a great sense of relief that I heard, when I told her of my return to England being again postponed, that she had promised her mother not to prolong her stay in America beyond the autumn of this year. What will become of me without her I do not know, but that is an after consideration, and in the mean time it is a comfort to me to think that she is going home to her mother, and I trust to fulfil her promise to the worthy fellow to whom she is engaged, and to recover some health and strength, and enjoy the rest and happiness in a home of her own, which she so richly deserves. My keeping house in this most troublesome of all worlds, when she has left me, will be impossible. Besides, my whole household is breaking up; my little English cook goes home with her, my worthy man-servant goes back to Ireland, and I should find it a task quite beyond my powers, to gather together another household out of the horrible material that supplies American establishments here, or, if I could do so, to conduct and govern it myself. Housekeepers are not procurable for love or money. . . .

I cannot spend another summer like the two last, without stirring from this place, the heat is more than I can endure, so I suppose I shall go either to Lenox, among the hills, or to the seaside for the hot part of the summer, and after that, *che sarà sarà.* I cannot leave America while all my children are here, and may eventually take up my quarters in a Philadelphia boarding-house, in order to remain near them as long as the L——s continue here ; but, indeed, the future is a complete mist before my eyes, and I endeavour to think about it as little as possible.

You are mistaken, my beloved H——. I should have infinite satisfaction in seeing you again, even as you now, alas! describe yourself. It is not in the power of life so to change you as to make my being with you anything but a happiness to me, especially if I were able to minister to your sad infirmity, and help your dear E—— to cheer you and brighten your darkness. I cannot bear to dwell upon this, or to say how very often I long to be with you and hear your voice again, my dear first and lifelong friend.

S——, on her return from the South, gave a very good account of her sister, who, she says, is undoubtedly in her element on the plantation ; but I think it much more important that her husband should be in his proper place, sphere, and element, than even that she should.

I do not know Mrs. Algernon Sartoris, the young princess, Nelly Grant, of these United States, but I hear from those who do, that she is an amiable, sweet-tempered person, and my sister writes she is kind, dutiful, and affectionate to her. The newspapers speak of the young people returning to this country in April.

Our weather now has become early spring-like, with high winds and chilly rain, and the trees are budding, and the birds beginning to sing. I do not long for the summer at all ; the heat is my dread and detestation, and the longer it keeps off the better, and the better pleased I am.

God bless you, my dearest H——. Give my very affectionate love to E——, who will take it as she reads this to you.

Ever, as ever, yours,
FANNY.

York Farm, March 27th, 1876.

MY DEAREST H——,

I have been a very much longer time than usual without hearing from you, and conclude that I have lost some letters of yours, because the one I have received to-day begins by saying that you had already told me that you never received F——'s missing letter. Now this is the first word I have had from you upon that subject, and, therefore, either you have thought you had mentioned it before, when you have not, or the letter in which you said anything about it has miscarried. There have been violent storms, by sea and land, and some vessels are known to have been lost, and some may have been lost that are not known of; but it is evident, I think, that I have missed a letter of yours. F—— got the one I wrote her, and that I fancied I had misdirected to you, a day or two after she ought to have received it, I then found out that I had made only half the blunder I thought I had been guilty of; but it was the one I should have preferred not making, as it kept your letter from you.

F—— never alludes to public affairs in her letters. S—— and her husband are miserable at the moral degradation which their government is exhibiting. I think if it was not for their boy they would willingly leave the country; but Dr. W—— says he does not know where they would go, for that there is no part of the world in which he should not just now be ashamed to acknowledge himself an American. All decently honest people are bitterly mortified at the disgrace which is being brought on the country by the low blackguardism of its public men, and the feeling of indignation and shame is becoming so strong and so general, that the evil will undoubtedly be checked and remedied.

I wrote thus much to you last night, having received yesterday your letter of the 14th of March, by which it was clear that I had missed a previous one. This morning's post brings the one dated the twelfth, so that, though I have not lost a letter, there has been some curious irregularity in their arrival. Perhaps, however, at this season of the year that is not much to be wondered at; it is at this moment blowing a hurricane and pouring in torrents, and it is terrible to think of vessels on the sea in such frightful weather.

As for Mr. L——'s clerical duties, he is zealous and indefatigable in his discharge of them where he is. He not only has the charge of all the religious services on the island, which are duly and regularly performed, but he has a church in the small town of Darien, distant from them a mile by water, which depends almost entirely upon his ministration. He labours incessantly among the coloured people, carrying on Sunday schools, night schools, schools for the children and the adults, and the influence of his teaching and his devoted work among the people, and of his admirable and most amiable character, is felt and acknowledged in the whole region, he is really and truly doing missionary work with all the zeal of a missionary, so that though I cannot help deploring his protracted stay in this country, because I think his proper place is in England, I feel well assured that he is working with all his mind, heart, and soul, in God's service and man's service where he now is.

Thank you, my dear E——, for your few kind words. I am grievously disappointed at not seeing her for yet another year.

York Farm, April 2nd, 1876.

MY BELOVED HARRIET,

I am glad you liked my school-boy's verses ; I think them remarkably good, because of their simplicity and singleness of purpose, the absence of all matter foreign to the theme, such as abstract thought or generalizing sentiment or feeling, the *concrete* quality, in short, which is an important element in all really good poetry, and very rare in that written at an early age. I approve of the verses, too, for the accuracy of observation of natural objects and facts of natural appearance in this description which prevents vagueness, and gives a character of pure poetic truth to it. Of course one feels the Burns and Shakespeare and Milton, with which the lad has just begun to make partial acquaintance, but there is enough individual observation and feeling of nature of his own, and grace and spirit of expression and diction to make it, I think, a very satisfactory specimen of school-boy poetry.

He is unusually gifted, for he has a lively poetical

imagination, and keen sensibility to beauty with strong and steady reasoning powers. His most decided tendency is to scientific objects and mechanics, all great works of engineering enterprise, all good and fine machinery and its results; and his most remarkable gift is a real talent for music, which seems to me to approach to original genius. This is an unusual combination of different capacities, and cannot fail, I think, to make him a remarkable person in his day ; he is at present, of course, a very chaotic and heterogenous *bundle* of *beginnings*, but the natural endowments are full of promise — a promise profoundly interesting to me, though I can only look to see his earliest entrance into manhood, if even that.

Alas! my dear Harriet, my triumph and your congratulations were premature as to the hope of filling my ice-house, the pond did not freeze hard or thick enough to admit of the ice being cut, and we shall have to depend upon the daily supply left at the door by the cart of the great Knickerbocker Ice Company.

You speak of living entirely in the past, but it seems to me that no one, not even you, can do so more entirely than I do. My existence in the present, as far as its events are concerned, is like the endless winding of a skein of grey-coloured wool. However, I have the variety of change of place and mode of life in prospect, and with the end of the month of June, I shall be shaken out of my present monotonous existence into conditions that may make me look back to my peaceful life here with great regret.

The L——s are to come to me at the beginning of May, and stay with me the whole of that month, and as much longer as they find it convenient, though that is at present all they speak of. Whenever they go away I shall give up this dear little place, for there is some idea that it can be profitably let during the summer to sightseers coming to the Centennial Exhibition. Whenever my children leave me, I shall go to Champlost and pay M—— a visit of a week or two, and then fly somewhere, away from the heat, either to the seaside or the hills, but I have no definite idea where.

At the end of the summer, Ellen and my cook and man-servant all return to England, and at present I think there is every probability of my spending next winter in a Philadelphia boarding-house. If all my children are on this side of the Atlantic, I cannot go away to the other, at the same time that I have fully determined not to undertake the intolerable task of housekeeping in this country, when once my English servants and my invaluable Ellen have left me.

How often when I write to you, my dear friend, I wish I had anything, the smallest thing to tell you. I envy Mrs. St. Quintin the variety of her life, which enables her to put something into her letters to cheer and amuse you. To-day, what have I done? It is Sunday, but it is my Sunday for staying at home—that is to say, that in order to give all my servants in turn their Sunday free, and also to contrive that the house shall never be left without the indispensable supervision of either Ellen or myself, every third Sunday I am obliged to stay at home and keep the house, and this is "my Sunday in," as the housemaids say.

After breakfast I clipped and arranged some
beautiful hyacinths M—— gave me at Christmas, in a
china box, that fills one of my windows, and which
have been putting forth a lovely succession of purple,
and pale blue, and pink, and deep rose-coloured blossoms
ever since. You do not like the perfume of hyacinths,
I remember, but I am very fond of it, and my little
book-room is very agreeably fragrant to me with these
charming spring flowers. Then I cleaned the keys of
my piano, which I do not trust to the housemaid,
and which every now and then are the better for a
damp dusting. Then I caught and caged my canary
bird, an admirable songster given to me on Christmas
Day, a year ago, by my grandson, and who every
Sunday morning is allowed an hour's liberty in the
greenhouse, which he enjoys immensely.

Then I read my prayers and my Bible, then I
worked hard in my greenhouse, shifting the places of
various pots, so as to bring the greatest possible number
of plants in bloom immediately opposite to the glass
door of the drawing-room, which stands open into the
greenhouse all the morning. I do not sit in my
drawing-room in the morning, but in my tiny book-
room, which communicates with it by a door which is
never shut, both the rooms being very small and warm,
and bright and sunny, and from the place on the sofa,
where I sit to write, I see through the drawing-room,
immediately opposite to me, the scarlet flush of the
geraniums in full bloom in the greenhouse, and on the
wall by the door the pretty portrait of S——, with
her sweet flower-soft complexion, and dreamy eyes,
and dress of pale sea-green ; a graceful, Venetian-

looking picture, which I gave F—— for her wedding present, and which she and Mr. L—— have been kind enough to leave here with me, to adorn my room and keep me company. Having tired myself a good deal with my greenhouse work, I lay down on the sofa and read a paper, called the *Nation*, the only American paper I ever see. It is published weekly, and contains about half as much matter as the *Spectator;* it is political, literary, and critical, and full of general information, both on public events and books in Europe and America. It is an enlightened, able, and high-toned paper, and I believe Arthur Sedgwick, the son of my friend Theodore, is one of the editors of it. Whoever manages the paper certainly does his duty manfully, exposing the evils of the present administration, and the abuses of the existing system of government in this country. It is really a valuable publication both for the interest and accuracy of the information it contains, and the excellent spirit in which it is conducted. Every week, as soon as I have read it, S—— sends it up to her boy at school, so that I always make haste to get through with it.

After this I read a book which S—— has lent me, a collection of the letters of the two French authors, the Ampères, father and son, the latter of whom, a charming person and very delightful and distinguished writer, was among our most intimate friends in Rome during the last winter I spent there.

[In speaking of the distinguished, eminent, and remarkable men I have had the pleasure and privilege of knowing, I might have said they were all agreeable in society. In speaking of Ampère, I should say he was pre-eminently agreeable in society, lighter in hand, and better company than any one I ever knew. He was a poet, an essayist, a scholar, a philologist, a traveller, a cosmopolite, but, above and before all, he was a charming member of society. Graceful, easy, free, and refined in his manner, brilliant and sparkling in his conversation, courteous, cordial, kind, and sympathetic, gently genial and perfectly well bred—the representative man of the very best society.

During the last winter, when my sister and myself were in Rome at the same time, we had an excellent custom of going on alternate weeks to spend a morning in the Campagna, always accompanied by the same party of our intimate friends, and carrying with us our picnic luncheon. Browning, Ampère, Leighton, Lord Lyons, the sculptress Harriet Hosmer, and a friend of hers, both known to me since their school girlhood, and two English sisters, our dear friends, the one like a rippling brook in sunshine, the other like a still lake in moonlight,—with these, our invariable companions, we drove to Tore, Nuovo, or Tor San Giovanni, or Lunghezza, or some other exquisite place in the flowery solitude of the magnificent desert that stretches on every side of Rome. We used to leave our carriages, and stray and wander and sit on the turf, and take our luncheon in the midst of all that was lovely in nature and picturesque in the ruined remains of Roman power and the immortal memories of Roman story. They were hours in such fellowship never to be forgotten. Alas! few now remain to remember them!

Lockhart was sometimes with us on these expeditions; but, sick and sorrowful and sad at heart, he oftener came with my sister and myself when we were alone.]

When I speak of reading, I must tell you that the time I pass with a *book in my hand* is always spent (at least half of it) *asleep*, so that out of three hours in the *attitude* of reading, one and a half is passed with closed eyes. I do not feel sleepy when I am doing anything else, but as on Sunday I neither print my manuscripts, nor copy old journals and letters, nor touch my piano, nor work with my needle, I read (that is sleep) a good deal. Somebody said sleeping in church was a religious exercise; I hope sleeping out of it may be a moral one.

God bless you, dear, good night. My empty day has made a full letter and my paper has room for no more. In the afternoon I walked round the garden, in the evening I played patience, *read, and slept.*

Ever, as ever, yours,

FANNY.

York Farm, April 11th, 1876.

My beloved Harriet,

You did not complain of the effort of dictating, but from some expressions in one of your letters I feared, as I often have done, without any such indication on your part, that it might be too great a tax upon you. Though God knows it would be dismal to me to get no more of your dear, very dear words, I could not bear to think of your making an exertion that was painful to you for my sake. I am only too thankful to get your precious tokens of constant affection, your love and remembrance, dictated by yourself to dear Eliza, which still prolong our close heart communion (now of how many years duration!) with each other, as far as that is possible.

I do not hear often from Fanny Cobbe. She sent me some time ago a short satirical essay, called "Science in Excelsis," upon the vivisection abuse, and a catalogue of all the eminent names she had enlisted in her compassionate crusade, in behalf of the poor brutes, in a volume of her collected magazine papers.

I have written to her twice since, and hope she has got my letters, though I find that I put a wrong number on her address, directing it to 8 (eight) instead of 24, Cheyne Walk; but I thought the postman would be wise enough to rectify that blunder.

She certainly may take the credit and the comfort of having forced upon public attention a question of humanity which, but for her, might still have long escaped effectual notice, and I think she is to be congratulated upon having undoubtedly, by her active energetic benevolence, begun a moral reform in a direction where it was much needed. Anybody who has achieved one such result, may consider that they have made good use of their life.

You ask me if Dr. W—— is a keen politician. No, not otherwise than that he feels very *keenly* indeed the present disgraceful character, conduct, and condition of the American government. It is really deplorable, and both he and his wife are profoundly grieved and indignant at the national disgrace.

I was much obliged to you for the *Standard* you sent me. The article on American affairs was very good. The public feeling here is becoming intense upon the subject of the audacious rascality of the government officials and their friends, and radical reform will, I have no doubt, ensue ; but the fact is that the machinery of the government is so complicated and intricate that it will not be an easy thing to reach and punish the evil and provide effectually against a repetition of it.

Everybody's comfort here is more or less impaired if not destroyed by the incompetency and unmanageableness of their servants.

An elderly lady of the W—— family came to see me the other day, bringing her little granddaughter, a child of about four years old, with her nurse. The latter, when her mistress was taking leave of me, literally pushed herself before the old lady as she and I were about to go out of the door of the room (I escorting her to her carriage), and I was obliged to tell the rough, coarse, ignorant German she-boor (much more like a cow than a human creature) that she ought to stand back and allow her mistress to pass, instead of thrusting herself before her and all but knocking her down. She was not insolent, and did not resent my rebuke, which, if she had been low Irish instead of low German, she infallibly would, and probably then and there have thrown up her situation and *discharged* her old mistress on account of my "impertinence."

Another lady of the W—— family, a cousin of my son-in-law, whom I have known very well and liked very much for a long time, speaking upon the subject of servants, said that for the last year she and her sister, who live together, had had a perfect state of domestic anarchy in their house, sometimes no servants at all, sometimes such servants that they *envied themselves when they had none.* To give you a notion of the sort of creatures they are, she said that their last parlour-maid, upon her sister's complaining at dinner that the potatoes were cold, had flounced out of the room, and returned bringing from the kitchen *one* hot potato stuck upon a kitchen fork. Just imagine the class of servants from which the households here are furnished! But, indeed, nobody who has not lived here can form the slightest conception of what it is. Of course when Ellen leaves me I shall have nothing further to do with housekeeping, and shall at once take a room in some boarding-house for the rest of the time I may stay in this country.

I am having the outside of this cottage painted, as I wish to leave the little place in better condition than when I came to it. There is a greenhouse that runs along one whole side of the house, and that and the shutters and windows and frames, etc., are all being fresh painted. The process is making the place very uncomfortable for the present, and giving me constant headache with the disagreeable smell, but it is a very considerable improvement to the appearance of the tiny tenement, the exterior paint of which had not been renewed for a great many years. The painting of the house was begun with the first appearance of settled fine weather, and the first coat of milk-white paint had hardly been put on everywhere when we had a perfect hurricane of wind that lasted more than twenty-four hours. We live, as I have told you, all but *in* the high-road, and the soil is so light and dry that, except immediately after the heaviest rains, we are always powdered with white dust. Under this sudden furious wind (a half tornado), the whole air was perfectly thick with dense clouds of dust, and the fresh paint received such a covering of it that it was black and begrimed and gritty like sand-paper, and the workmen have had to *scrape* it all off and begin the job all over again.

I expect F—— and Mr. L—— at the beginning of next month to stay some weeks with me, I do not know precisely how long. After they have left me, or I have left them, as the case may be, I shall go to Champlost for a fortnight, then to Lenox for the rest of the summer. In October, Ellen leaves me, and I shall then take up my abode in Philadelphia.

Good-bye, my dear friend; my desire to see you once more has been far more earnest than I have cared to express, my disappointment at not doing so this year is much deeper, too, than I can say. God bless you.

Ever, as ever, yours,
FANNY.

York Farm, April 17th, 1876.

MY DEAREST H——,

I have just come home from my regular Monday evening and dinner at Champlost. My friend M—— has an income of about seven thousand pounds a year. She has five women servants, but her own maid is just now disabled by illness, and not one of the others could be a decent competent attendant, even for a time, upon her mistress, or supply for a day the place of her maid for her—so little can wealth do, in this country, to procure the ordinary comfort and convenience that it commands everywhere else.

You speak of my contemplating without dismay my coming winter in a Philadelphia boarding-house, and without the comfort and help of my dear Ellen; but I cannot say that this is quite the case, though it is of very little use saying anything about the dismay I do feel at the prospect. I wish Eliza could send me out a decent good girl, to take Ellen's place; it would be doing me an infinite service.

You say you should like to know my view of the general political aspect of things in this country, but I really have no *view* about it. The present state of political dishonesty and depravity is not at all worse than that which prevailed in England during the reigns of George the Second and George the Third (and that among our highest aristocracy). We have emerged from it, and I have no doubt at all that this country will do so also. The extremely complicated machinery of government here, with all the wheels within wheels of state rights, state interests, and state sovereignties, is not easy to explain to you. The processes adopted to ensure purity of voting and elections are so exceedingly intricate, and have become themselves such complete systems for facilitating and promoting corruption and political fraud, that the business of reform will be extremely difficult. The sense of the people is, however, strongly aroused and excited by the present turpitude of the professional politicians, by whom they are now governed, and I have no doubt that measures will be found to check the present abuses, and restore something like decent honesty to the conduct of public affairs. The disgraceful character of the present administration is felt so keenly throughout the country, that the general indignation and disgust will undoubtedly lead to some effort at reform. I see no cause for despondency about the future here, though much for profound shame and sorrow at the present condition of things.

I do not understand anything about our Indian politics, or take the slightest interest in them, but it seems to me that to be Viceroy under Lord Salisbury must be rather a difficult and unpleasant position. I regret the addition of Empress to our Queen's title. It seems to me vulgar (*flashy*, like every one of D'Israeli's inspirations), and far less *royally respectable* than her present style.

I suppose, however, to a descendant of the patriarchs (the shepherds of Chaldæa, in whose time Egypt itself may have been young), like our Jew Prime Minister, the descent of a Guelph Queen of Great Britain and her style and title must alike seem modern, trivial, and insignificant. I dare say he thinks what that insolent Duc d'Angoulême said to Lord Dacre of Baron Grefuhl's name, "Est ce que *cela* a un nom?" Lord Dacre having asked the Bourbon Prince how the Swiss financier's name was spelt, Monsieur Grefuhl being one of the most remarkable men of his day in France, not only for wealth, but various accomplishments and great ability, and moreover (which always gave wonderful point to Lord Dacre's story to me), though a born, or perhaps because a born Swiss Republican banker, a devoted aristocratic worshipper of the exiled princes, the branch *comme il faut* of the Bourbon House, and an infinite despiser of the Orleans bourgeois branch of the same, King Louis Philippe, the bourgeois king included. I am surprised the English peers did not make a stand against the imperial innovation. Does the Queen herself wish to be called Empress? That, I should consider, a piece of bad taste in our Queen and *Lady*.

That Italian story you speak of, "A Carnival in Rome," seems to me a full length sketch of Madame M——, the famous Princess C——, the heroine of that extraordinary story my sister used to tell so funnily, but the author of the "Carnival in Rome" positively denies any intention of making it such. The Contessa di Rocca Diavolo is certainly not a bad likeness of Madame M——, and on one occasion wears a gown of hers; but, of course, the things I like in that story are the descriptions of Rome and the Campagna, which are done *con amore* and seem to me admirable.

I am very sorry, dearest Harriet, to hear of Mrs. St. Quintin's illness. I am sure it must have grieved and made you anxious. I often think what a much happier and pleasanter life hers must have become since she has been restored to her own family. She must have had a fund of inexhaustible cheerfulness to have endured her existence at St. Leonards with such unvarying sweet serenity.

I suppose the unusually powerful activity of your

mind, during so many years of your life, is what constitutes to you the peculiar hardship of the gradual
blunting of your faculties of which you complain so
sadly. It is curious to me how comfortably I endure
the sense of gradually losing my faculties and becoming *stupid*. My memory is quite gone for any
useful daily purpose; I muddle up names of places
and people, and cannot be trusted to tell the truth
about anything, or deliver a message without spilling
it a couple of hours after receiving it. I hardly know
what I read, and invariably fall asleep, no matter at
what time of the day I take up a book; and when
I have dozed through one of my solitary evenings,
am as well satisfied with the employment of my
time as if I had been working logarithms.

I do not like my physical decay quite as well as
my growing imbecility. I have not been able to
walk more than two or three times in the last six
weeks, fearing exposure to damp and cold, and wet
and wind, and dry and dust, as I have never done
heretofore; and I am very sorry to think that I
must soon have abiding falsehood in my mouth, as
all my large front teeth are more or less loose in their
sockets, *ma che!* as the Italians say, all this has to be
so. The one only thing I regret to have lost is my
voice and power of singing.

God bless you, dear, dear Harriet; my speaking
voice is not changed, and tells you

I am ever, as ever, yours,

FANNY.

York Farm, April 25th, 1876.

My dearest Harriet,

I am very sure that my conclusion about leaving this house is the best I could come to, for there is now some talk of trying to let it during the summer to some of the visitors coming to Philadelphia for the Exhibition; and, if that cannot be done, it may perhaps be sold.

To-day is S——'s reception day; that is, the day in the week when from twelve till four o'clock she remains at home, so that such of her friends as like to come from town to visit her may not be disappointed in finding her, as she is frequently very much occupied in writing, and very frequently also in town, and does not like morning visits on any but this appointed day. I generally go over at twelve o'clock, and sit with her for an hour or till some of her visitors come.

I am sorry to say that in F——'s last letter she mentioned a circumstance which is likely to operate very unfavourably against either the sale or lease of their rice plantation. F—— says that the New Orleans and Louisiana planters are now to a great extent giving up the cultivation of cotton and sugar, which have been hitherto the staple products of that state, and are taking to cultivate rice upon a scale which will be seriously injurious to the Georgia rice-planters, and greatly diminish the value of the rice growing estates there. I believe I am superstitious about that Georgia property. I have a feeling that it is never to be prosperous or profitable to those who own or inherit it. I shall rejoice when Mr. L—— has turned his back upon it, and resumed his own proper position and vocation in his own country, though I am afraid as long as it is theirs F—— will never be contented anywhere else, and unless the plantation is absolutely parted with, I fear she will always be desiring and endeavouring to return there.

The American International Exhibition, in honour of the Centennial Celebration, which takes place in Philadelphia, and is to open early next month, is occupying everybody here entirely.

I take very little interest in it. I have seen our own two great London exhibitions, and the great Paris one, and thought them all oppressive, overwhelming, distracting, and fatiguing, and, with all their wonder and beauty, unsatisfactory to the last degree. And the disgraceful character and condition of the present American government is so distressing to all who really love and respect the country, as I do, that I cannot help regretting this challenge, sent abroad to foreign nations, to come here and admire this country, when it seems to me essentially less admirable than it has ever been, and to be really in a humiliating and degraded position, morally, whatever its material prosperity may be.

There is a railroad now all the way to Halifax, which shortens the Atlantic passage by two days. I shall surely go that way whenever I do go back to England.

York Farm, April 27th, 1876.

MY DEAREST HARRIET,

I am shocked and very sorry to hear of poor Dr. Trench's accident, and of his being disabled as you describe him. I am surprised that only one of his daughters is near him to help her mother in her attendance on him. He had eleven children, and I believe the larger proportion of them was girls, so that I should have thought some of them would always have been with, or near, their parents. During the last winter I spent in Rome, the Archbishop and Mrs. Trench were there with, I think, two unmarried daughters, who used to come sometimes with their mother to S——'s evening parties, and with whom Dr. W—— occasionally rode in the Campagna. I wonder if it is one of those young ladies who has gone as a missionary to South Africa. Has she married a missionary clergyman? or gone out alone to convert the African natives? She is very brave in either case.

[Richard Chenevix Trench was one of my brother's college contemporaries and early intimate friends, one of the most remarkable of that circle of brilliant young men with whom I had the great good fortune to be in frequent intercourse in my girlhood. He came to our house whenever he was in London, and was admired there for his personal beauty as well as his charming character and uncommon intellectual gifts. It is a matter of regret to me that the two likenesses of the Archbishop of Dublin, in his lately published memoirs, should give so unfavourable an idea of his very fine and noble countenance. I have myself a head of him, by Samuel Lawrence, which does far more justice to his refined and sweetly serious face—the very face of a poet.

My American marriage separated me from my family and all our early friends, but whenever I

returned to England I found myself unforgotten by
them, and received kindly proofs of Dr. Trench's
constant and friendly remembrance. I stayed with
him at his living at Itchenstoke, while reading at
Winchester, and in Dublin, after his episcopal elevation,
was honoured by his courteous notice and invitations.

These circumstances rendered not a little distressing
to me a letter which I received from Dr. Trench, after
the publication of my "Record of a Girlhood," in which
he expressed himself displeased and hurt at my
mention of his participation with John Sterling and
my brother in their Spanish adventure and sympathy with the unfortunate revolutionary attempt of
Torrigos. Dr. Trench referred both kindly and re-
proachfully to our mutual regard of so many years
duration, and complained of my having (as he appeared
to think) held up the Spanish enthusiasm of his youth
to ridicule, saying most truly, "It surely was not an
unworthy cause." No, indeed! had it been so I should
neither have held it nor my brother or his best friends
up to ridicule in my account of it. I compared them
to Don Quixote, the pearl and flower of noble mad-
men, not to Sancho Panza, who was a sensible fellow.
But it was Dr. Trench himself who was ashamed of
the young Englishmen's Spanish crusade; for, while I
thought all their contemporaries as well acquainted
with it as myself, I found, to my extreme astonish-
ment, that Dr. Trench had made such a complete
secret of his part in the affair that, until the publication of my book, his own family and children knew
nothing of that episode in his life, and my full reference
to it was an absolute revelation to them, and caused

them considerable amusement, and him, I am sorry to say, much annoyance.

A curious circumstance of rather a comical nature occurred to my daughter, who, dining at the Deanery in Westminster with Dean Stanley and Lady Augusta, found herself, to her great pleasure, seated next to the Archbishop of Dublin, of whose early friendship with her uncle and partnership in the romantic Spanish expedition she had often heard me speak. When, therefore, Dr. Trench said courteously, " I think on these occasions it would be an advantage if neighbours at table were furnished with a sort of conversation *menu*, slight hints of the subjects by which they might interest each other." " Yes," said my daughter, with smiling acquiescence, little suspecting on what unwelcome and forbidden ground she was treading, in appealing to her neighbour's youthful recollections, " for instance, my lord, your early Spanish adventures." Dr. Trench was dismayed and *not* delighted by the young lady's familiarity with that carefully, silently suppressed Spanish secret, and much surprised at it till he found out who she was, and how she became acquainted with it.

All our knowledge of my brother's experiences in Spain reached us through his most uncertain and infrequent letters, and his friend Richard Trench's personal report, who immediately upon his own return to England, came most kindly to give us information about my brother, for which we were so painfully anxious.

And now that I trust it can offend and hurt nobody, I will mention a circumstance at once pathetic and ridiculous, which I did not speak of before, because I could not bear to *appear* to cast any ridicule upon what was, as the Archbishop truly said, "assuredly no unworthy cause." Like doughty knights of old, the young English partisans of Torrigos vowed not to shave either beard or moustache till their attempt at the liberation of Spain had succeeded. By degrees the razor triumphed over the sword, beards and moustache fell with their hopes, my brother retaining hair and hopes longer than any of his companions. This I was told by Richard Trench himself on his return from Spain.

This little incident has, I think, never been mentioned, though the whole episode of the "Spanish Tragedy" (or comedy) has, of course, found its due record in the lately published memoirs of the Archbishop.]

No, my dear Harriet, you can never be so altered that I shall not desire and long to see you; but my chief thought in wishing to be once more within reach of you has been to help to minister to your infirmity, to read to you, to talk to you, to be with you, to share and lighten E——'s charge of you. I cannot write of this. Sometimes I have felt that you wanted me so much more than my children do, that I must go to you; but I cannot speak about this, and while all my family are here, it seems to me most unnatural that I should not remain here with them.

To-day has been one of the first pleasant spring days we have had, and I walked to Champlost, going by the road, and returning through M——'s woods and our own farm fields. One of the meadows I crossed was almost sheeted with the exquisite little blue-white china-looking blossoms of the *Euphrasia,* eye-bright; tufts of violets were in bloom along the road-side, and the woods are full of bloodwort, wild anemones, speedwell, and a diminutive bright yellow star, which belongs to a species of wild strawberry here. It was all very sweet and lovely. The mis-fortune of this climate is that the heat comes so suddenly that everything rushes into bloom at once, and then the fierce summer sun dries and withers them almost as quickly as they blow, and there is no pleasant temperate season for the vegetation, any more than for us; it is all parched, and dessicated, and choked, and buried in dust, before it reaches its full perfection of flower or leaf.

I wonder if you have heard talk of a marriage which is much gossiped about here—Lord Mandeville, the Duke of Manchester's son, to a New York young lady, whose mother has been in England, and to whom (the mother) the Duke giving Lord Mandeville a letter of introduction, begged she would not allow any designing American girl to "snap him up," so her own daughter "snaps him up," a very pretty, and, I suppose, very rich New York girl, who is now Lady Mandeville, and will be Duchess of Manchester.

Good-bye, my dearest Harriet, how I wish my letters were better worth looking for. Oh, do not, for pity's sake, invoke pain to make you patient, believe God knows what is best in sparing you that bitter teaching, and sees you do not need it.

Ever, as ever, yours,

FANNY.

York Farm, May 16th, 1876.

My dear Harriet,

I have now got F—— and her husband and baby with me, and am expecting in less than a month to leave them in possession of this small residence, of which I have become very fond, and where they now think of spending the summer. I shall be thankful when Mr. L—— is once more in England, for which move they now seem really to be making some serious preparation. Their present plan is to spend the summer here, F—— merely running to the seaside, not far from here, for a week or two, if the baby should appear to suffer from the heat.

At present we are all rather suffering from cold, the spring having turned within the last fortnight rainy and chilly, and extremely like our orthodox spring weather at home.

You express surprise that M—— was unable to provide herself with a temporary substitute for her maid, during the illness of the latter, which only proves how little I have succeeded in giving you any notion of the difficulty and discomfort attending everybody's domestic arrangements in this country.

The better an English servant is, and the more fitted for their particular position in England, the less are they calculated to give or receive satisfaction in any situation in this country, and the more certain to become utterly spoiled for all service anywhere, in the shortest possible time. I once *imported* a lady's-maid, a German woman, warranted to be a paragon, who proved such a disastrous failure that I never repeated the experiment, and I am quite sure that, bad as the material from which one has to choose one's servants here is, one had far better make one's choice from that, than send for people entirely strange and un-accustomed to the modes of living and ways and manners here.

I am trying to get a decent young woman to come to me, when Ellen leaves me, and have to offer her *forty* pounds a year, absolutely ignorant as I know her to be of the duties of her situation, having never been in service, and knowing no more of a lady's-maid's work than I do of that of a groom. I could not get her or anybody of any kind to come for lower wages than that. (This young woman came with her mother to speak to me about the situation, and sent me up their names on printed visiting-cards, " Mrs. and Miss Daly.")

York Farm, May 21st, 1876.

MY DEAREST HARRIET,

I received from you yesterday two letters, dated the 8th and 9th of this month. In the first you request me to write to you, in the second you acknow-ledge the receipt of two of my letters. I have no settled rule about writing to you, but always write once a week, and generally twice. The irregularity in your receiving the letters I can in no way positively account for. The fault may lie with our extremely careless postmaster, or the weather may be answerable for delay at one time, and then for the arrival of two mails at once. Absolute regularity can hardly be expected in the delivery of letters that have to cross the Atlantic, and it really seems to me wonderful,

upon the whole, how few letters miscarry or are
materially retarded among those that are sent in
such millions across that vast ocean. The amazing
facilities, both in punctuality and speed, that modern
science has produced, have made the world exacting
both as to swiftness and sureness of communication.
Only think what it was when first I married and
came to live in America, the weeks and weeks we had
to wait for each other's letters, carried by those excellent sailing-packets, depending upon the capricious
will of the winds for their progress! Why, I remember
in our own first crossing, a whole week spent in a
dead calm, within a comparatively short distance of
New York, rocking to and fro on that tedious water,
like raw recruits practising goose-step without taking
one step onward.

Your idea of there being any difficulty in my
keeping out of the uproar of the Centennial Exhibition
made me smile. You probably know a great deal
more about it than I do, for you have read something
about it, which I have not, and not feeling any particular interest in it, and being by nature extremely
incurious, and now by age very reluctant to make
any unusual exertion, I have not been near it, and
do not suppose I shall go near it, which, as it is six
miles distant from me, and on the other side of the
Schuylkill River, will certainly not be difficult.
Neither M—— nor our intermediate neighbour, Mrs.
T——, have been to it, and beyond hearing it talked
about pretty constantly, we are as innocent of it as
the " babe unborn," or as if it was in Hyde Park.

S—— went with Mr. L—— to the opening, but

she did not see anything that particularly interested her, or was half as striking as the immense concourse of people and their admirable general good behaviour. She has been once or twice since, I think, with friends, but I have not heard much from her about it. F——— has not been to it yet, and seems in no particular hurry to go. Mr. L—— asked me the other day when I was going, and I said I would go whenever he would take me, and as he is active and energetic and genially sympathetic, and likes running about to see things, I dare say he will make me go some day or other.

I pass Champlost every Sunday on my way to church, and as M—— only goes to church once a month, on Communion Sunday, I not unfrequently stop on my way back and pay her a short visit. You asked if she purposes remaining at Champlost during the "hubbub" of the exhibition; but Champlost is two miles further from the exhibition than York Farm, so I have already explained to you its "hubbub" does not come near either of us, and we are in no hurry to go near it.

I sometimes wish M—— would leave Champlost for some cooler place during the great heat of the summer, but the luxurious comfort of her own home makes the wretched accommodation of the hotels she stops at in travelling so intolerable to her, that I believe upon the whole she is better and really suffers less from even the terrible heat at Champlost than she would anywhere else.

I had the great pleasure of a visit from Longfellow this morning, who is in Philadelphia just now. I had asked him to lunch with me to-morrow, but he was unable to do so, and had written to tell me so, and say he should drive out to see me this morning. The post-office, as usual, did me one of its vile good turns. I never received his note, and was out when he came. Luckily, I had only gone to take the dogs to swim, a distance of half a mile, and as he and his companion, a young lady of my acquaintance, asked to come in and wait for me, I found him on my return home, and was most delighted to see him.

[Longfellow was my friend for a great many years, and one of the most amiable men I have ever known. His home being near Boston, I saw him oftenest (and always when I was there, but for two summers he took a charming old-fashioned country house on the outskirts of the beautiful village of Pittsfield, six miles from my own summer residence in Lenox, and during those seasons I saw him and his wife very frequently, and was often in that house, on the staircase landing of which stood the famous clock whose hourly song, "Never—for ever; ever—never," has long been familiar to all English-speaking people.

Fanny Longfellow, the charming Mary of the poet's "Hyperion," had a certain resemblance to myself, which on one occasion caused some amusement in our house, my father coming suddenly into the room and addressing her as "Fanny," which rather surprised her, as, though it was her name, they were not sufficiently intimate to warrant his so calling her. She was seated, however, otherwise he could not have committed the mistake, as, besides being very much handsomer than I, she had the noble stature and bearing of "a daughter of the gods, divinely tall."

On one of my visits to Boston, I was honoured with an invitation to read to the gentlemen of Harvard College (the Cambridge of New England), Longfellow was then Professor of Poetry and *belles lettres* there, and led me through the student audience to my reading-desk, and from it, when my performance was over, to his own house, to an exquisitely prepared supper-table, where, seated between him and his wife, and surrounded by kind friends, I received from her a lovely nosegay, and from him the manuscript copy of the beautiful sonnet, with which he has immortalized my Shakespeare Readings.

This delightful evening was not only a great pleasure, but saved me from a great pain. Dr. Webster, the Professor of Chemistry, having offered to lead me to my desk, which proposal I declined, having previously accepted Longfellow's proffer of the same courtesy, but for which I should have put my hand in that of a murderer, and remembered my reading at Cambridge with horror ever afterwards.

The murder of Dr. Parkman, of Boston, by Dr. Webster, who had borrowed money from him, and so endeavoured to cancel the debt, created the most terrible sensation in a society of which all the members were related, connected, or acquainted with each other. The unfortunate man was sentenced to death, but escaped the disgrace of public execution by taking strychnine, which was said (I know not how truly) to have been conveyed to him in prison. The penalty of the law (hanging) would, in this instance, have had an unusual element of horror, for it was then carried out by the personal action of the high sheriff, who, surrounded by the government officials, stood himself on the same platform opposite the criminal, and by the pressure of his foot loosened a spring and drop in the plank on which the condemned man stood, and so fulfilled the sentence. Dr. Webster had been intimately acquainted with the gentleman who would thus have been his executioner.

At this time I gave a reading of Macbeth, at which all the gentlemen engaged on each side in this dreadful suit were present, and was more impressed, as many of my audience told me they had been, by the awful tenour of the play, than I ever was before or since. A deep groan from one of my listeners, a most distinguished and venerable member of the Boston bar, having been the only sound that broke the breathless silence of my audience in the terrible murder scene. The graceful and delightful supper with my dear friends, the Longfellows, spared me the cruel associations which might have haunted that evening, instead of those with which I shall always remember it.

After reading the sonnet on my readings, I told Longfellow that the next time I read in Boston, it should be something of his, a promise which I fulfilled by reading his exquisite poem of the "Building of the Ship," copied in some measure (but as genius only can copy) from Schiller's noble "Casting of the Bell." Among an audience of more than two thousand hearers, Longfellow and his wife sat near, and just in front of me, his sweet and bright countenance beaming, I hoped, with pleasure, and her fine eyes raised towards me, while tears, which certainly were not

" drops of sorrow," fell from them like glistening dew in bright moonlight.

Not long after this the sky was darkened over my friend's head, and the light of his home put out for ever, by the tragical death of his beloved wife, the partner of that ideally happy marriage, which had never known a shadow or a cloud. Robert Mackintosh (Sir James Mackintosh's son) had married Mrs. Longfellow's sister, and in so doing had become the husband of a dear friend of mine, and my friend himself. He came to America and stayed with me at my home in Lenox, on his way to join the Longfellows at Cambridge. During this visit, he spoke one day at length of the unusually fortunate and happy life of Longfellow—the blessed home, relations, the devoted wife, the dear and lovely children, the affectionate esteem and admiration with which he was regarded throughout his own country, the general appreciation and favour with which his writings were received in Europe, as well as in America, his distinguished social position and ample fortune, an existence which, with his own most amiable character, certainly combined all the elements of happiness possible in this world in a most unusual manner and degree. A week after this conversation, after Mackintosh had left me for Boston, I got a letter from him recalling it to me, and telling me that Fanny Longfellow was dead, burnt alive while playing with her children in the next room to the one where her husband was sleeping.

It was a considerable time before I again visited Boston or saw Longfellow; the first time I did so, he threw his arms round my neck, perhaps my face recalled her's to him, perhaps only my love for her, and his bitter loss.

After another lapse of time, on the occasion of my last visit to Boston, I was staying with a dear friend, who asked Longfellow and others that I loved to meet me. The "strong hours" had done their appointed work with a grief that, though still unconquerable, was no longer conqueror of his life. His children had grown up, and sweet serenity smiled once more in his, beautiful countenance. I sat by him at dinner, and he told me he was preparing a volume of extracts from various poets, descriptive of places, which he thought would form a collection of pleasant pictures, and that he had done me the honour to place in this selection some lines of mine on Venice, which token of his approval gratified and touched me deeply.

Since that, Longfellow asked me to join him and his family for a winter at Palermo, a delightful proposal, which I should have accepted eagerly, but the plan was given up, and I never saw him again after my last meeting with him in Boston.

Dining one day in Paris, with the distinguished painter, Ary Scheffer, the latter, in his enthusiastic admiration for Longfellow, maintained that he was a greater poet than Byron, by so much as he was a better man. To this I could not agree. Longfellow was not a great poet, but he was among the first of those who are not the greatest, and I doubt if any of the noblest lines of Byron will be remembered longer than some of the sweetest of Longfellow.

He asked me once how I liked his " Evangeline." I told him I did not like the measure in which it was written, that I did not think the hexameter suited the genius of our language. "Oh! but have you read, it?" said he. "Three times from beginning to end,' said I, with perfect truth, admiring it extremely though I did not like the metre. He smiled sweetly, and said, "Oh, then read it just once more, and then you will like it."

He told me a curious anecdote of his own literary experience. One day hearing me sing the "Ballad of Bonny George Campbell," he said that he had first known it as a *German* ballad, which he had thought original, not being acquainted with the Scotch song; and that the German adaptor of it had translated the second line, "Low upon Tay," (not knowing what it meant, and that Tay was the name of a river) by "Tief in den Tag," which Longfellow again, in his ignorance of the original song, had rendered, "Far in the day," and only found out long afterwards that he had translated into English a German translation of a Scotch ballad.]

We are having already very oppressive heat, and I am sitting writing to you in my nethermost garment, though it is past midnight, and but for respect for you should be quite willing to dispense with that.

York Farm, May 23rd, 1876.

MY DEAREST HARRIET,

I wrote to you last night till half-past twelve, when the heat was so intolerably oppressive that I could hardly bear to keep a single garment on. I was really (though in such undress) so much too hot. This morning at seven o'clock, when I opened my window, it was so *cold* that I was obliged to wrap a thick woollen shawl round me during the few minutes I stood cleaning my bird's cage. We had to have large fires in all the rooms, and until they had burnt well up, we were all shivering, and shuddering, and shaking, and half perished. " *Figgerez-vous*," as Mrs. H—— used to say, what a climate, my dear !

With regard to the entailing of property in this country, it is left like any other testamentary disposition, entirely optional with the testator. It is a mistake to suppose that a man is compelled by law here to divide his fortune or estate, equally among his children. It is custom stronger than law, which in almost all cases makes this the usual distribution of a man's property. But there is nothing but general opinion to prevent his making the division as unequal as any individual may choose.

When a man dies intestate, a third of his property goes to his widow, and the rest is equally divided among his children ; but that entails are legal and can be, and are made, I can assure you, from my own experience.

With regard to Butler Place, there seems to be an insuperable difficulty in the way of the sale or alienation of any part of it, arising from the terms of the mortgage, by which the estate was made liable for my annuity. The property is by that document entailed on my children's children, and nobody of the present generation can alienate any portion of the estate. And hitherto the obstacles to the present joint owners parting with the property, or any portion of it, to each other or any one else (a contingency contemplated in the drawing up of the deed for my settlement) have proved insuperable. Of course an entail can be got rid of, here as in England, with the joint consent of all parties concerned; but as my grandchildren, on whom Butler Place is entailed, may yet possibly be unborn, and those who are born are a boy of sixteen and a girl of two years old, on whose children it is also entailed, there appears to be no solution of the difficulty. So you see we enjoy the privilege of entailed property in this republican country more than some of us find desirable. I believe a Bill in Congress might be obtained that would perhaps relieve our dilemma.

My little Alice is backward in teething, not having yet achieved her eye or stomach teeth, and backward, I think, too, in talking, though she is beginning to string her words together, and makes her will and wishes distinctly and imperatively understood. It is a very great privation to me that I shall lose my grandson's whole term of holidays, as he will not come home till after I have gone to Lenox.

I shall now be glad when the time comes for my leaving this place, the pleasant little house is too small for our large party to be comfortable in it. F——, and Mr. L——, and the baby, and three servants, make a considerable addition to our population, and I shall not be sorry to leave the dear tiny abode to its future occupants, and resign the bustle and responsible dignity of providing and ordering matters for so large a family, especially as Ellen, upon whom of course I entirely depend, has not been at all well lately; she is very much worn out, and I shall rejoice to have her in tolerable peace and quiet, with only me to think and care for during the summer.

You will remember, I dare say, the account I wrote you last year of the horrible pest of Colorado beetles, or potato bugs, as the country-people call them here. It was said that after eating everything before them they burrowed in the earth, and would reappear again this spring. About a month ago, the farmers and gardeners, turning up the ground, began to find them again, and they have now come forth and are laying their eggs, and we are again in expectation of being overrun by them. I cannot help hoping, however, that the unusual quantity of heavy rain we have had lately may prevent their overwhelming us in such disgusting multitudes as they did last year.

We are reading Macaulay's life and letters, which we find extremely interesting, and I particularly so, from my acquaintance with him, and his great intimacy with Mr. Ellis, to whom so many of the letters given in the book are addressed.

George Trevelyan seems to me to have compiled the book extremely well, with good taste and good feeling, and in a style worthy of his uncle's nephew. I find it charming reading; but I cannot help thinking that if Macaulay had understood French better, he would not have recommended Paul de Kock's "Sœur Anne," as a book for his sister's reading. It is surely a good deal coarser even than our own novelists of the last century, which seem to me intolerably so.

York Farm, May 31st, 1876.

MY DEAREST HARRIET,

I have just come from over the way, where
S—— has been giving a sort of garden party to a
number of people, and where I have been talking, and
listening, and standing, and curtseying, till I am very
tired, and shall surely be obliged to go to bed before I
can finish this letter.

It seems that little in the way of social hospitality
is being done in Philadelphia for the number of
foreigners and visitors from the other states of the
union, who are collected in the city just now in consequence of the Centennial Exhibition, and S—— has
felt rather indignant at what has appeared to her a
want of kindly courtesy towards the strangers in the
city, and so she has made what has been for her a
great exertion, and asked three hundred people to
Butler Place to dance and walk about and play croquet,
and otherwise amuse themselves as best they could.
Not many more than half that number came, the
weather was extremely fine, and the party was pronounced very successful, and I am very glad it is
over. . . .

York Farm, June 8th, 1876.

MY DEAREST HARRIET,

F—— told me to-day that the twentieth or
twenty-eighth of January was the date on which she
believed Mr. L—— intended to sail for England. He
particularly desires to go by one vessel, I think the
Britannica, which belongs to the Irish White Star
Line of steamers, in one of which we came out here

three years ago. The season at which we are to sail is of course a very undesirable one, yet occasionally good winter passages are made, and the whole event of my departure is mixed up with such heavy sadness, that the more or less physical misery of the passage does not occupy my thoughts in the least.

You ask me if I am interested in the presidential election? Yes, indeed, deeply interested; not so much as to which of the candidates is to succeed, but in the closeness of the struggle itself, and in the extraordinary patience, forbearance, and law-abiding attitude of the people throughout the whole of this vast country, where every other man almost is a voter, and where every single vote is of vast importance in the issue in which every individual throughout the United States feels a passionate personal interest.

Certainly it is the very strangest political position any country was ever in, and the general good sense and good feeling of the people seem to me unparalleled, unless by the bad faith and daring dishonesty of the politicians, technically so called, a formidably numerous and unscrupulous class of men, who have got the whole government in their hands and are wrestling in two desperate factions, each for the nomination of the man who is likely to be biassed or influenced after his election in favour of them and their interests. It is come to so complete a deadlock with the elections, in consequence of the withholding, falsifying, and *cooking* the returns of the votes in the three states of South Carolina, Florida, and Louisiana, that the question of which of the two men, Hayes or Tilden, has really been elected will in all probability have to be decided by an appeal to Congress. All business is at a standstill, every interest in the country is suffering from this prolonged struggle, which may be protracted for two months still, in which case it seems difficult to imagine that some violent demonstration of popular feeling will not take place, and the parties being so nearly equally divided throughout the whole country, a general *electoral war* would seem to be among the possible results. It is at present really quite impossible to foresee the course of events from day to day, and men's minds are filled with no other subject.

My dearest Harriet, the letter I have just received from you is terribly sad. I cannot but hope that I may yet embrace you once more, nor have I the faintest doubt that in spite of your loss of sight you will recognize the human being you have loved so tenderly and constantly, and who has loved you so dearly for so many years. I do not believe that my voice is much changed, and though the falling of my teeth makes me lisp slightly occasionally, my power of speaking distinctly is not so impaired but that I trust to make you hear and understand what I may say and read to you, if it pleases God that we should meet.

I am beginning to speculate upon where I am to look for a house in London, and feel attracted to Mrs. St. Quintin's neighbourhood. I like that part of London, and I think that I could find without difficulty somewhere about there, a house that would answer my purpose and not exceed my means; but the idea of beginning a new chapter of housekeeping with a new set of servants, and without my dear maid and housekeeper Ellen, seems to me very formidable, even in England.

My present hope is to spend a month in Dublin, near you, my very dear Harriet. After that F—— wants me to go with her in search of clothing to Paris, and after that *che sarà sarà.*

M—— will grieve at our parting, and certainly miss me very much, but she has an older and dearer friend than myself living within a stone's throw of her, who will not make up to her for my departure, but will certainly help her to bear it. It is no use thinking about it, it is wretched all round.

Champlost, June 13th, 1876.

MY DEAREST HARRIET,

Your letters had better now be directed to Curtis's Hotel, Lenox, Berkshire, Massachusetts, as my visit to M—— will not be a long one, and that will be my place of abode till the end of August.

I left my small house at Branchtown yesterday with a profound sense of heartfelt thankfulness for two years and a half of peace and pleasant comfort which I have enjoyed there, and for which I do not think I have been half grateful enough while they lasted. The little snug rooms have already put on something of a different appearance and no longer look *mine.* How completely characteristic of its habitual inhabitant a room becomes in its order and disorder, its look, its sound, and its smell. Russia leather, you know, is always an element of the atmosphere of my rooms, as all the shades of violet and purple are of their colouring, so that my familiar friends associate the two with their notions of my habitat.

I left the place, the dear little York Farm, without any poignant sorrow, which I am becoming incapable of feeling about any such circumstance as a change of residence, but with sincere regret. There was really no beauty of situation, cultivation, or prospect about it to lay hold upon one's imagination or charm one's memory, but the hours I have passed there contemplating Butler Place, the home of my early married life, under the altered circumstances of my present old age, have sunk deep into my heart, with the mingled emotions they excited. The residence had many advantages for me, besides the supreme one of its nearness to S—— and its delightful neighbourhood to my dear friend M——, and I am not likely to find what will suit me better in any house I may light upon now, either here or in England. Besides being in all essential respects comfortable, it was quaint and pretty and cheerful in an unusual degree.

Thanks to my kind English servants, too, and to Ellen's incessant labour of love, I had passed my time of housekeeping there without any of the constant change and turmoil and distress that all housekeeping in this country involves, and in that particular my daily existence was fortunate and quiet far beyond that of most people here. I am very glad the L——s are going to live there till they return to England, as I think, now that they have the house to themselves, they will be able to make themselves comfortable there. He has the talent of making every place he inhabits look charming, and she is a good and energetic housekeeper, and between them both I think they will make their temporary home there, in spite of the small rooms and rather narrow space, satisfactory.

I have a feeling of rest and relief this morning in finding myself free from all domestic duties, cares, and responsibilities. No breakfast, no lunch, no dinner, no nothing to provide for and order, and myself fed like the fowls of the air by Providence and M——, only a great deal better than any fowl that ever flew. Neither have I my own peculiar feathered bipeds, my mocking-bird and canary to clean and attend to, for I left them with F—— at the farm, and I have an astonished, surprising sense of nothing to do and unlimited leisure to do it in, consequent, I suppose, upon all abdication; but I have lost my dear little granddaughter Alice's trotting feet in the nursery above my head, and her sweet little bird's voice calling at the head of my dressing-room stairs, "Go see Ganny," which she used to say very plainly.

I think American women, compared with others, deficient in natural animal love of offspring. I think many things in their climate, education, and modes of life produce this result; morally and intellectually, they are very good mothers, but not physically, and they and their children are the worse for it.

I had a very sad letter from my sister two days ago, telling me of the death of her little grandson— A——'s child. My sister writes that the baby's death is a great loss to her; he was ten months old, and she delighted in him. A—— sent me by his mother a very tender message in the midst of his affliction, which touched me very much. He and his wife are gone to Italy for a while.

You ask me if my daughters take much interest in the exhibition? F——, I think, not much, although she has announced her intention of paying it several future visits. She and Mr. L—— escorted me thither very kindly about a fortnight ago, and by dint of going about in a wheel chair, and only looking at a small number of the objects particularly worthy of observation, and only remaining in the building a couple of hours, I came away well pleased and not over-fatigued. I shall be perfectly satisfied not to return again, and equally ready to do so in the same manner, if anybody invites me thither.

Mr. L—— and F——, having succeeded so well in their charge of me, undertook to pilot M—— in the same manner to the show, and I think the expedition was equally successful with her.

The exhibition, as far as I had time or means of observing it, bears no comparison whatever with the Great London and Paris ones, both of which I saw, except in the one particular instance of the Chinese and Japanese goods, which by reason of some special mitigation of duties in their favour had been brought over in great quantity, and are extremely beautiful, tasteful, and magnificent. The immense duties which the European exhibitors have to pay for bringing their goods into this country have very much interfered with the quantity and quality of what they have brought, because, unless they find a sale for all, or a large proportion of the things they exhibit, they will be obliged to carry them back again, having not only

incurred the expense of their transport to and fro
across the Altantic, but the enormous custom-house
duties, which purchased their entrance into the ports
of this country.

S—— has been from the first much more interested
about the exhibition than her sister. She had no
sympathy or enthusiasm about the original plan, and
rather regretted that any such project should be entertained; but the thing having been called into existence,
and a challenge having been given to the whole civilized
world to come and admire the hundred years achieve-
ments of her country, she has felt an extreme desire
that the thing should not prove an ignominious failure
upon a gigantic scale, which she feared it might. She
has gone very often to the exhibition, and professes
her intention of going as often as she possibly can,
visiting each section and division of the whole exposi-
tion in regular order and succession, and making, as is
her wont, a thorough systematic study of its contents.
Her pleasure, of course, in this process will be greatly
enhanced by the companionship of her boy, when he
arrives, which will now be in a few days. He, however, will probably take up his abode in the machinery
department, and find no charms in any other, and in
that I sympathize with him entirely.

Nothing stirred me so much (or I might comparatively say at all) as the huge, ingenious, *wise* engines,
for every conceivable purpose, collected in the vast
machinery department. But especially was I fascinated
by the silent, swift, steady, sure, tremendous labour
of the magnificent giant of a steam engine which,
stationed in the middle of the vast hall filled with

machinery, furnished the motive power for all their several processes. This noble two-armed (one would have thought, he should have been Briareus) iron Titan enchanted me, and I felt idolatrous, and as if I could have fallen down and worshipped *him*. The impression made upon me vividly recalled that which I experienced at the sight of a similar stupendous creature, which moved every wheel, and spindle, and pully, and crank, throughout one of the Marshalls enormous factories at Leeds. That beautiful steam engine had a room all to itself, a sort of circular boudoir, lined with green baize, where it lived, working in perfect silence and solitude the thousand whirring, whizzing, twirling, twisting, crashing, clattering, voluble, noisy engines throughout the whole building. How I did wish and beg to be left alone for a little while with that great power in its solitary temple. I was not allowed to be so, however. No one is ever allowed to stay there, I suppose lest attempts should be made to injure the machine. I think I might have watched the motion of its shining arms till its monotony, like the falling of a waterfall, mesmerised me, and I flung myself into them, an English victim to an English Juggernaut.

The triumphs of science affect my imagination the same way that the most beautiful creations of art and nature do; and when I read, in the account of the Mont Cenis Tunnel, how those two engines, working their way from each side of the mountain mass, encountered in its rocky heart so accurately, according to the calculations of the engineers, that their steel finger-tips met, and their iron hands touched each other, I burst into tears of enthusiasm such as the finest poem might have called to my eyes.

Good-bye, my dearest Harriet. I told M—— this morning that I would make you laugh by the only fault her friends find in her supremely luxurious housekeeping, that the cream from her Alderney cows is too rich and thick to mix well with the tea. God bless you, dear.

Ever, as ever, yours,
FANNY.

Champlost, June 19th, 1876.

MY DEAREST HARRIET,

Your letters had better now be directed to Curtis's Hotel, Lenox, Berkshire, Massachusetts. I have already been here a week, and have written you two letters since I came. I go up to Lenox this day week for the next two months, and after that have decided nothing at all as to my future movements or residence.

I think the idea of letting York Farm during this summer has been given up, and the L——s seem inclined to remain there themselves, only going to some sea-bathing place for temporary refreshment if the baby should appear to suffer much from the heat, or to require change of air.

Yesterday I walked through M——s woods to York Farm, to profit by my remaining short period of vicinity to my printing machine, and get ready another instalment of matter for my next month's article in the *Atlantic Magazine*.

I have found this printing machine an immense

relief from the quantity of tedious copying by pen, but I cannot carry the little iron stand and apparatus about with me, for, though not very bulky, it is heavy, and easily jarred out of order by being shaken. I have had the benefit of it ever since last autumn, and have now left it to Mr. L——, who originally persuaded me to buy it, not only for my own use, but as likely to be of great assistance to S——, who has more than once seriously over fatigued her hand by her incessant use of her pen. She, however, finds it impossible to make use of the printing machine, the working of which causes her intense impatient nervous irritation; nor can she be persuaded to try if this would not wear off with habit, which I think it would, because Ellen, who now uses a sewing machine without any disagreeable sensation or result, told me that when first she tried to work with it, it irritated her nerves to such a degree as almost to make her sick, and oblige her to lie down after using it for any length of time. So yesterday I printed my last sheets till I return from Lenox.

Champlost, June 23rd, 1876.

My dearest Harriet,

I wrote to you three days ago, and yesterday despatched to you the last printed number that I have received of my " Gossip." It had been my intention to have terminated the publication of these papers with my appearance on the stage, but the proprietors and the editor of the *Atlantic Magazine* are desirous to continue the series, and I am quite willing, as that is the case, to do so. The trouble of printing or copying the original is not pleasant, to be sure, but the addition to my income from the price of the articles is a very great consideration to me just now, and so for the present I go on. I find it difficult to imagine that much interest can be felt in such a chronicle by anybody, but, of course, that is not my affair, and the proprietors and publishers of the magazine are the only people to determine that question. Hitherto, it appears to pay them, since they are willing to pay me; and, both parties being at liberty to cry "Hold! enough!" whenever it suits them, "I go on gossiping."

S—— seems to me entirely free from the order of sentimental associations about family descent, family possessions, family importance, of which the Americans are proud and tenacious in proportion as there are few among them with reasonable grounds for them, few in whom such pretensions are not ridiculous, or whose claims to any distinctions of the sort are not of the slenderest description. The Livingstones and Van Ransselaers, of the State of New York, who were among the early settlers in the state, and brought family descent of ancient date in their native countries to dignify great territorial possessions in America, have long ceased to occupy the peculiar social position which those advantages gave them for many years as aristocratic members of this democratic community. The Patroon was, in fact, the title borne at Albany and in the State of New York, by the head of the Van Ransselaer family. Of course, I am not now speaking of southern planters and great landholders, but only of the northern aspect of the question.

Large estates, where slavery does not exist, almost
necessarily involve tenancy; a man owning thousands
or even many hundreds of acres must, if they are
cultivated, have tenant farmers. The objection to
such a position here, and a general conviction and
custom that a man should own the ground he tills
is so irresistible, that long ago the great northern
properties of the Livingstones, Van Ransselaers, and
Wadsworths (the latter, however, being an estate of
infinitely less extent and more modern ownership),
succumbed to the pressure of public opinion, and
were sold and subdivided in compliance with it, till
nothing special remains to their present representatives, and the only properties in the whole country,
not absolutely cultivated by their owners, or the
persons employed by them as mere cultivators were
(until the enfranchisement of the slaves) the great
estates of the southern planters.

[Lately, or within some few years, large tracts of
grain-growing land, have become the property by
purchase of foreigners, Englishmen, who, without
becoming American citizens, have become landed
proprietors in the United States, and I cannot help
thinking it doubtful how long this ownership of their
soil by aliens will be tolerated by the Americans.]

On the small property of under two hundred acres,
where I have been living, York Farm formed one of
the rare exceptions to the old but universal preference of ownership over tenancy of land here. For
nineteen years, I think, an Irish farmer was content
to rent as a tenant that part of the Butler Place
Estate, and was much admired, in the old sense of

being wondered at, by all his friends and acquaintances for so doing.

Dr. W—— is not, I think, much interested in the Centennial Exhibition, and has not yet been to see it. I should not wonder if he did not go near it.

I am afraid there is very little probability of the southern property being sold. I think both F—— and Mr. L—— are disinclined to part with it. Mr. L—— has literally recreated the place, and put it not only into the most admirable working condition, as a fine agricultural property of its peculiar sort, but has made it attractive and pleasant as a residence, and altogether so improved it, that it is matter of marvel to those who knew it before he went there, and of admiration to everybody. His life there may, I can easily imagine, be agreeable to him in many ways; the agricultural pursuit, farming, in short, and constant activity out of doors, in all the processes of cultivation must interest and occupy him from morning till night, and the care of the people, the religious services of the small churches on the plantation and at Darien, and the zealous teaching in his evening classes and Sunday schools, give him enough work (of his own peculiar professional kind of duty) to prevent his feeling that he is neglecting his special vocation.

I shall leave my dear M——s house with great regret, but the terrible heat has come upon us within the last two days, and I must profit by my rooms, which are engaged at Lenox, soon, if I am to escape thither unboiled and unbroiled.

Lenox, June 28th, 1876.

MY DEAREST HARRIET,

I arrived here yesterday, having left
M—— and slept in New York on Monday. This
divides the journey, not, indeed, at all equally, but the
whole would be more than I could undertake in one
day. The distance from Philadelphia to New York
takes but two hours' and a half to perform ; from New
York here is eight hours' journey, and that is as much
as I care to travel at once. It is a particularly
fatiguing journey, for the train by which I come stops
at every small wayside station, loitering away, I am
sure, two hours upon the whole time by these tedious
pauses, and then between these endless stoppages we
made up for lost time by tearing at a furious pace
along the sharp curves, by which the railroad follows
the windings of the Housatonic river, a beautiful
stream, the narrow valley of whose course affords the
only tolerable level approach to the hill country of
Berkshire. The violent swinging and shaking of the
train was such that Ellen and myself both arrived in
Lenox with sick headaches, and almost shattered to
pieces.

The village itself is not so much altered as improved. Side walks and small patches of grass or
turf are tidily kept and trimmed, the trees have grown
and spread till the place is quite embowered in them,
and all round the village in every direction handsome
country houses are growing up on the hillsides. It is
a very charming place, and the whole region in which
it lies is picturesque and lovely. Without being at all
sublime in the character of the scenery, it is very like

the tamer parts of Switzerland or the Black Forest, near Schaffhausen.

The spring has been temperate, with a good deal of rain, and the vegetation is magnificently full and fresh. I do not think I ever saw this part of the country in greater beauty.

None of even the younger members of the Sedgwick family are now in Lenox. B—— lets her large pleasant house in the village during the summer, and betakes herself with her children to a cottage on the lake side between Lenox and Stockbridge. I have one Boston and one New York friend, who have pretty country houses near the village, but they do not yet know of my arrival.

I felt a good deal of sadness at leaving Champlost. The closing of my two years life at Branchtown, the breaking up of my household, and leaving all my children and my friend M—— gave me again a feeling of the solitary wandering in which so large a portion of my life has been spent. No other arrangement, however, was possible. The L——s wanted York Farm, and I did not wish to pass a third summer in the dreadful heat of the neighbourhood of Philadelphia. Ellen's leaving me puts an end at once to all possibility of my keeping house in America, and an entire change in my mode of life was unavoidable.

I already perceive the relief of coming to this cooler climate, especially in the night atmosphere, which in Philadelphia is really almost as oppressive as the day. Ellen looks better already, and will, I trust, recover soon from the miserable nervous depression she has been suffering from since we left Branchtown, which was undoubtedly the result of over-work and over-worry. What I shall do without her or where I am to get any one to fill her place I cannot imagine; but whatever *must* be done, always *is* done, somehow or other, and so I shut my eyes to the probable discomforts and annoyances of the future as much as I can.

Lenox, July 5th, 1876.

My dearest Harriet,

You ask me if the " Perch " still exists, and I can answer that question particularly accurately, for it was on my return from walking down thither that I found your letter on my table. A very violent thunder-rainstorm had so cooled the air and laid the dust this morning, that I determined to go down to my old little estate and see how it was looking. The whole country is in unusual beauty, the spring having been temperate and rainy and much more gradual in its development into summer than is its wont in this climate. The vegetation is ,in the freshest, fullest beauty, and the woods and fields of this whole picturesque region quite exquisite. It is astonishing how like Switzerland it is; not the Alpine, magnificent side of Switzerland, but the whole of the valley of the Lake of Neuchâtel, looking towards the Jura. It is like the neighbourhood of La Jonchere and all that family of Jura valleys. The village of Lenox itself is immensely improved. The beautiful trees along its two streets, which cross each other at right angles on the top of a steep hill, have grown tall and thick, so that on looking down on the small table-land, where

the houses are clustered together from a considerable
height, on which stands the oldest village church
(whose clock, with which I endowed it, still shows
the inhabitants the time of day). The whole place is
embowered in foliage, and with the deep valleys
below it, and the blue distant hills rising up almost
to mountains beyond, is a most charming piece of
scenery.

The side-walks have all been widened and made
regular, partly paved, and, where not paved, smooth
and tidy and well-kept. Trees planted by my dear
friend Elizabeth Sedgwick, along the roadside-path
leading to her house, have grown into sheltering shade
which I blessed to-day as I walked under them towards
the Perch.

The injury I did my foot at Stoneleigh, the year
that I was laid up in Dublin, when I came to see you,
has never entirely healed. A small bone in the instep
was broken, and though it subsides almost into its
place, and seldom gives me very serious trouble,
occasional accidental treading on very uneven ground,
or unusual exertion, starts it into inconvenient pro-
minence, and makes it undesirable that I should use
it much, which matters little, however, during my
American summer, when the heat alone makes much
walking for anybody impossible. At starting this
morning I felt my instep painful, and went rather
lame, but only for a minute or two, after which I
walked (slowly enough to be sure), but without inconvenience, the whole mile, as it used to be reckoned
(I do not think it is near so much), to the cottage.

It is still the property of the person who bought it

from my daughters. I ventured inside the gate and walked up the carriage-road, which I myself had made, when first I bought the place, through a very pretty strip of wild woodland, until I came within sight of the house. It did not appear to have undergone any alteration, but looked pretty and tidy and much as it used to look. The single trees about it, and scattered over the sloping ground in front of it, had grown and spread and become handsome oaks and maples and chestnuts. It is a pretty little place, and I cannot help feeling sorry that my children parted with it, for the increase in the value of land in the village and neighbourhood of Lenox has been such that, having sold the property when they did for twice what I gave for it, it would now undoubtedly fetch more than twice the sum they received for it.

I came back to the hotel greatly pleased with the aspect of my former tiny estate, and with the sheltering screens of what had been quite young trees and plantations, when I lived here, and which are now thick handsome belts of wood.

Lenox, July 16th, 1876.

MY DEAREST HARRIET,

I have written no letter to you this week, and you will wonder at not having heard from me, and you will be sorry to hear that I have been too unwell to do so. I have not been seriously ill, but enough so to be incapable of the exertion of even writing a letter. I am well again now; that is to say, I am no longer ill, though a good deal pulled down and weakened by a sharp succession of physical troubles. Ellen, about whom you kindly ask, is, I think, already decidedly the better for change of air and scene, and relief from the wearing worry of her three years' housekeeping in America. The change in coming up here has not been so favourable to me, as the severe attack I have been suffering from appears to have been immediately brought on by the hot, hard, long day's journey from New York; the change of diet, the strongly lime-impregnated water of this district, and the generally unwholesome food, which all sojourners in country inns in America are compelled to poison themselves with; tough and ill-cooked meat, unfresh fish and vegetables, sour milk and cream, and, worse than all, bread prepared with soda, salleratus (sceleratissime) and every species of abomination to spare the use of proper yeast, which can seldom be obtained, and the necessary kneading for good rising, which can never be obtained. I hope, however, I have now gone through my seasoning, and shall be able to benefit by the greater coolness and lightness of the air of Lenox, compared with the atmosphere of Branchtown. There, indeed, the heat has been frightful. S—— writes me word of the thermometer standing between ninety and a hundred night and day for a week past, and tells me that the L——s have fled with their baby to the seaside, unable to endure their existence any longer at York Farm, which does not surprise me, after my two summers' experience of it.

You ask me if I take any interest in the election of the president? Yes; surely a very sincere and lively interest in the question of whether this great country is governed by a parcel of scoundrels, or whether something like an intelligent endeavour after common honesty is to guide the counsels of the nation. The nomination of Governor Hayes, of Ohio, as the most likely candidate for the presidency, relieves one's mind from the apprehension that a downright dishonest man or a mere miserable peddling politician was to be chosen. Mr. Hayes is known to be an honest, upright man, of unblemished character and integrity, who has kept himself aloof from all political intrigues, and though I believe he is not supposed to be a person ef exceptionally brilliant capacity, honesty is so decidedly the best of all policies in this country just now, that the nation is gasping for it, and, I think, will elect Governor Hayes as its representative with quite an enthusiasm for this strange order of merit.

You certainly would not rejoice more than I should if the Georgia plantation was sold, and York Farm sold, and all F——'s territorial possessions in this country turned into a few thousand pounds, with which she might go and begin housekeeping in some quiet parsonage in England, but I am afraid one might as well wish for the moon. The southern life of simple half-savage independence has an immense charm. I felt it keenly myself, in spite of my horror of the slavery by which I was surrounded ; and S——, in her late winter's visit to her sister, experienced its fascination, and spoke of it as almost irresistible.

Lenox, July 19th, 1876.

MY DEAREST HARRIET,

I have received your first letter directed to Lenox, so that now I know you have my precise address.

The news of Harriet Martineau's death had not reached me until I got your letter. It caused me a sort of retrospective emotion, for I had at one time known her very well and liked and admired her very much, having still in my possession letters of hers, beginning "Dearest friend," which I valued and preserved, as remembrances of an intercourse which had however ceased for many years.

She was extremely clever and excellently conscientious, and thoroughly good and more conceited and dogmatical than any person I have ever known (but one). That exquisitely simple and humble Christian soul, Lady Georgiana Fullerton, complained, as of almost a physical pain, of the distress the absence of all humility in Harriet Martineau's mind and books occasioned her. I think her change of opinions towards the end of her life almost the strangest that I ever neard of, and her curious deference to that Mr. Atkinson, under whose influence, I think, she professed to have become an absolute disbeliever, even in the existence of God, was a prodigious instance on the part of the author of "Life in a Sick Room" of the *refuges* to which the believing *necessity* of our nature will betake itself when wrested from its legitimate object and natural direction. To be sure, Shakespeare says, "God is a good man;" but Mr. Atkinson, for as good as he may have been, seems to me a poor succedaneum for Harriet Martineau's earlier objects of veneration. This extraordinary revulsion, convulsion—what shall I call it, of opinion in her?—shocked and grieved me so much that it was long before I could prevail upon myself to read her unchristian recantation and new profession of unfaith; and when at last I did so, I sat by the sea at St. Leonards a long time, crying very sorrowfully for her and for all those to whom she had been a speaker of vital truths, and whom her late denial of them must wound and perhaps injure, and for all those, alas! for whom her great abilities would thenceforward have no value or influence for good. I was very miserable because of these thoughts, and, if I, then I suppose many others who must have thought them too. The last time I ever saw her was while I was staying with you and dear Dorothy at Ambleside, when I remember going with F—— to call upon her, and when she received me with very kind cordiality, but talked chiefly of Mrs. Gaskell's "Life of Charlotte Brontë," which she had been reading, and of which and its author she spoke in terms of such denunciatory reprobation that I thought F—— would be terrified by her vehemence of blame.

I think with great pleasure of some of her books, which appear to me among the best of their kind ever written, "The Crofton Boys," "Feats on the Fiords," "Ella of Garvelock," and some of her Political Economy stories, one of which you gave me, I remember, the heroine of which had been on the stage, and had been suggested to her, as she told me, by me. She must have been a very old woman when she died. I suppose there will be some notice of her in the *Spectator*.

Madame George Sand, too, is lately dead—a woman of uncommon powers, one of the great geniuses of the present day, and one of the best writers of the finest French of these later times. It is a pity that she had not *clean hands*, and could hardly touch the picture of a woman without smirching it. [If Madame Sand's novels, with very few exceptions, cannot be read without regretful reprobation for her treatment of womanly character and the relations between the sexes, it is impossible to read her letters without the highest admiration for the fine moral sense, the true artistic sense, and the perfect good sense with which they are pervaded. It is difficult to conceive how a mind so clear, upright, and just on all other subjects should have suffered such lamentable eclipse in treating of the qualities and duties of her own sex.]

The American female politicians have been getting up a *womanifesto* (as Thackeray called the Stafford House Anti-Slavery Protest), in opposition to the famous Declaration of Independence of their ancestors and fellow-countrymen, protesting against that celebrated document as worse than meaningless, while "woman," as they call *us*, remains in her present position of political non-existence. At the head of the signers of this female Declaration of Independence appears the name of the celebrated Quaker preacher, abolitionist, and philanthropist, Mrs. Lucretia Mott, who is upwards of eighty years old, but takes energetic interest in this public demonstration of her country-women. I suppose my own individual superabundant sense of independence, and the unfortunate circumstances which have given full scope to its exercise, prevents me from sympathizing, as I ought, with the clamorous claims of the unfair sex in this particular.

Our weather is tremendous, though the air on these charming hilltops is never without some vitality.

You say you wonder if the Sartorises will give up Warsash. I have heard no intimation of any such intention; and though I believe they have taken a house with a long lease at Kensington, I do not think my sister would be at all happy without some place in the country, where she could take refuge from London, which she hates, just as I do, and my mother always did.

Good-bye, my dearest Harriet; God bless you. I think you think yourself a great deal more stupid than you are. Most people think the contrary; but I know that against the prevailing oppression of your painful circumstances it is of little avail to remonstrate with mere words. The shoulders that bear the burthen alone can tell how heavy it is and how weary they are. God help you to support yours, my very dear friend.

Ever, as ever, yours,
FANNY.

Lenox, July 22nd, 1876.

MY DEAREST HARRIET,

Hitherto Lenox has not treated me very well, because, as I have already written you word, I have been indulging in all sorts of attacks, more or less unpleasant, none of which have tended to make my sojourn here as agreeable as the relief from the dreadful heat at Branchtown and the charming hill country I am so fond of would have done, but for these objectionable physical experiences.

I am not a little amused at finding myself, quite without premeditation on my part, under homœopathic treatment. When I was suffering a great deal, Ellen asked me if I would not send for a doctor, and, as I thought my doing so might not only relieve me from pain, but her from anxiety, I gave her the name of a medical man in the county town of Pittsfield, six miles off, whom I remembered to have heard well spoken of as a physician; and so he came and prescribed for me, and then I discovered, to my amusement, that I was being treated homœopathically, which would certainly have diverted my allopathic son-in-law very much.

I do not think that my habits have altered with increased years, except that this summer I have left off getting up at six o'clock and walking before breakfast. The only change in my habits, of which I am conscious, is that I now hardly walk at all. The extremes of heat and cold of this climate make doing so in summer or winter here almost impossible for old people.

Your old Leamington acquaintance, Dr. Jephson, came to lunch with the L——s, when I was staying with them at Stoneleigh a few years ago. He was quite blind, but very cheerful and gossipy, and talked a good deal about Mrs. Kemble, who, you know, was a patient and great crony of his in her Leamington days.

My last letter from F—— reported them still at Branchtown; but, unable to endure the heat, they have gone to a seaside bathing-place, not far from

Philadelphia, which I rejoice at for all their sakes, especially that of the little child.

I miss my darling printing-machine very much, and have had again to have recourse to an amanuensis in order to escape the intolerable tedium of copying my own lucubrations, and also to spare the poor printers' eyes, to whom my vile handwriting will be doubly trying after the delightfully clear printed sheets I have been supplying them with for some time past. I am sorry not to have been able to send you my last October article; I cannot get it here, and have sent to Pittsfield, the county town, to obtain it for you. As soon as I get it you shall have it.

Lenox, July 26th, 1876.

MY DEAREST HARRIET,

I have now written to you, I think, four letters from Lenox, and have received two directed to that place—one this morning, written on your birthday, telling me of your being eighty-one. My dearest friend, if I avoid as much as possible in my letters dwelling upon, or even referring to the sad and depressing conditions of your life, it is not, as you must well know, because I do not feel them much more deeply than any words could express, or because they are not often and often present to my thoughts and imagination with most acute and unavailing pity. God sustain you, my friend, in the path He has appointed you to tread, and still mercifully spare you acute physical suffering, and preserve to you the noble mental faculties, the decay of which you so frequently deplore, but which you certainly exaggerate to yourself, unless Eliza invents, as well as writes, your letters for you, which I do not in the least suspect her of doing.

I am staying now in the same old inn which has always had the monopoly of lightening the travelling public ever since I first came here. Many years ago it was bought by the son of the village baker, who, when a lad of about eighteen, used to come out with me on my fishing excursions on the lake to manage my boat, let down and haul up anchor, and otherwise make himself useful as my attendant. I remember a droll and characteristic conversation which once took place between us while we were sitting on the bank eating our luncheon one day. After gazing round him for some time at the charming landscape far and near, my companion said to me, "Now, Mrs. Kemble, I want to know" (the invariable Yankee form of interrogation) "what would be the difference between all that we see here now if we were in England instead of America?" I thought awhile what feature of difference would be at once the most comprehensive and the most striking to him that I could name, and, looking round at the fair hillsides, the meadows, orchards, woods, and farmsteads, all cultivated and inhabited by their owners, I said, "Well, William, in England, all that we see here now would probably be the property of one man." "Oh, my! that's bad!" was his sole reply, as with a solemn shake of the head he bit a huge mouthful out of his bread and cheese. "Well, now I want to know," are the words oftenest in the mouths of these people. This fellow was as ignorant as it is possible for a Massachusett's man to bè; but think of the intelligence evinced by both his question and answer.

He was absolutely ignorant and desperately idle, but good-tempered and good-looking, with a sort of coarse likeness to my brother Henry, which was a recommendation to me. As he grew up he took to working about a livery stable which his brother estab-.lished in the village, and, having the liking for horses that most idle fellows seem to have, he became one of the finest drivers I ever saw; so that on all her mountain expeditions with her school-girls, my friend E. S—— invariably had him to drive the huge four-horse omnibus, which, what with its freight of scream-ing, gabbling girl-geese, and the terrible dangerous roads he often had to go over, was a very considerable proof of skill as well as of steadiness and courage.

He was recalling to my memory the other day a day's drive he had taken this lively freight, when I was one of the party, when he brought the whole caravan safely down a steep and execrably bad mountain-road that skirted a precipice the greater part of the way, and towards the end of which day the daylight was beginning to fail him, and said that when he arrived safe at the bottom of it, at the village where we stopped for the night, his hands shook so that he could hardly use them—not with the effort of driving his team, but with the nervous tension of the anxiety he had felt during the whole descent.

Well, this Jehu contrived to captivate the good will of a very pretty Lenox young woman, refined and delicate, and of so much more education and better breeding than himself, that she was a teacher in Mrs. S——'s school; and my friend E—— considered her marrying him quite a *mésalliance*. He had had perception enough, however, of her superiority to fall in love with it; and I think her name being Evelina must have had something to do with his admiration for her. However, he presently purchased the Lenox Hotel, and has gone on thriving and prospering ever since; and one fine day was sent up by his fellow-citizens as their representative to the Legislative State Assembly at Boston, where he took his place by the side of one of the best educated, best bred, most refined, and every way distinguished men that I have ever known anywhere. Now E—— will be sure, if you do not, to echo my Yankee lad's exclamation, only probably not in his vernacular, "Oh, my! that's bad;" but it isn't so bad for reasons which I have now neither time, space, nor inclination to give you. . . .

Mr. Curtis has gone on thriving and prospering and becoming a well-to-do "hotel" keeper—a position supposed in this country to require administrative faculties and a certain intelligence of no common order, the familiar saying being, in speaking of a man's abilities, "Oh, well, so-and-so's smart enough, couldn't keep a hotel, though;" but my friend William walks about with his hands in his pockets, while his pretty ladylike wife lives retired in her own apartments, the house being managed by three grown-up sons and two daughters; their father only occasionally condescending to give a sample of his former skill by driving a four-horse omnibus full of gay summer visitors, who throng his house from Boston and New

York, to some of the especially beautiful points of view, hills or lakes, of this picturesque region. . . .

The beauty of the place and the temperate healthy summer atmosphere bring more and more visitors every season; and as the house is really thriving, though there are occasional complaints of want of progress in the establishment, and even sometimes threats of the opening of a rival Lenox house, I dare say there will before long be set up by the young people some horrible, *modern*, big, new, fine, city-looking building, which will keep pace with the times in all the latest "improvements" (six stories high, with *alleviators*, as the Irish servants wisely and wittily call elevators), which will give more general satisfaction, and supersede the old-fashioned red-brick, ugly, dear old house, which I loved for its memories of many years, by something really much uglier, but which will be an object of pride and pleasure to the Curtis's family and the whole neighbourhood.

The Perch, my former property and home in Lenox, is called a mile from the village. It never seemed to me more than three-quarters of that distance, if so much. I walked down there and found it looking very pretty, the trees grown, and the whole place much improved. It is the only place in all this neighbourhood where there are any oak trees, and there are about half a dozen fine ones scattered round the house, and I was assured the other day that it was always supposed that my English love for the English tree had made me select that particular place; whereas, it was bought for me, without my eyes having seen it, or knowing whether oaks or willows grew on it, but merely because it was a ready-furnished house for sale, which I wanted at once. . . . I find myself, however, in consequence of that purchase, invested with a dignity which none of my more distinguished kinsfolk achieved.   Not only is the little "Perch" designated as the Kemble place, but the road that leads from the village to it is set down in the maps of Lenox and its neighbourhood as Kemble Street or Road, which struck me as strange and comical and melancholy enough.   Good-bye, my dearest H——.

Ever, as ever, yours,
FANNY.

END OF VOL. I.

PRINTED BY WILLIAM CLOWES AND SONS, LIMITED,
LONDON AND BECCLES.

J. D. & Co.

www.ingramcontent.com/pod-product-compliance
Lightning Source LLC
Chambersburg PA
CBHW021256050726
47498CB00003BB/870